Married to a New Orleans Savage:

AN IN LOVE WITH A NEW ORLEANS SAVAGE CONTINUATION

By: Londyn Lenz

© 2017
Published by **Miss Candice Presents**

Prologue

(Kylee)

A year later

We were all outside clapping and congratulating Brandon and Tiff as they got in their black Phantom. Tiff looked beautiful with her long white dress on and her flower veil. Her belly looked like it was about to explode.

They were having a baby girl and naming her Brandy. Tiff had a glow that made her skin look flawless. Brandon brought them a new four-bedroom house with a huge backyard. That was where they were on their way to because Tiff was due any day. She made Brandon promise to give her the honeymoon she wants once the baby gets here. Brandon was so overprotective of Tiff that they left their own wedding reception at 8pm because he said she needed to rest.

Myself, Kimmora and Tiff graduated from the university last June and we had a huge party. That same night is when Kevin proposed to Kimmora. Of course, she said yes. We all were thrilled especially our dad, Italians love weddings. It made dad even happier when they said they wanted to have their wedding in Italy in the same church dad and mom were married at.

Kimmora just had their baby boy Keion Kaine Royal last month. I cannot believe my sister is a mommy. Kim was in love with Keion, he was gorgeous with curly hair and big brown eyes like ours. They have a new home as well which is beautiful. Kimmora even opened her hair store that was doing great. I was so proud of her.

Keira and Kalvin spontaneous asses eloped in Vegas. We all were happy, at first my dad felt some kind of way. But he could never stay mad at any of his girls for long. Keira was due any day just like Tiff, they were also having a girl they are naming Kyra Stella Royal. We all went to Italy to visit our family and our Nonna (grandma) told us before she even knew that she was pregnant. Nonna always said she could just look at a woman and tell if she was with child.

Kelly and Kaylin were the fun couple. They traveled so much we could not keep up with them and their crazy destinations. The pair just got back from Paris last week. In another week, they will be going to Puerto Rico. Kelly moved in with Kaylin and they loved it. You never saw one without the other. Kelly does not know but when they go to Puerto Rico Kaylin is popping the question. He already asked our father for his permission and everybody knew but Kelly.

Karlos pulled into our drive way and we got out the car. A wedding will exhaust you especially when you have a pregnant bride. We walked in our new home and I plopped on the couch. Karlos ass refused to move me back to his condo because he said it was where I left him and he did not like the thought of that. We now lived in a five-bedroom house that he had built from ground up and I decorated. After we showered together I was laying on Karlos chest playing with his hair while I watch HBO show Shameless. He picked up the remote and turned it to NFL Network.

"You hate when I do this shit don't you?" Karlos asked while laughing. He knows it annoys me when he takes over the TV in here because he can watch all the sports he wants in his man cave.

"You know I do." I rolled over off him.

"Kylee get the fuck back over here." His deep ass voice boomed through our bedroom. I rolled over back on him holding an ultra sound picture. He looked at it and gave me the biggest smile.

"No fucking way baby! You bullshittin' me!" He sat all the way up.

"I found out yesterday. I am 9 weeks, remember when you kept saying my insides felt different. That's why." He grabbed me making me straddle his lap.

"I fucking love you Mrs. Royal. You know that shit? You brought yo' chocolate ass in my life changing my shit for the better. This is the second-best thing you have done for me, the first is giving me another chance." I smiled and kissed him.

Me and Karlos got married three months after getting back together. My dad let us have it in his backyard and it was gorgeous. Karlos cried in front of everybody when he recited his vows. There was not a dry eye present. He threaten everybody's life if they mentioned him crying after that day. We went to London for a week for our honeymoon. I loved this man with all that I have in me.

I was heartbroken when he hurt me but with time I was able to heal. He has gone above and beyond to show me that he wants to keep me in his life. He did not even have a bachelor party with strippers. They went to the casino, and gambled all night. Karlos and Brandon won $25,000 apiece as if they needed it. Both ended up giving that shit to me and Tiff.

I had a bachelorette party that my sisters and Tiff threw for me. I had no idea there would be male strippers at my party but I was cool with looking at some fine ass men. One of our friends recorded it and posted it on Instagram. Word got back to the crazy ass Royal's and these fools showed up with Karlos in front and guns blazing.

I was so mad, nobody was hurt but still it was unnecessary. I wanted to call the wedding off but we all know how Karlos is if he even thinks I am about to leave him. I did not talk to him until our wedding day. This man called me, my sisters and my dad phone so much it was ridiculous.

"Boy, I am marrying you stop calling I am trying to get ready," I finally answered my phone after the 100th call. We had our wedding which is one of the days I will never forget.

Now here I was telling my husband that we are about to be parents. I cannot believe I am a wife and about to be a mother.

"So, what do you want to have?" I asked Karlos still straddling him.

"I want a little me, I do not need a girl. Hell naw! I trip when a fucking male waiter takes your order," he said making both of us laugh.

"I don't care what we have as long as it's healthy and has your gorgeous eye color." I smiled at him.

"Come ride somewhere with me baby." He got up and put his basketball shorts on.

"What? Karlos I'm tired," I whined. Tiff's wedding drained me of all my energy.

"Come on baby, I will carry your ass. Ride with daddy somewhere, we will come right back and I can murder that pussy," he said biting his lip getting me hot. I got up and slipped a maxi dress on.

"Remember this?" he asked me as we walked off the elevator. We were at the sky scrapper building where Karlos first took me when we met. My emotional ass had tears running down my face.

"You are always crying." He teased me and I looked at him with shock. Referring to our wedding day when he cried like a baby. But it made me love him more.

"Don't even say it." He mean mugged me and I kissed his lips soften him up instantly. He pulled me in front of him with my back facing his chest and arms around my waist. The New Orleans air was warm and comforting.

"I have not been up here since I brought you. Seems like you been my roof top baby." He kissed my neck.

"I love my Mr. Royal, so much." I could feel his smile.

"Nowhere near as much as I love you." We both shared a laugh and just watched the clear sky and stars. I love the shit out of this crazy man. My Los.

Kylee

(The Present Three Months later)

Ugh! I cannot believe Karlos is taking this long at McDonalds. All I asked for was a double cheeseburger, a large fry, vanilla milkshake, two apple pies and come chocolate chip cookies. It does not take this long to make my food. Why the hell is it called fast food it takes all day to make?! Plus, I was missing Karlos like crazy. I cannot wait until this pregnancy is over. I ate like a pig and all I wanted to do was be under Karlos. Y'all remember how much me and Karlos were obsessed with each other? Well turn it up about 100 notches on my end. This baby had me so emotional when it came to him.

If I wasn't stuffing my face then I was hugging and kissing all on my husband. Oh, that's another thing. I absolutely loved being Karlos wife! Now please don't mistake our lives as perfect. That couldn't be farther from the truth. Sometimes I wanted to punch him or vice versa. But we worked so well together. It's like we are in tuned with each other on every level. But as good as we are together there has been a feeling that I have been having lately. I just can't shake the shit off no matter how hard I try.

When I chose to marry Karlos it felt natural almost like breathing. I never even talked to anyone about these feelings because I can't even form the words to explain. For now, I just wanted to have a stress-free pregnancy. Anyway, his cocky ass was loving me all over him. He told me it felt good for me to be thirsty for him for a change. Smart ass!

I heard our alarm alert us the front door opened. I knew that was my baby coming home with my food. I left out the nursey and walked down stairs. I had just turned 5-months and in three days we find out what we are having. As long as I was not having twins I was cool with whatever sex the baby was. Karlos wanted a boy! He talked shit all day and said he could only make boys. His ass claimed he couldn't handle a girl.

"Ky why the hell are you walking down the stairs? You know I would have brought your food to you." He put his car keys in our bowl we had by the door. Sitting our food on the table he hugged me. He smelled so good as I closed my eyes and take in his scent.

"You missed daddy baby? Was I gone too long for you?" he whispered in my ear. Not even wanting to give him the satisfaction I rolled my eyes and grabbed my food.

"Imma take the eye roll as a yes," he said as he grabbed his bag of food and drink. I smirked and started eating. That was pretty much the only time I was not all over my husband. Sitting on the couch I felt some eyes on me. I turned and Karlos was muggin' me. I shook my head and smiled while leaning over and kissing him.

"Thank you for my food baby and your right. I did miss you." He smiled big and we ate while watching TV. I don't know if I am the only pregnant person that does this. But my movie that I have to watch every day is Look Who's Talking. I laugh and cry at this old ass movie.

"You ready to find out what we are having baby?" I asked him while getting up to throw our trash away. That food was bomb but once I burped I know I will be hungry again. Walking back to our living room I set between Karlos legs. He started rubbing my belly.

"Hell yea I'm ready! I need my boy to flash that Royal dick so you can start buyin' some blue shit." We both started laughing. Laying there watching TV both of us fell asleep for about an hour. When I woke up Karlos was still sleep looking so sexy. I snuck some kisses in on his soft ass big lips. He does this to me all the time so it felt good to get him back. But his eyes popped open as soon as I was getting my second kiss in.

"You tryna be on some creep shit? Come here." He

pulled me up with his strong arms and kissed me. Our tongues made out together and my hormones kicked in right away. While we were making out the doorbell rang.

"Who the fuck is fuckin' up my nut! Hold on baby let me get rid of whoever this is." I sat up so he could stand to his feet and get the door. When Karlos opened it, I heard Kaylin and Kelly at the door. They had been in Paris for three months and came back two days ago.

"There is my pregnant big sister." Kelly ran to me after she hugged Karlos. My pregnant ass started crying. Me and my sisters have never been apart from each other for more than a day. I missed the hell out of Kelly.

"Aww stop crying Kylee. I missed you to sister." We hugged again and she bent down and rubbed my belly.

"Hi in their niece or nephew. I love you and I will be your favorite." We both laughed and I hugged her again. After I hugged my brother in-law me and Kelly went up-stairs.

"So, are you next on the pregnant train?" Grabbing my bag of mini Reese's cups and sitting next to her on the love seat we had in our room.

"Please don't say that shit loud. Kaylin might hear you and make me take a test." She shook her head and grabbed one of my Reese's. Annoying!

"Kel if you're not ready for kid's just talk to Kaylin about it. He is your fiancé, he will understand." I stuffed some candy in my mouth.

"I know and I will just not right now. We just had a blast together in Paris I don't want to ruin the mood. But I am on birth control and he doesn't know so don't tell anybody Kylee." I nodded my head and promised not to say anything.

I went to pick up my phone. It was on the charger on top of my pillow. Unplugging it and walking back to sit down I noticed I had a message on Facebook messenger. It was from Tony again. I exit out of it and traded my phone for my candy.

"What's that face for? Who was that?" Kelly asked

trying to get some more of my candy.

"Umm no one. Just someone who liked my picture." I chuckled and turned on the TV hoping my baby sister would not press. A girl can dream.

"Stop lying Kylee your terrible at it. Now who was that? Don't lie." I sighed and spoke.

"It was Tony. He messaged me when I post the picture of me and Karlos on our wedding day. And before you talk shit no he is not on my friends list. And no, I have not been talking to him. I delete his messages." When I looked at my sister he mouth was on the floor.

"Ok there are a million things wrong with all of this. But I'll just give you the first three. Karlos. Karlos. Karlos. Kylee if Karlos finds out he is going to kill Tony and everyone who he has met since birth. The nigga might even go kill the fuckin' doctor who pulled Tony out his mama's pussy. Why haven't you blocked him? Unless—

"No! I do not want Tony. I-I j-just deleted his messages. I didn't think to block him." I kept my head down as the words stuttered out my mouth. Kelly grabbed the candy out my hand and set it on the side of her.

"Kylee talk to me. I know your older but I am smart and I am not going to judge you. We are sisters and I promise this will stay between you and me. Now what's up?" Kelly looked at me and waited for me to talk.

"I don't know what is wrong with me Kelly. I love Karlos with every fiber in my body. After God he comes next. I love our life together and I love how he treats me. Kelly, we are so in tuned with each other we both know when the other is going to say before they say it. But he did cheat on me. I forgave him and had my time to heal but Kel sometimes when I look at him I see Zena. I see her fucking and sucking him. I see him enjoying it while I was somewhere being faithful. I have no feelings for Tony what so ever that's why I have not responded to his messages. I don't know a part of me feel like keeping Tony in the corner just in case. Like I would never be with him but just to boost my ego if---"

I couldn't even finish my sentence. I realized how foolish I sound now that I was saying it out loud. Kelly looked at me with sadness and she hugged me tight. I broke down in her arms and I knew this cry was not because of my pregnancy. She wiped my face and kissed my cheek. I lightly smiled at her. It was nice to see my baby sister comfort me because I was the oldest. I was usually comforting them.

"Kylee, let me tell you what I think. I think you are very smart book and street wise thanks to daddy. You would have NEVER married Karlos no matter how much you love him if you thought he would hurt you again. That's why you couldn't even finish your sentence Kylee. You know how crazy you sound. Sis if you are really feel like you cannot trust Karlos then let's swallow this shit up as a loss and get you a divorce. Of course, we are going to have to hide your ass on a remote island. Because Killz is going to hunt yo' ass down and kill all of us for helping you." We both started laughing and I instantly felt better. My sister was right, I just was afraid. The only thing I need to do is sit down and talk to Karlos about it. Even though I do not have any feelings for Tony. I still do not want anything to happen to him. So on that note, I will not be telling Karlos about the messages. I do however need to block Tony from my Facebook and Instagram. Pulling my phone out I did just that.

"Thank you Kelly I feel so much better. I have been holding this shit in longer than a fart.," I chuckled and shook my head.

"You're welcome big sister. I'm always here, now let's go eat. I know yo' ass is hungry. Practically tore my head off for one tiny ass Reese's cup." We laughed and got up to walk downstairs. My purpose of blocking Tony was to stop any kind of trouble that could await me and especially him. Little did I know nothing was going to stop the shit that was about to rain down on me.

Karlos

I walked my brother and sister in-law to the door. My baby pregnant ass was hungry again so we warmed up all the food she cooked yesterday. Kylee made fried chicken, spaghetti, mixed salad, garlic bread and a caramel cake. I asked her did she want me to warm her up a plate earlier instead of having fast food. She started crying and saying she didn't want those nasty leftovers. Now a half an hour later her ass was smashin' the leftovers and damn near the whole cake. My son had my baby eating everything in sight! When she wasn't eating she was all over daddy and I was loving every minute of it.

I never doubted Kylee didn't love me. But let's be honest with the shit and say that my love for her was on another level. I craved the fuck out of that girl all day every day. She was on my mind more than money! There was nothing Kylee could do that would make me leave her or not love her anymore.

Last year I fucked up and cheated on my baby and she found out. My stupid ass actions crushed her and myself in the process. When Kylee found out she erased her entire existence from me. Her ass moved, changed her number and left school. I did everything in my power to find her and I couldn't. I was so lost without my baby I stooped to a low that I didn't even knew existed. Ok I'm done talking about that shit! On to the present Kylee forgave me months later and became my wife. Now she is about to have my baby boy and I could not be happier. The only thing that would make this perfect is if my parents were here.

My pops and mama were murdered last year by my pops bitch ass half-brothers. Shit fucked me and my brothers up real bad and had my ass locked up in my crib for a month.

Me and my brothers handled them bitches the best way we knew how. Avenging my parent's deaths felt good as hell but what I really loved was killing that bitch Zena. That's the hoe I cheated on Kylee with last year. I didn't have feelings for her or nothing. She just caught a nigga slippin' one night high off some good weed and drunk off that that dark shit. Well that hoe was fucking my uncle Ricky and got knocked up by his ass. Between me and you, Zena was going to die either way. After I nutted on that bitch face I knew I was going to kill her. She would have always been a walking reminder of what I did to Kylee. Before we tracked my punk ass uncles down I had already killed her entire family. Call me crazy but I warned that bitch! I told her if she ran her mouth I would kill her and everyone she knew.

I didn't stop at her family either. I killed that rat ass bitch she was always hanging with. I know y'all think I'm crazy as hell. But obviously y'all love a nigga or Londyn wouldn't have wrote this part 2! Anyways after I put all them six-feet under I came home and got my baby back. Kylee was dating some flake ass dread head. They didn't fuck but he took her out and they kissed. Shit pissin' me off even thinkin' about it so you know I put a hot one in him. Once I got my baby back three months later we got married.

I have no idea why God felt I was worthy of something so beautiful inside and out. But I loved him even more for making her for me. I was so connected to this woman the shit didn't make no damn sense. I even knew when her fuckin' period was about to come on. My fucking stomach would hurt as if I bled every month! That's how I knew some shit has been off with her for a few weeks now. I knew it was not pregnant related because I kept all her cravings within her reach. And she never had to go a day without being under me.

If Kylee wanted to lay in bed and cuddle all day we could. If she wanted to watch that girly ass Sex in the City shit she loved all day we would do it. Anything my baby wanted she could all ways get from me and she knew that shit. The only thing I wanted from Kylee was her heart. As long as I had that I could breath and continue being in this fucked up ass world.

I was downstairs cleaning up the kitchen while my baby took her shower. I made sure Kylee didn't have to stay on her feet all day. She was mad as hell at me when I told her to put her time off in from her job. She was working at this publishing company called Ink. After she graduated I was so proud of my wife. I told Kylee I would buy her a whole building so she could start her own publishing business. My pops always told me to be your own boss. But Kylee wanted to get some experience first. She told me Ink was one of the best publishing companies in Louisiana. Her boss loved Kylee so much they set it up so she could work from home. I turned one of the bedrooms into an office for her. Happy wife happy life!

Once I was done cleaning up the kitchen I straightened up the living room and secured our house. Walking up the stairs I could hear Kylee rappin' along to Drake- Passionfruit. I was sick and muthafuckin' tied of that nigga. When I reached our bedroom, my mood changed when I saw my wife pretty ass. She was sitting up with her back against the headboard and her laptop on her lap.

When she looked up and saw me she smiled showin' them deep ass dimples. *My fuckin' Ky.* I smiled back at her and started taking off my clothes so I could take a quick shower. Ass naked and walking into our bathroom I always laughed to myself. Kylee designed our bathroom peach and gold. The shit looked fit for a king and queen I just wasn't a peach nigga but what baby wants baby gets. The hot water felt good as hell when it hit me. reaching for my shampoo so I could wash my hair I realized I was out.

"Fuck!" I said out loud with frustration. I knew I would have to use some of Kylee fruity shit. I don't fuck around about my hair being clean. I would just have to suck the shit up and do a Walmart run tomorrow. We had a 24-hour

Walmart but if I tried to leave this house tonight my wife would start crying.

After my shower, I dried off and hung my towel back up. Walking out the bathroom still naked Kylee looked up at me and her eyes traveled to my dick. My shit was hangin' like Mr. Cooper and her eyes lit up. I smirked at her sexy ass makin' her blush and look back at her laptop. She didn't even have to say shit. I was dickin' her down tonight after we talk. Drying my hair off I went to my drawer and grabbed some boxer briefs.

Kylee hated the smell of my Old Spice deodorant so I had to switch to Degree. Finally done I climbed in to bed and turned on the TV. She rolled her eyes and turned Drake off on her laptop. I knew that would make her turn his wack ass off. Funny thing is I fucked with Drake music but knowing my wife was crushing on him made me hate his ass. Kylee worked for about twenty more minutes while I watched Power since she already saw it. She would have cussed my yellow ass out if I watched an episode without her.

"You still have not seen this episode baby?" she asked as she closed her laptop. I shook my head no. Once Kylee put her laptop on the night stand she laid under me. Instantly Power was no longer interesting to me. I turned it on NFL Network and put the remote on the night stand. Looking down at my pretty ass wife I pulled her up and kissed her. Y'all know I hate that peck shit. After she pulled away I looked in those big brown pretty eyes.

"You know I love you so much baby. Right? You know how happy I am with you as my wife?" I had my hand on the side of her face. Kylee nodded yes but looked down. See that shit right there! She never did that shit before. Kylee would look in my eyes like she was searching for a lie. Then she would look down or away as if she didn't believe what the fuck I said. Enough is enough of this bullshit!

"What's up with you Ky? Some shit is off with you lately and it's not the baby." I grabbed her chocolate ass up. I made her straddle me as I sat up in the bed with my back against the headboard. Kylee soft skin felt good as hell on my skin. My baby kept her head down and would not look at me.

"Ky all you gotta do is tell daddy what's wrong so I can fix it. If shit is not right with me and you then that means I won't breath right. Not breathing right means I won't think right and that's a lot of bloodshed." Please talk to me baby." We looked at each other and for once she didn't look away.

"I don't know what is wrong with me lately. It's like this pregnancy does have me hormonal and greedy. But I don't think it has me wanting to be up under you the way I have been." She put her head down and tears fell from her eyes. Hell no!

"Karlos I forgave you when you cheated on me and we have moved on from it. The best decision I ever made was becoming your wife. I just feel like the happier I get and comfortable I get with you the more scared I get. You came into my life and made me fall in love with in a matter of weeks. I got comfortable and thought things were ok but you cheated. Now it's like I'm pregnant, gaining weight and emotional all at once. It's making it hard to think you won't stray off again." Kylee tears were falling down her face back to back. The shit had me fucked up on the inside. Never in a million fuckin' years I would've thought she felt this way.

Not being able to see my baby cry I grabbed her and hugged her tight. We sat in silence for a few minutes while I hugged her like a newborn. Even though Kylee was a grown ass woman in every sense. She still was my baby and I was her protector. I thought about what I did last year a few times. I always caught myself because I never wanted to feel down about something she forgave me for. But I feel if you truly love someone you would never hurt them. When I told Kylee, I would spend the rest of my life making up for what I did. I meant that shit and I tried to do it every day. I guess maybe me trying too hard to not fuck up was makin' me fuck up either way I needed to fix this shit with my wife.

"Kylee look at me." She pulled slowly away from me and looked in my eyes. This girl had the most gorgeous face I ever seen. Every fuckin' thing was perfect in its place from her forehead size. To her ears and pretty ass nose. Those big, brown pretty eyes which lit up whenever she was excited about some shit. Then those sexy ass lips that moved out the way to reveal her white straight teeth when she smiled. Oh, and how the fuck could I forget them dimples. Them fuckin' dimples! They were so deep and placed perfectly on her face. And whoever the fuck said chocolate girls not winnin' is a fuckin' dummy. Kylee skin reminded me of a Hershey's bar and a nigga had a sweet tooth. Ok let me focus on the damn matter at hand because I could go on and on about my wife.

"I apologize for inflicting this pain on you. I honestly didn't know you felt this way baby. I don't think about the fact that the shit is forgiven but not forgotten. The only way I can fix this is to continue to do what I been doing. I'm going to tell you some shit you probably have heard from other people. But now you can hear it from my mouth." My eye contact was intense as I stared into her eyes. I wanted her to feel my words and know I was spitting' was straight facts.

"When you left me Kylee I drove to you old condo every night hoping I would catch you there. Even though I knew you had moved it was still your last home. Your sisters were still staying there and I thought I would eventually see you. I went to every condo and apartment building I thought you would have moved to. I even went to your pops and talked to him. The knowledge yo' pops dropped on me made me respect him more. I was a fuckin' reck without you baby to the point my parents had to step in. My pops and mama told me to give you some space. They said I had nobody to blame but myself for you leavin' me. At the time, I was not trying to hear shit. I was being selfish and wanted you back for me. I never even thought about the shit you were going through. Someone who you thought loved you and would never hurt you did. Kylee, I didn't make you my wife just to trap you. I asked you to be my wife because you are the other half of me baby. I have NEVER wanted anybody else but you. It took you to leave me to know this shit. I mean like really know that I do not want to exist without you. Baby I promise I will never hurt you ever again. I can only show through my actions that I can keep this promise. Please try to believe me Kylee and know I need you baby. I ain't scared to say that shit out loud. I fuckin' need you all day every day even after death." I grabbed her pretty ass face and kissed her deep as hell. I needed her to feel a niggas soul, heart and everything was hers. All of my yellow ass belonged to my wife.

"You can come to me about anything baby. No matter what it is I will try my best to fix it. Please don't keep shit from me Kylee. You're my wife and I don't want secrets between us." I rubbed the side of her face and her bottom lip.

"Anything else you feeling baby?" I waited for her to answer. I did not want her bottling anything else in. I wanted her and my baby boy happy and at peace. Kylee bit the side of her lip and shook her head no. Now I could have pressed on that I knew she was lying. But I did not want to add more pressure to her. This was going to fuck with me because Kylee was keepin' shit from me. Suddenly my mama's words came to my head. I need to stop focusing on me and give Kylee some space. My baby knows I am here whenever she wanted to talk to me.

"I love you Kylee. I swear there is nothing I wouldn't do for you. Believe that shit wife." She smiled so big at me showing those deep dimples. Makin' a niggas heart pound fast as hell. Her eyes stayed locked on mines. Kylee didn't look away not once. It made me feel good as hell.

"I love you more my Los. I will always love you baby and I don't regret becoming your wife. Sometimes I just get in my feelings." I was done talking. I needed to physically show my wife how much I love her. Over my dead body was I ever losing her again!

*

So, you think Kylee is hiding something from you?" my baby brother Kalvin asked me.

"Hell yea she is and it's pissin' me the fuck off. My wife knows she can talk to me about any fucking thing. I looked at her face and could tell she was holding back something." I threw the body down on the concrete. We were in the basement of the funeral home we owned. Me, Kalvin and two of or workers were down there as well.

"I think maybe you are being paranoid nigga. You fucked up last year bad as hell but she forgave you. Not only did she forgive you, she became your wife. You know Kylee is not a fuckin' door mat. Hell, her sisters ain't either." I heard every word my baby brother just said to me. I went and grabbed the saw from shelf on the wall. Bending down I began cutting the body up. This was my favorite part of being a savage. Killing a muthafucka always made me feel good. I always killed with a purpose so I never felt guilty.

"Sam was one of the guys that just got put on the money team last year. Why the fuck are you sawin' his ass up?" Kalvin asked as he gave me some trash and Ziploc bags.

"The nigga was picked up by the police. He said some shit he shouldn't have and thought I wouldn't find out. Stupid ass forgot we got boys on the inside. I personally wanted to pop this fool and saw him up. Plus, I need a stress reliever." I was working on cutting Sam's left arm off. Then his torso and legs starting at the knees. I loved the sound of bones cracking. The skin and tissue made squishy sounds when the saw cut it. A person with a weak stomach could not handle seeing so much blood. My ass loved it! I should have gone in the medical field but then I wouldn't be able to kill.

"You are a fuckin' lunatic bro. If you were not my brother I would have yo' ass committed to a physic ward." I looked up at my brother and smiled at his funny ass statement. I was far from crazy. Now it was time to separate Sam's head from his neck.

"Aye you know I am about to open up this gym next

week. I just designed the website for it. Shit looks dope bro." I felt my chest sticking out. Y'all know a nigga loved computer shit and making money. Everybody was into working out lately so I decided to open a gym. Ripped is what I named my gym. My ass was excited about this new money in the bank venture.

"That's what's up bro. See, look at all this good shit around you. And here yo' ass come stressin' because you think Kylee is being secretive. Tomorrow you find out if you are having a mini you. Count yo' blessings bro." I nodded my head at my brother statement. He was right, maybe I did need to chill out. I was beyond blessed and I didn't even deserve it.

Finishing up sawing Sam black ass up I stood to my feet. I bagged all the body parts up except his head. I put that in the giant Ziploc bag and gave it to one of our workers.

"Aye go give this to Sam bitch at his crib. That hoe about due maybe this will make her water break."

"On it boss." Me and Kalvin left the other workers to handle the other body parts. I took my gloves and my disposal hazmat suit off. I threw it all in the ~~boiler~~broiler and burned it along with my black shoes. After getting dressed me and Kalvin walked outside towards my truck.

"I know you geeked as hell about tomorrow my nigga. I know I was nervous as hell when me and Keira found out what we were having," Kalvin said as he opened the passenger door and got in.

"Naw I'm good bro I don't get nervous about shit. I already know it's a mini me in Kylee's stomach. I keep tellin' y'all I don't make girls." I started my Escalade up and pulled off.

"Nigga how the fuck do you know what you can make? This yo' first kid fuck boy! All the shit yo' ass been talkin' I bet money yo' punk ass have a girl." With humor in his voice Kalvin lit a blunt and took a puff.

"Ok bitch let's bet $500 I have a boy," I said while Kalvin passed me the blunt. We agreed and cracked jokes on the way to drop him off. Lil nigga talked royal shit I was going to enjoy takin' his money.

*

Nervous was just one of many of the emotions I was feeling. Anxious and excitement were a few more. Me and Kylee were in the waiting room of Touro Infirmary Hospital. I was rubbing Kylee's round belly while she murdered some cherries.

"Kylee Royal." We both looked up at the short white nurse with the clip board. Me and Kylee stood up hand in hand and followed the nurse in the back.

"Room 3 is all set up for you. Get undressed and put the gown on and the doctor will be in with you in few." The nurse smiled at us and closed the door. I watched Kylee take her clothes off and I had to remember where we were. Even though my baby boy was rounding her stomach up, Kylee's body was still a work of art.

"Don't look at me like that Karlos. We are in a doctor's office and she can come in at any minute," Kylee said to me with a sexy smirk on her face. I bit my lip as I eyed her sexy ass body. I helped her put the gown on and helped her get comfortable on the bed.

"I'm sorry baby but you know I cannot resists your body. You carrying my son make me love you even more if that's even possible. Thank you Kylee for everything baby like for real you are life to me." I was sitting in the chair next to the hospital bed holding her hand as I talked to her. Kylee sensitive ass smiled at me big with teary eyes. I leaned forward and kissed her soft ass lips. I got lost every time I kissed my wife. The feel of our tongues swirling around in each other's mouths made my dick hard.

"Stop Karlos before you get some shit started you can't finish." Before I could get in her ass a light knock came on the door. Kyle's doctor walked in smiling as she closed the door. I had already told my wife she better get a female doctor. Wasn't no man about to look up my wife's pussy.

"Hello my beautiful Royal family. How is everything?" she asked as she took a seat on the rolling stool by Kylee's stomach.

"Everything is fine Dr. Raju. I'm just eating everything under the sun." I chuckled at Kyle's confession to the doctor. My baby was eating like crazy. But as long as her and my son were healthy I was cool with it. I didn't give a fuck if she got as big as a house. I would love every pound of her chunky ass.

"That's normal for your appetite to increase. You and the baby are doing excellent and I have no concerns of your eating. You are well aware of what you should and should not be eating. Now, for the fun part! Let's see what we are having." I couldn't help but smile big ass hell. I was about to see my son reveal his gender. I kissed Kyle's had the whole time as the doctor put that jelly shit on her stomach. Turning the machine on Dr. Raju looked at us and said.

"What are we hoping for?" she asked while putting the transducer on Kyle's belly.

"I just want a healthy baby," Kyle answered then she pointed at me.

"But he swears up and down that we are having a boy." I nodded my head while still kissing Kyle's hand.

"Well a healthy baby is already without a doubt. Baby is doing fine and growing very well." Dr. Raju printed us out some pictures of our baby's head, arms and legs.

"Looks like baby Royal is being stubborn and not opening its legs. I am going to aggravate the baby just to get it to move around. Hopefully baby opens them legs." She smiled at us and started moving Kyle's belly around with her hand. I sat up and kept my eyes glued on the screen but still holding my wife's hand.

"Oh my God!" Kylee shouted with joy in her voice.

"Wait a minute is that a----"

"Yes it is dad! Looks like you two are having a little princess." Dr. Raju beamed at us. Kylee was crying hard as hell.

"Hell naw man! I can't believe God gave my ass a girl." I didn't even mean to be that loud as I started laughing and clapping my hands. My eyes still did not leave that screen until I heard Kylee sniffle.

"Come here baby." I went to my wife and kissed all on her salty face. I hugged and kissed my baby.

"Yo ass dun gave me a girl! You know I'm already crazy as hell when it comes to you. Now I will have two of you. I'm going overseas to get all kinds of weapons now!" Me and Kyle laughed as I kissed her again. I kept thanking her and telling her how much I love her and our daughter. Wow! I'm having a fucking daughter!

Kalvin and Keira

"Hell yea bitch! Run me my fuckin' 5 Franklin's nigga! Told yo' dumb ass you were having a girl!" I was on the phone with Karlos. This nigga called me ready to cry and shit because he was having a girl. Told this fool to shut the hell up talkie' shit. God gave that nigga exactly what he needed. If he would have had a boy his ass would have had a junior savage. Naw, my big bro needs to calm down. This was what he needed. Just my opinion. I chopped it up with him for a minute then hung up. I was pulling in my driveway coming from Toys R' Us. My stuff I ordered arrived today and I went to pick it up. I couldn't wait to see my munchkin's face glow when she sees what daddy got her. I had to make two trips from my hummer to the house.

Walking to our living room I set the big boxes in the living room. Every time I stepped in our living room I smiled. I purchased this bad ass cherry brick home for my bae. I knew once Keira met my parents that I wanted to be with her forever. The way my mama took to her made me happy as hell. I miss my mama and pops every day and it killed me that they will never meet Kyra. I swear if it wasn't for my wife and daughter I don't know how I could function. Back to what I was saying. I brought Keira to this house the day after I brought it.

It was empty as hell just waiting for my baby to decorate it. The 5 bed bedrooms were waiting for us to fill them with kids. When we pulled up Keira looked at the house in awe. We walked around the back yard and she lost it. My bae fell in love with the pool, patio and the gazebo with wooden swing I had built. We walked in the inside and I took her to each room. Even the finished basement and my man cave. Once I was done giving my bae the tour I dropped to my knees and told Keita that this house was all hers.

I told her it came with me and a lifetime of happiness. All she had to do was put this ring on her finger. My Ke broke down and said yes making me the happiest nigga ever. We eloped that night in Vegas. Our families were not happy with us doing that but with time they forgave us. Now we both are still going strong and my boo blessed me with our baby girl. Kyra Stella Royal made me experience a new type of love. I never wanted to protect someone so much.

While in the same breath wanting to give them the world and protect them from it. That's why I am happy Karlos was having a girl. Watching this nigga do soft shit was going to be so funny. Picture Karlos crazy ass having tea parties and playing dress up. Kylee already had him in a trance. His daughter was going to be ten times worse with him. I know I was going to do it all with Kyra if she wanted me to.

Walking in our master bedroom Keira was sitting on the couch we had in our room. Kyra was laying in her arms eating from Keira's breast. They both looked beautiful as hell. The sight of them made me stick my chest out with pride. This was my beautiful family. I walked to our bathroom and washed my hands and took my shirt off. My wife had hand soap and hand sanitizer all through our house. You could not even say hi to Kyra unless your hands were clean. After I washed up I turned the bathroom light off and walked out.

"Hey baby. Where did you sneak off to this morning?" Keira asked while she eased Kyra off her breast. She put Kyra on her shoulder and began patting her back to burp her.

"I had to pick up some stuff for Kyra." Keira started laughing at me. I had become so obsessed with buying our daughter shit every fucking day.

"Bae, she does not need anything else. You have already set her up until her sixteenth birthday." Just as I was about to respond Kyra let out the loudest burp. Me and Keira twisted our faces up and laughed.

"Yo what the hell is in that titty milk you feedin' my munchkin? Got her burpin' like she just finished a 40." I was cracking my own self up. Keira walked over to our bed and laid Kyra on her pink donut pillow. She walked over to me and put her arms around my neck. I returned the affection and wrapped my arms around her waist. My hands automatically went down to her round ass. Keira's shape was slim thick with a round ass and flat stomach. Her body bounced back like a fuckin' ball off a wall.

"I missed you bae love. Don't be leaving me in that big bed anymore." I bit my bottom lip and looked at my fine ass wife. Gripping her ass in both my hands I brought my lips to hers. Her warm ass tongued danced with mines. My bae breath always was on point which made me never want to end our kissing.

"Come on and show me the damage you have done now." I turned her loose and grabbed her hand leading her downstairs.

"Oh my goodness Kalvin Shamar Royal! What the hell is a four-month-old going to do with all of this?" Keira looked at the boxes and shook her head.

"Bae before you know it Kyra will be running around the house and playing with all of this." Shit I was proud I had the bread to spoil my wife and munchkin. There was nothing that I would ever deny my ladies.

"Bae love I feel where you're comin' from but bae look around. You have become obsessed. A pink Hummer power wheel truck. A Blu-ray DVD player and a 55-inch TV. You are insane." Keira laughed at my ass while looking at the Hummer box.

"You just gone crack jokes on your husband like that? You supposed to love yo' nigga for better or worse." I faked looking sad so she could feel bad.

"Aww come here bae love." Keira poked her lip out and walked towards me hugging me.

"I do love you for better or worse. But bae you are crazy for buying a four-month-old all this shit." We both laughed and I kissed her.

"I made you a plate it's I the microwave." See this is the shit I love about my wife. Beyond keeping me happy and complete. She also kept my stomach full of good food. After warming my plate up, she sat the food in front of me. My bae cooked blueberry pancakes, eggs with hash browns and turkey bacon. I don't fuck with the swine.

"Thank you bae this shit looks bomb as fuck." I said my grace and wasted no time digging in. Keira set a cup of orange juice in front of me. While I was eating she sat in on the stool in front of me. I know this was some weird shit but I loved when Keira watched me eat. Don't know why or have a reason the shit was just so cute to me.

After I murdered my food I downed the cold orange juice I cleaned up my mess. Walking in the living room Keira was staring at the baby monitor looking at Kyra. My bae was just as obsessed with Kyra as I was. Keira was sitting on our giant suede bean bag. This big ass thing cost $400.00 but like I said earlier. I would never deny Keira of shit. She wanted it; she got it without question. I plopped down next to her turning so her ass was pressed on my dick.

"Bae love I have something I want to talk to you about," Keira said while biting her nails. Even though she kept her nails done like clock works she still bit them when she was nervous. I don't know why she was nervous when Keira knew she could ask me anything.

"What's up bae?" I asked while kissing her neck to calm her nerves.

"So, me and Kelly want to open a braid shop. Like any kind of braids you can think of including dreads and locs." I looked at Keira's face beam and she talked about her and Kelly's business. Lately Kelly and Keira had been braiding their friend's hair a lot. I thought the shit was just a hobby. Keira and Kelly both graduated from college with bachelor degrees in social work. But seeing my bae's face light up. Knowing how good her and Kelly's braid skills are I figured why not. Call me petty but one thing did hit my dome.

"You said all braids. So, that means if a nigga walks in your shop wanting his hair braided then what?" The look Keira gave me said it all. She must have lost her fuckin' mind.

"Ke please don't play with me. You and you hot ass twin sister want to open up a shop and braid hair. Have you fuckin' seen you and your twin. Nigga's gone be growin' hair on their heads just for the fuck of it." My nostrils flared and she put her soft hands on the side of my face. Damn her touch.

"Kalvin this is something that me and Kelly really want to do. I know we both have degrees in social work. But this shop will be such a success and our looks won't have anything to do with it. We both are going to go to Vanguard College of Cosmetology and get licensed. Kalvin, I am not letting something so petty as nigga clients stop me you need to get out your feelings." She rolled her eyes at me and went back to watching TV. That shit pissed me off.

"Keira, you are my wife and you are not braiding nigga's hair. What about childcare for Kyra? There is no way in hell she is going to a day care. Just so her mama can braid nigga's dick hairs." As soon as the stupid shit left my mouth I regretted it. Keira got up with a scowl look on her face.

"Fuck you Kalvin. I am doing this with or without your support. And as far as Kyra goes, just know she will be fine." Keira turned on her heels and walked up stairs.

I knew I had hurt my wife with my smart-ass comment. I just was not ok with her braiding niggas hair. As much as I wanted to go after her I had business to take care of. Kevin decided he wanted to make me a partner in his barber shop, Royal Trim. Since cutting hair was a side hustle I was good at, I figured why not. We were interviewing new barbers today and I needed to get up to the shop. I will for sure be linking up with Kaylin later today. I know he ain't about to let Kelly braid niggas hair.

I parked my silver Bentley GT in the parking lot of Royal Trim. Royal treatment was what you thought if you came to a shop with this title. But that was the complete opposite when you stepped in the shop. Don't get shit twisted you were going to walk out with top of the line service. But the inside was not like any other barber shop. Stepping in the shop the color scheme was midnight blue and silver checker pattern.

There were search lights on the ceiling and mirrors all on the wall. Kevin had a 75-inch TV on the wall and two poles by the DJ booth for Friday's. We had vending machines, a full bar and two glass pool tables. Shit felt like you were at a kick back instead of a barber shop. But because of our name Kevin pulled in bank every week. Even though he had an accountant to handle his books. He still wanted me to handle them which resulted in me becoming a partner.

I went to barber school with Kevin and got licensed but it was just a side hustle. I started enjoying the shit and Kevin gave me my own chair. Now a year later shit is still poppin'. We had to let two barbers go because they were stealing money and supplies. And them fools were selling weed like we would not find out. We had to fire they asses and send a message to people. Damn shame they had to cut their lives short at 23.

"What's good bro!" Kevin yelled over ESPN playing on the TV. Never taking his eyes off the dude whose hair he was lining up. Bro had mad skills and stayed booked.

"What up nigga! What up Nick. What's good with you Bari, Dru my nigga what's poppin'." I dabbed my brother up and the rest of the barbers who were working. I went over to my chair and set down. I didn't have any appointments today and there was no one waiting on a cut.

"Aye so how many people are we interviewing?" I asked while playing Temple Run on my phone.

"Shit Melissa said she set up five for today. I'm hoping

out of the five we at least get one we can the payroll," Kevin said as he brushed the hair of his customer.

"Aye so listen to this crazy shit. Keira tells me that her and Kelly want to start a business. Now I'm all for giving my wife what she wants. But the business they want to start is a braid shop." My brother and boys looked at me like I had spiders in my head.

"Nigga how is that crazy shit? Keira and Kelly got mad skills! The money train gone roll right the fuck in. Ya' feels me?" Kevin joked while dabbing Dru up.

"Nigga, they not just doing them Beyoncé braids. They talkin' about doing all kinds of braids. Meaning niggas can come in to and get there shit braided. No fuckin' way is Keira braiding niggas hair. They already bad as hell and their twins. That shit alone gone have niggas growin' hair any way they can. Just so they can thirst for my wife! Fuck'outta here with all that crazy shit. Y'all know damn well my reason for trippin' is legit." I felt like a pouting child but I didn't give a fuck. I was right about this shit.

"Man, you sound like a legit bitch! Is your last name Royal or not bro. Where the fuck this insecure shit come from. You right, yo wife is lit as fuck. Shit her sister, my wife, is bad as fuck to. But I would never let my own insecurities get in the way of Kimmora's dream. Like fa'real fool you straight trippin'. Keira don't trip on you go to Royal and work. Our fuckin' club is crawlin' with naked bitches. Them thirsty hoes dick ride us like a mechanical bull. But Ke never gave you a problem about that shit. Plus, nigga her and Kelly got mad skills braiding. I know you want them to stop settin' up shop at yo crib." Kevin gave me and earful. He got up and grabbed a Pepsi out the vending machine.

"I don't know man. I gotta think about this shit. I know I would grow my hair out if some fine ass twins would be braidin' my shit. I will fuckin' lose it if I see niggas flirtin' with my wife." Kevin and the fellas laughed and shook their heads at me.

"Mr. Royal your 1'o clock will be here in ten minutes," Melissa said walking towards the bathroom. All the guys drooled over her because she was thick as hell. Melissa was a plus size girl but it was all in the right place. Now even though I'm married I am a man first. I must admit that in my single days. Melissa squishy ass could get the goods from me.

"Let's take this shit to the office." Kevin suggested. We got up and walked to the office in the back. It was a huge ass room with a blue steel round table and silver steel chairs. I turned the 55-inch TV off that was mounted on the wall. We used this room as a break room as well. There was a stainless-steel refrigerator in there. The shit stayed stocked with food.

I went to the fridge and grabbed a few bottles of water and set them in the middle of the table. Kevin was making sure the place was clean and the bathroom was on point.

"I'm ready to get this shit over with. I hate having two empty chairs in the shop. Good lookin' out bro on becoming a partner with me if anything, I always trust my brothers," Kevin said while sitting next to me at the round table. We slapped our hands together and I kissed his forehead. Feel how the fuck you wanna feel but me and my brothers loved each other.

"Shit you know I got you bro. Thanks for the words you dropped out there. I gotta think about this shit with Keira. I said some stupid shit and pissed her off before I came here. I gotta fix this shit soon as I get home." I meant what I said. I never wanted Keira mad at me it's just I felt strongly about this.

"Yea bro get yo' shit in check and make your wife happy," Kevin said while texting. This goofy nigga was smiling big as hell. So I knew he was texting Kimmora. It made me want to hit Keira up but I knew she wouldn't respond. I tried my luck anyways and texted her I love you.

Putting my phone back in my pocket the office door slowly opened. Melissa walked in with her face red. I figured it was because her and Nick were flirting like always. I don't know why they wouldn't just hook up already. Me and Kevin didn't give a fuck as long as drama was not brought here.

"All your interviewees are in the waiting area. Taylor Hamilton is up first." Melissa moved and let in the first candidate. Had my wife not already had the throne this bitch would be in the spot. She was fine as hell and thick as fuck. I know my brother could not deny how bad she was. Melissa nodded at us and closed the door.

"Nice to meet you Taylor. I'm Kevin and this is my brother Kalvin Royal. We both are the owners." She shook his hand smiling then she shook mines. Her skin was soft as hell and the color of honey.

"Nice to meet you both as well. I am a little nervous but thank you for the opportunity." She smiled them full lips showed her white straight teeth. Taylor had brown almond shape eyes. They stood out because her hair was jet black and stopped at her shoulders. We took a seat and she set across from us. Finally, I had to open my mouth as speak.

"Do you have a resume or portfolio?" I asked her. She smiled and answered yes while giving us the folder in her hand. Kevin looked at her resume and I looked at her pictures of her work. Shorty was bad as hell with clippers. She did line-ups, designs, trimmed bears. You name it shorty did it. Me and Kevin switched and I read her resume. I saw that she was from Washington D.C.

"So, what brought you to Louisiana?" I asked her while looking at her resume. As she was about to speak I looked up at her. Our eyes connected and for a second I was lost and she was too.

"Umm well I stayed with my aunt and uncle from middle school until now. Me and my parents did not get along and the move was best. I have always loved cutting hair so I went and got licensed. I missed home and my parents so I came back. I saw your profile on Facebook and started following. Then I saw you post the help wanted and it seemed destined." As she spoke her words her eyes never left mines. I was stuck and so was she. I felt a hard kick on my foot and I snapped out of it. Kevin kicked my foot and when I looked at him he had a grim look he was giving me. I cleared my throat and tried to play it off.

"Well your resume is good as hell and your portfolio is even better. How would you like to do a three-day trial here? You could get a feel of the shop and see if you like it. Because you are new you should post your work on the shop's Instagram page. That will get you some clientele and some followers." Kevin told her and her face beamed with happiness. She pulled her Galaxy S8 out and went to Instagram. Taylor and Kevin added her pictures on the shop's page and I could not keep my eyes off her. After they were done we talked a little more than we wrapped it up.

"Well Taylor it was nice meeting you and we will see you tomorrow." We all stood up and shook hands again. Once again, her soft as skin rubbed against mines.

"What does everyone call you bosses?" She smiled and looked at both of us.

"You can call us Kalvin and Kevin. None of that formal shit here unless you hear Melissa call us Mr. Royal. She goes back and forth but our first names are cool." I responded and at that moment I realized I was biting my bottom lip. She noticed it to because she blushed and looked at my lips.

"Ok well I will see you two tomorrow Kalvin and Kevin." Taylor smiled and walked towards the door. Me and my brother could not help but look at her big ass booty in some True Religions. When the door closed and she was gone I felt like I snapped out of her trance.

"Nigga you need to breath and control yourself. What the fuck was that Kalvin? You and her eyed each other like y'all wanted to fuck on the table." Kevin went and set back down at the table.

"Bro I don't fuckin' know what the fuck that was. I think I was just caught in lust for a second. But on the real Kevin, she bad as fuck." I laughed and so did Kevin. I knew his ass could not deny that.

"I ain't gone lie shorty is bad as shit. Did you see her ass in them jeans? Dammnn! She will get high clientele from that ass alone." We both fell out laughing.

Yea Taylor had it but if she was my woman she would have to pick another line of work. Niggas most definitely be drooling all over her. Keira came to my mind and the shit pissed me off. No way in fucks hell was this braid shop happening. We finished the rest of the interviews and found another potential employee. Thank God it was a nigga.

I left Royal Trim and headed to the florist shop. I wanted to pick Keira up some flowers and apologize to her for how I reacted. The little flirt shit that happened between me and Taylor sealed my decision. Keira was not opening a braid shop I just had to find a respectful way of telling her.

<u>Keira</u>

"Wait a damn minute. Kalvin really hit the ceiling when you told him about the braid shop?" Kelly asked me while she held Kyra. She came over to chill with me and her niece. I loved all my sisters to death. But me and Kelly were twins so the connection was a little deeper.

"Yes twin. He all the way tripped out on me like I didn't even recognize him. Kalvin has always been so supportive of everything I wanted to do.

"I cannot believe sweet Kalvin can be such an ass. Well I am on your side and if you want to move forward then we will. Registration for school is next week and we can go together." Kelly was talking to me but she was looking at Kyra. My twin eyes lit up whenever she saw Kyra as if she was hers.

"You must be ready to have one because you look at Kyra like she is yours. You and Kaylin would be great parents." I smiled at her and her smile disappeared.

"Umm no I am not ready for this. Kyra is just so beautiful and she reminds me of us when we were little. The pictures daddy has of us looks like we could be triplets." I looked at my munch and smiled. She was gorgeous and a spitting image of me and Kelly. Looking up at Kelly she had tears in her eyes.

"What's wrong Kelly? Why are you crying? Does Kaylin not want to have kids Kelly? You know you can tell me?" I had tears in my eyes seeing my twin cry.

"It's not Kaylin, it's me. I don't want kids Keira." She sniffed and wiped her face. Still holding Kyra, she laid her down in her crib. We were in Kyra's room because she woke up crying.

"Well it's not that I don't want kids. I'm just scared as hell to deliver a child. Look what happened to mommy. She died and every day we think about her. Daddy has a sadness in his life since she has been gone. We never had a mother only mother figures. I don't want that to happen to me or any of you. I watch all of you with your babies and I would love to give Kaylin his first child. But Keira I am terrified to give birth." I got off the purple sofa that was in Kyra's room and hugged my twin. I hugged her tight and we cried together. I never even thought of our mother's child birthing problems. I don't think any of us did unless we didn't share it with each other.

"Kelly you cannot think of things like that. Look at things like this. You get to give you children the motherly love we have always wanted. God will give you a healthy pregnancy and a healthy delivery. Don't let fear stop you from living your life twin. Ok? I love you." I smiled at her and hugged her again.

"I love you to twin." Kelly smiled back at me and went to pick Kyra back up. I laughed and shook my head at Kelly. I could tell she is going to have my baby rotten. We chilled and hung out for a few more minutes.

After my sister left I went and played with my munch

for a minute. Then her little chunky butt wanted to eat. I fed her some Gerber spaghetti and green beans with some bananas for dessert. You know her chunky ass ate all three jars then drunk a 4oz juice bottle. Her and Kalvin gave me so much joy. I really did not want this braid shop to mess things up between me and my husband. But I was not about to let this go. I have never given Kalvin any reason not to trust me or think I could not handle myself.

His rude ass comment he said really hurt me and pissed me off at the same time. I put Kyra down for bed in her crib. Turning her baby monitor on I walked to our master bedroom. Looking at my baby on the camera I stripped out of my clothes. Walking to the bathroom I turned on the shower and stepped in.

Lathering my body up with Olay body wash I washed myself from head to toe. I grabbed my Tresemme curly shampoo and washed my hair. Drying off I put Dove Almond lotion all over my body. Yes, I was a Dove girl even down to the deodorant. I put on a tie die muscle tee and a black thong with my pink furry socks.

Walking down stairs I was hungry as hell. I went to the kitchen and turned on the stove. I wanted a bacon burger and I did not feel like going to get one. While my burger cooked I heard the keys in the front door. I rolled my eyes because I knew it was Kalvin I went to the fridge and grabbed a slice of Kraft cheese to put on my burger. Kalvin walked in the kitchen putting the stuff he had on the counter. My back was still to him as I flipped my burger over.

"Hey Keira bae. I got you something," he said to me and I heard him go in a paper bag. I turned around with my arms folded.

"Hi Kalvin." That was all I had for his ass. A simple hi because I still felt some type of way about his behavior earlier. He pulled out a bouquet of red roses and handed them to me. I usually smiled at the sight of roses. Or at the sight of my husband. But material shit or my husband good looks was not a factor. I placed them on the counter and looked at him with my arms back folded.

"Ok Keira look, I fucked up. I shouldn't have said that rude ass shit earlier. I apologize for disrespecting you bae for real. I love you so much and never want you to feel disrespected." I turned around to check on my burger and put the cheese on it. I could feel his eyes on my body manly my ass. I smirked to myself. Turning back around I was right about him eye fucking me. He was biting his lip hard as hell and I swear I saw some drool.

"Kalvin, I was hurt by how you came at me earlier. You fuckin' exploded on me and thought an I love you text would fix shit." I turned back around and took my burger out the pan and put it on a paper towel.

I could smell Kalvin Burberry cologne before I felt his touch. He put his arms around my waist and squeezed tight. I could feel him closing his eyes as he buried his face in my neck. I can't front on how good his embrace felt. My back was to his front and I closed my eyes for a second.

"Bae please forgive me. I am so sorry I never want to hurt you wife. I swear on that shit." He kissed my neck and my ear. My body was giving in on me when them soft lips touched my skin.

"Ok Kalvin just don't do me like that again." My voice was low because he was still kissing my neck and ears.

"Turn the fuck around and kiss your husband bae." I slowly turned around and kissed him like he requested. Kalvin grabbed both my arms and placed them around his neck.

"Put yo hands all over me when you kissin' me Keira. Act like you know." Aggression was all in his voice. He pressed his lips back on mines making me juice up between my legs.

Kalvin reached behind me and turned the stove off. He grabbed both my legs and lifted me up. he set me on the kitchen counter and looked me in my eyes.

"I love you so much Keira." I smiled at his confession and said.

"I love you to bae love." He smiled big at me and kissed me again. I did love him so much. As mad as I was at him Kalvin always will be my weakness. Even though my body was taking over my thinking. We still were going to have a talk later.

Kalvin looked on the counter to make sure Kyra's baby monitor camera was on. Once he saw that it was he bit his lip looking at me. I smirked and pulled his shirt over his head. Anytime we had sex Kalvin liked to be ass naked. No matter where we were he would strip out of everything including his socks. I didn't mind because my bae love body was like a Picasso painting. After I took his shirt off and threw it on the floor.

He undid his pants and took his shoes and socks off. I almost came then and there just looking at him. Naked and dick hard as steel he hurried and peeled my clothes off. Once I was naked Kalvin went straight for my titties. He sucked on them as if he was breast feeding. I knew for a fact milk was coming out but he never cared. Kalvin bit and pulled on my nipples driving me fuckin' wild. My back was arched and legs were wrapped around his waist. His mouth felt so good on my skin my body was on fire.

"I promise when we go up-stairs I am going to lick yo' pussy like a sundae. But right now, I need to feel them walls." As he spoke he was stroking his dick. I felt my juices slide down my leg. Yea Kalvin would get me that fuckin' wet. I nodded at his remark and he slid his dick in making me gasp. We both paused and took in the moment. Kalvin thick 10-inch felt so good! My pussy muscles immediately gripped his dick. He started moving slowly with his head down watching his dick go in and out of me. I threw my head back and let him slow stroke the fuck outta'me.

"Look at me Keira." Shit! I hated when he made me look at him while we fucked. I couldn't take his sexy as love faces.

But I did what he said and looked in those gorgeous light grey eyes. Damn! The lust mixed with love was all in his eyes and I felt my orgasm building up. Suddenly Kalvin put both my legs in the crook of his arms and lifted me of the counter. My arms locked around his neck and his dick was still inside if me. Kalvin began slammin' me up and down on his dick while standing in the kitchen. Now, we have fucked all kinds of ways but never standing up. This shit felt so good all I could do was roll my eyes to the back of my head. Kalvin had me straight lookin' possessed while slamming me hard as fuck on his dick.

"Ugh! Kalvin shiiitt bae" My arms were so tight around his neck I don't know how he could breath.

"Take all this dick Keira! Imma make this pussy gush juices all on the fuckin' floor" His voice was husky and sound so good in my ear. All you could here was the TV from the living room. Mixed with my pussy slapping against his pelvis. I felt like Kalvin's dick was going to come out of my throat. And I didn't want him to stop! Kalvin was fuckin' me so good I wanted to carry his dick with me everywhere I went after tonight.

"Kalvin bae I'm about to cum! Arrgghhhh shitiitt" My neck gave out and my head fell back with my pupils in my head.

"SHIT KEIRA! FUCK!" Kalvin came all in me as he slowed down his pounding. My pussy was aching but still held on to his dick.

"I love you so much Keira bae. You and Kyra mean everything to me and I never will hurt you like that again. Bae if you want this shop then you have my support one hunnid." I looked at him and smiled. Still standing with my legs in his arms Kalvin was still slow stroking me. Making me get wet all over again. I barely got my next sentence out.

"Thank you so much bae love. That means everything my husband supporting me like I will always do him." I kissed his soft ass lips while he still was slow pumping me. I pulled and sucked on my husband bottom lip.

"Come on let's go up-stairs," Kalvin said. As he walked with me still in his arms. I heard his feet his something wet on our black marble floors. He looked down then back up at me smiling.

"I told you I was makin' that pussy cum all on the floor." I laughed and shook my head. Seems like life was back to being perfect.

Kelly & Kaylin

I had our whole kitchen smelling like cinnamon. I flipped the french toast I was cooking over in the skillet. I walked over to the thermostat and turned the air on. It was the middle of August and hot as hell. You couldn't go pass noon without turning some A.C. on. I went back to the stove and took the last two french toast out the skillet. Putting them on a plate with two other ones. I sprinkled some powder sugar on them and cool whip. Kaylin hated syrup on his french toast and waffles. His weird ass like cool whip, not whip cream.

It had to be cool whip with his picky ass. I had another plate with some scrambled eggs and cheese, turkey sausages and sliced strawberries. I loved cooking for my fiancé especially while he slept. I had woken up early as hell for no particular reason. I was just an early morning kind of person. Kaylin stayed sound asleep when I crept out our master bedroom. I watched Daria on the firestick in the living room. All you old school heads know exactly what Daria is. Shit is a classic! Anyways after I watched some TV I went to make some breakfast.

Putting the food on a wooden tray I headed up-stairs to wake my King Kay up. I slowly pushed open the door with my back. When I walked in the bedroom was empty. I knew exactly where he was at. I walked over to our balcony we had in our bedroom. One of our favorite things about this condo. When I walked out he was sitting on his black stool shirtless looking yummy as hell. He had his canvas up and was painting the sunrise. I loved watching Kaylin paint he had a calm persona anytime he did.

He was so talented and I'm not just saying the shit because he was mines. He really could have his work in a gallery. Up for auction or however those painters get exposure. But Kaylin never told anybody he could paint. Not even his parents, only me. And he didn't tell me until he proposed in Paris and showed me a painting of me sleeping. I thought he bought it but he surprised me and said he did it himself.

It took me a while to believe him until he did a live one for me. He painted a picture of me and my mother. Even though she died when me and Keira were born. He still took my baby picture and a picture of her and painted it as if she was holding me. The details of my mother's beauty were captured and looked like me and her posed for him.

I cried like a baby when he was finished. From then on, I wanted him to make his work public. But he refused, he said painting is soft and will make him look like a punk. He couldn't be further from the truth. Hell, Karlos loved graphic designing and Kalvin loved numbers. Nobody fucked with them because of their passions.

I set the tray on the table we kept out there. Kaylin had his Beats in his ear and didn't know I even came out. I placed my hands around his waist and kissed his neck. He didn't even jump he just smiled. I looked at his painting and fell in love with it and him even more. I'm tellin' y'all this man was that damn good. He pulled his headphones off and leaned his head into my neck.

"Good morning King Kay. I made you some breakfast," I whispered in his ear and kissed it. Kaylin aggressive ass grabbed my arm and within a blink of an eye I was straddling him.

"Good morning to you honey love. I smelled the breakfast as soon as you opened the door." He leaned forward and kissed me. Kaylin's lips were so soft and warm. After we kissed for a minute he got up and set at the table. I sat next to him and watched him eat. He didn't even look up once he just stuffed his face. Watching Kaylin eat was some of the funniest shit! He ate like he had a damn tape worm in his stomach. After he was done he downed the orange juice I gave him. Sitting in the chair he rubbed his stomach and looked at me.

"Come here." I got out my chair and went to sit on his lap.

"You cook my food that good again I'm gone beat yo' ass." We both started laughing. I rubbed the side of his face and kissed his lips.

"That is a gorgeous painting Kay. Captured by a true artist." I looked back at him and smiled. He laughed and shook his head.

"Kaylin you cannot keep hiding this gift. I just don't understand you wanting to keep this on the low. Look how good you are." I kept my eyes on him and pointed at his painting. This shit was starting to annoy me.

"Ugh! Ok honey love I'll make a deal with you. I will think about makin' this shit public. If you think about giving me a baby." He looked at me with a serious face. I didn't see this shit coming at all.

"Kay that is two completely different things. A baby and a painting don't even hold the same value." He smirked and shook his head which means he was about to get mad.

"Yo I don't fuckin' get you. How the hell do you agree to marry me. Let me put that fat ass rock on your finger. But don't want to give me a baby? What type of shit is that?" He was starting to raise his voice but he knew that didn't shake me.

"Kaylin you better lower your damn voice. The last time I checked this was my body and I decide what to do with it. If you don't like it then you can have your fat ass ring back." I stood up and was about to walk away. But Kaylin jumped up and grabbed my arm not hard but enough for me to stop.

"Kelly shut the fuck up talkin' that stupid shit. Your

body has not been yours since we met at Royalty. I bet my last breath you have my fuckin' baby. Go in the house and get fuckin' dressed. We are meeting Kevin and Kim in a few." He roughly kissed my lips and walked in the house. I stood there mad as hell but turned on at the same time. I knew I was going to have to be honest with Kaylin. I needed to tell him about my fear of having kids and the birthing process. But right now, some things were happening between my legs. I needed some of my King Kay lovin'.

<u>Kaylin</u>

I left Kelly on the balcony looking stupid as hell. I loved the fuck outta her but right now she was pissin' me off. How the fuck she gone come at ya boy that way?! Talmbout it's her body shit to me. Yea in the physical sense it is. But emotionally, mentally and any other way that fuckin' body belongs to me. I knew the moment I met Kelly she was going to have my kids. And I have told her this shit.

Now all of a sudden she wanna act new. Then her little ass not even telling me why she don't want kids. Kelly knows she can come to me about any fuckin' thing. I'm either gone put a bullet in it. Or I'm going to fix it in any kind of way. Y'all already know I'm a Karlos number 2. I don't play about Kelly and she knew that shit. If her giving me kids was a health problem. We could always adopt or get a healthy bitch to carry our baby. Kelly didn't want to hear shit about us having kids. That shit was hurting me bad as hell.

I walked in our bathroom and took off my basketball shorts. I threw them in the hamper along with my socks. I looked in the mirror at my goatee and hair. I needed to hit up Royal Trim and get a line-up. After brushing my teeth, I turned on our three-head shower and stepped in. The glass door fogged up quickly. I stood under the water letting it hit my body and my face. Kelly came to my mind. I wanted nothing more than to fix this shit between us.

Her ass hasn't even set a date for us to be married yet. I'm starting to think she does not want this life with me. If that is the case I swear I am going to fucking lose it. Kelly is every fuckin' thing to me and the thought of us being apart. That shit made me fire hot with rage to the point of murder. As I stood under the water I heard the door slide open. Kelly stepped her sexy ass in the shower naked and lookin' good.

I turned around and looked down at her ass with a mug. Even though she was sexy as fuck I still was pissed. She looked back at me with sad puppy eyes and like a bitch I soften up. Kelly placed her arms around my waist and hugged me tight. I wrapped my arms around her whole body and hugged her back. This was my honey love right here. She lifted her head up looking at me. I lifted her chin to my face and kissed her deeply.

I wanted her to know how much I loved her through this kiss. Kelly was mines all fuckin' mines! That fat ass ring was staying on her pretty ass finger. The hot water was falling over both of us making me kiss her more intense. I dug my fingers in her ass cheeks and lifted her up. I slammed her against the wall with her legs wrapped around me. I still was kissing her hard and deep making her heart beat fast against my chest. I pulled away to look at her pretty ass face.

"I love you so fuckin' much Kelly. When you are ready to talk to me about this you know I'm here. Just don't push me away honey love because I can't be shit without you." Kelly nodded her head and tears slid down her face.

I knew it was not water from the shower because her eyes got puffy. I did not even wait for her to say anything. I went back to kissing her deep and worked my way down to her neck. I made two passion marks on her neck then moved to them perky ass titties she has. Kelly had some round caramel nipples that got hard when I even looked at them. I licked her right one and flicked my tongue back and forth on her now hard nipples.

Trailing my tongue over to her left titty I did the same thing. Looking up at her our eyes met and she had that sexy fuck me face on. I dropped to my knees, like only Kelly could make me do and looked at her pussy. It was shaved like always and looking so damn tasty. I put her right leg over my shoulders and dug in. Like a cat Kelly arched that back against the wall bringing that tasty pussy more to my face.

Kelly's juices tasted like sweet honey to me which is why I gave her the name honey love. I used no hands this time. My mouth was going to do all the work and give Kelly a fuckin' ride. I swirled my tongue around her clit while adding pressure. I was tonguing that bitch down driving her crazy.

"Sssssss damn Kay. Shitt mmm." Kelly hands were in my head massaging my scalp while I ate the life out her pussy. Then I kneeled down under her some more and stuck my tongue in her tight hole. Those walls were so tight and wet. I swear I could separate her juices from the shower. I went in and out and around and around in her hole.

"Oh my fuckin' God Kay! Stoppppp Kay" I didn't listen to that shit. With Kelly, no means yes all the fuckin' time when we were having sex. She started moving her nips and the way I was positioned under her. She was riding my face while standing up and her ass was loving in. Within minutes she was cummin' all in my mouth.

"Ughhhhhhhhhhhh Fuck Kay!" Because of how I was positioned under her, Kelly's sweet juices poured all down my mouth. I licked her clean like she was my morning breakfast. Her body was jerking against the wall. I love when I get her ass that way. That shit made me stick my chest out. I stood up and kissed her with her juices still on my face. I wasted no time shoving this dick in her tight ass pussy. Kelly held her breath so long I thought she was going to pass out.

"Breath honey love," I told her as I started moving in and out of her. The shit felt so good I almost became a minute man. Kelly was moaning so loud sounding so sexy I had to stick my tongue down her throat. Between her moaning and good ass pussy I was going to shoot triplets in her ass. Oh y'all thought I was pullin' out? Naw! I fucked the shit out of Kelly against the wall and she was luvin' all of it. I know my back was scratched up because them nails of hers were grippin'. But I didn't give a fuck what she did to my body because it was hers. As long as she stayed away from my ass then we were good.

"Kelly I'm never leavin' you no matter what. You my fuckin' honey love and always will be. Say it Kelly! Ugh! Say you will always be mine!" I pumped faster in her driving her crazy.

"Ugghh Kay I'll always be yours baby. Ughhh shiitt I fuckin' promise." Hearing Kelly say that shit made me smile like the Kool-Aid man. A few more pumps and we both came together.

"FUCK!" We both shouted in unison. My head as buried between her titties. I still was holding her up with my dick inside of her. She didn't even trip about me cummin' all inside her ass. After a few kisses we washed each other up and stepped out the bathroom.

Since it was hot as satan's balls outside I decided to keep it simple. I wore a grey muscle tank top, some black Nike basketball shorts. I took my grey and black high top Airforce ones out the box and put on my white diamond stud earrings. Kelly walked out of our walk-in closet lookin' sexy as hell. Her slim thick ass had on some cut up jean shorts and this plaid button up. She tied the front up revealing her sexy ass belly button piercing. Kelly kept her nails and feet done which turned me on even more. Her hair was in a ponytail showing off her full beautiful face.

"You look pretty as hell honey love." I put my arms around her waist and kissed the side of her face.

"Thank you Kay. You lookin' sexy as hell yourself. You better be lucky you're with me today wearin' them damn basketball shorts." I laughed when she said that. Her face was bunched up and she real life had an attitude.

"Kelly don't nobody get none of the dick but'chu. This yo' King Kay dick." I grabbed my shit and squeezed it while looking at her. She laughed and shook her head as we walked out the bedroom.

*

"Umm so this bitch can just put heart eyes under your picture?" Kelly looked from her phone to me. We were in my 2017 F-150 headed to meet Kimmora and Kevin at the mall.

"Fuck you talkin' about?" I turned my nose up because I had no clue to what she was trippin' about.

"Emily! She put heart eyes under two of your pictures. Why is this bitch still following you?" Kelly raised her voice at me like I was a damn child. Let me nip this shit in the bud.

"Kelly first off you betta watch yo' fuckin' tone. Second, I have over 50K followers. How the hell am I supposed to remember she following me? I don't give a fuck! Shit her ass keep watching me and you live our lives. If she wants to be miserable over some shit she will never have then so be it." My eyes went from the road to Kelly and she looked pissed off.

"I am not trying to hear that bullshit. You better unfollow her and block her ass!" She rolled her eyes and turned the radio on. I had to laugh because only her ass could get away with telling me what to do. My honey love.

We pulled into the Mall of Louisiana and I parked my big ass truck. I hopped out and went around to Kelly's door. Helping her slim thick sexy ass out the truck I stole a few kisses. I could tell she was not mad anymore because she kissed back. Hand in hand we walked into the mall. Kelly took out her phone and called Kimmora. She said they were in Aldo so that's where we headed.

"What's up bro. Hey sis in-law. Where Keion at?" I dabbed Kevin up, hugged Kimmora and kissed her on her head. I loved all my sister in-laws like they were blood.

"Keion is with dad and nonna(grandma)," Kimmora answered while hugging Kelly."

"I hate when y'all speak Italian in front of us. Don't nobody know what the hell that shit mean." Kevin teased. I laughed and agreed. The girls were always speaking that shit when they were around each other. Or when they were pissed at one of us. Kelly and Kimmora waved us off.

"So, what's up with this braid shop I heard about. I think that is such a good idea Kelly. You and Keira got some good ass skills so that's money in the bank," Kimmora said then she turned to me and Kevin.

"Y'all need to talk to Kaylin. He is acting insecure and got my baby sis feeling like shit."

"Sis you can't clown bro. You already know Keira got that nigga wide the fuck open. He will get on board give him a chance," I told Kimmora and she smiled.

"Boo please tell me you gettin' something in this boring ass store you got us in," Kevin said looking around. The girls tried on some shoes and each got two pair. Kelly got shoes and a pink sparkle book bag.

Walking around the mall the girls spent about a half an hour in each store. The minute one of them saw some cute shit. They had to try it on then get about five people opinions. I was so happy my brother was with me. Together we made two trips to the car. Now Kelly and Kimmora had us in GAP for kids. This nigga Kevin was just as worst then Kimmora when shopping for Keion.

I couldn't lie, I was a little jealous. I wanted to shop for me and Kelly's babies and overdo the shit like my brothers were. Kelly was helping pick clothes out for her nieces and nephews and she was glowing. A little hope beamed inside of me with hopes she would be this excited about our child.

"400 dollars in GAP for kids and we don't even have any." I joked making all of us laugh. We walked inside of Footlocker. Finally a store me and Kevin could take our time and enjoy. The girls had the nerve to complain about us trying on gym shoes. We had the worker order us four pair on-line that were not in the store. We left out with three pair of gym shoes apiece. Dropping them off in our trucks it was time to eat. Now we were walking in to Chick-fil-A ready to get our grub on.

"I'm going to the bathroom," Kelly said and Kimmora followed her. Me and Kevin were talkin' shit and looking at the menu when I heard my name being called.

"Damn Kaylin you lookin' good as fuck. Long time no see best friend." Emily and her sister walked in and stood behind us. I can't even front Emily was fine as hell! She had a thick frame and golden hair that touched her shoulders. On the outside, she was the perfect girl you wanted on your arm. But then she opened her mouth and that's when you realized she was a fuckin' air head. Emily needed to walk around with a helmet on her damn head. She was stupid as Forrest Gump but her body and head game was sick as fuck.

"What's good wit'chu Emily." I nodded my head at her sister and she rolled her eyes. Emily sister always wanted to hook-up with one of my brothers. But they were not interested because she was sixteen. Don't nobody got time for that bullshit.

"Since you here solo let's hang. My sister is about to go to work anyways," Emily said licking her lips. Before I could answer Kelly and Kimmora walked up both looking ready.

"Naw he fuckin' good on that desperate attempt to fuck. You and yo' little beetle can get the fuck on." Kelly was so deep in Emily's face I thought they were going to kiss. Emily kept eye contact with Kelly and said.

"Damn Kaylin this bitch got'chu trained like that? You can't even chill with old friends?" Or is it she knows five minutes with me and I will have yo' toes curlin'."

"Oh hell naw! Kelly slap that bitch and if her side kick wants to jump stupid I got her ass!" Kimmora yelled while looking at Emily's sister. I moved Kelly out the way and got in Emily's face.

"Emily, you need to get the fuck outta here with that bullshit. This my fiancée and I be damned if you disrespect her. Take yo' sister and get the fuck on!" Emily jumped at my voice. Then she started laughing.

"Did you tell this bitch we fucked after she caught us at the mall?! Uh! Kaylin, did you tell---" Before Emily could the rest of what she was saying Kelly knocked that bitch out of her sandals. Kimmora jumped on Emily's sister before I could react to Kelly fighting. Before you knew it people we gathered around and phones were out recording. Kelly was on top of Emily hitting her in the face like Mayweather. Emily had blood coming from her nose and mouth. I was trying to pull Kelly off of her. But she had a hold of Emily's hair for dear life.

"Kelly let this bitch go!" I yelled and pulled but it was no fucking good. I used all my strength prying Emily's hair out Kelly's hand. Finally, I succeeded and the look on Kelly's face was unrecognizable. She didn't have a scratch on her but she looked like a mad woman. Her pretty ass face was red and her mouth was bunched up. She had blood and some of Emily's hair all on her hands. Her nails were all over the floor so I know her hand was in pain. I looked over at Kevin and he had Kimmora thrown over his shoulders. This nigga was laughing but I did not find shit funny. I didn't want Kelly fighting over something that was dead and over. Emily ass was lying, I did not fuck her that day.

"Kaylin let me the fuck down!" Kelly screamed while I still was carrying her ass outside the mall.

"Hell no! Not until we get outside! All you wanna do is run back over there and beat her ass. Calm down Kelly." Once the four of us got outside we placed our ladies on their feet. Kimmora and Kelly were breathing hard as hell. Either of them had not one mark on them just their hair was out of place.

"Kim what the fuck boo! Why did you have to whoop her sister's ass? She didn't even do shit!" Kevin was laughing but he was mad to.

"I don't give a fuck! I don't like the way she was

lookin'," Kimmora responded while fixing her hair in the mirror. I looked at Kelly and she had the nerve to have her fist balled up mugging me.

"Why the fuck are you looking at me like that? I didn't do shit, yo' ass the one fighting." Kelly didn't say anything. She hugged my brother and her sister and walked towards the truck.

"Damn bro you in trouble." Kevin bucked his eyes out and said. I shook my head and said my goodbyes to them.

Driving home Kelly was quiet as hell. She stared out the window the entire time we drove. I kept stealing glances at her but she didn't budge. Because we didn't get a chance to eat I stopped at Popeyes and got some food. Kelly would not even tell me what she wanted so I ordered me and her usual.

Walking our condo Kelly put her purse on the table and went to the kitchen. She washed the now dried blood off her hands. I was getting tired of the quiet shit so I spoke first.

"Kelly I---"

"I don't want to hear shit you gotta say Kaylin. How the fuck did you sleep with her after you got caught up? Did you figure fuck Kelly I'll get her back later? And before you talk about that stupid ass date I was on save it. I didn't even know Jayla was setting me up until I got to the lounge. Really though Kaylin, that's how we do. I should have just fucked Marques then." That shit turned me up to the max. before I knew it I had Kelly pinned up on the refrigerator with her arms above her head.

"Say that shit again Kelly! Come on, be bold and repeat that again! Put a bullet in his head and everybody he loves!" Kelly turned her head with a scowl on her face. I pressed my face hard as hell against the side of her face. My next words I spoke calm to her.

"Fix your mouth to say you should have fucked another nigga. Be a big girl and say that shit again. Watch I have me and Karlos kill that nigga, yo' fuckin' friend and her punk ass nigga. Now, I did not stick my dick in Emily or her fuckin' mouth. When you caught me in the mall with that bitch I took her home. Yo' ass the one who disappeared that day and stayed out all night. I never once questioned you about that shit after we made it official. You wanna know why Kelly? Because if you were with a nigga then he would have signed his death certificate. Now stop letting that bitch knock you off yo' square. My heart belongs to you and only you. Yo' ass is mines and always will be. Turn around and kiss yo' man." I pulled my face away a little so she could look at me. Kelly hesitated at first but she finally looked at me.

"Kaylin please don't lie to me. Did you and her fuck that day or any day after." Her eyes watered. I let her hands down and rubbed the side of her face keeping eye contact.

"Kelly, I swear I did not touch that bitch. Not the day you caught me or any other day after that." I brought my lips to hers and kissed her. She kissed me back and wrapped her arms around my neck. I pulled away and looked back in her eyes.

"Have my baby Kelly. There is nobody else who I want to have my last name and my babies," I didn't even give her a chance to respond. I went back to kissing her and peeling her clothes off. This woman was going to carry my baby and my last name so she betta get hip.

Kevin and Kimmora

"Kim, you can't be all outside fighting and shit. We got lil man now so we gotta set an example." I talked to my wife while she fed Keion some baby food. I was cleaning our Ninja blender up in the sink. Kimmora did not do the store brought food. She pureed all Keion's food in the blender and juiced his juice.

"I know boo and I'm sorry but I had to have my baby sister back. You know damn well you or your brothers don't do one on one fights." I laughed because she was absolutely right. If one fought we all fought that included Brandon.

"Yea your right but I want my wife to be more mindful that's all. Give me my lil man." I dried my hands off.

Getting ready to take him out his chair since he was done eating. When I had him in my arms I kissed his cheeks. This lil nigga had me soft as hell. Not trying to brag but my son was so fuckin' cute. He had his mama pretty brown skin and a head full of jet black hair. I guess me and Kimmora hair mixed together. It was long and the ends were curly and soft. His cheeks always looked like he had them stuffed with food. He had my eye color or as I called it the 'pussy net! All me and my brothers had to do was look at a bitch. And just that easy, the pussy was in a net for us ready to go. This was my lil man right here and I loved him so much.

"I'm not gone front. Watching you beat ol' girl ass was sexy as hell. Reminds me of when you knocked Chrissy the fuck out. My sexy ass Lalia Ali wanna be," I joked while holding Keion. Kim laughed as she wiped his high chair down.

"You so annoying! How you mad but turned on at the same time? Can you wipe him down for me boo? He needs to be changed to and a new onesie," Kim said all in one annoying breath.

"Kimmora what the fuck I tell you about asking me to do shit for my son. I ain't no fuckin' nanny I know what my boy needs. Just go shower and I got him. Just like I will have him when you start work tomorrow. This my nut sack right her." I smiled at her making her laugh. Before I walked upstairs I kissed my wife on the lips a few times.

Keion had his own bathroom in his bedroom. Kimmora decorated it baby blue and brown. He loved the water and his little chubby ass loved splashing it. He was only five months but this lil nigga was a trip. I still could not believe I was a husband and a father. I wish my parents could have been here to see this. My mama would have all her grandkids spoiled rotten.

Some of the girl's family relocated to the states once the girls got married and started having kids. The Ricci's clan was big as fuck! Five uncles, fifteen cousins and five aunties. And their grandma and grandfather moved up here as well. They still had a shit load of relatives in Italy, there family took to me and my brothers as if we were blood. Me and my brothers appreciated that shit and felt it was genuine. Plus with family being here we did not have to worry about finding the right child care for our kids.

My father in-law told us he didn't play that strangers keeping his family bullshit. While Kimmora worked I would have my son. And if ever I had to work her pops said bring Keion to him. I was happy as hell when my boo graduated and got her degree in Nursing. I knew she would be putting her degree to use but I didn't think it would be this soon. Kim knew she didn't have to lift a finger if she didn't want to.

But she told me being a registered nurse was a dream. Who the fuck am I to get in the way of my wife's dream. Her first day was tomorrow at the hospital. I was so proud of her but I knew she would have a hard time leaving Keion. That woman was obsessed over her son. I loved how good of a wife and mother she was.

After I bathed Keion I wrapped him up in his blue teddy bear towel. I walked him into his room laying him on the changing table. His room was sweet as fuck. Kim decorated his bedroom as well. She wanted a helicopter themed baby room. He had clouds and helicopter wall decals all over. His crib was honey wood colored with helicopter sheets. Kim even had his ceiling looking like an airport with planes and helicopters taking off. The shit was nice as hell and Kim had some good taste.

I grabbed Keion's Avveno baby lotion and put it over his chuck ass body. He giggled and blew spit bubbles. His little ass was about to go to sleep while I dig in his mama guts. I wanted to put another baby in her so fuckin' bad. I was trying to give her some time in between babies. But looking at Keion and seeing what we made had me thinking otherwise. After putting a new diaper on him I put a green onesie over his fat lil body. He looked so cute with his fat ass legs and feet out. I kissed him and loved on him for a minute. Then his eyes started getting low. I rocked him in his rocking chair and within minutes he was sleep. I laid him on his back in his crib. Kissing him on his cheek I turned his light off. His ceiling lit up giving him some light. I made sure his baby monitor was turned on and I walked out.

Entering our huge master bedroom, I took my clothes off. I walked in the bathroom and Kim was stepping out the shower.

"You might as well turn right back around." I eyed her wet naked body.

My boo was so thick with a fat round ass. Chocolate skin that made me weak to the knees. And long ass thick curly hair. She smiled and turned the shower back on while stepping in. Kim lathered the sponge up with that NOIR body wash shit for men. She brought it from that Bath and Body Works store she practically lived in. The shit smelled good as hell though. She washed my entire body like I was a fuckin' baby which I low-key liked. Every nigga wanted to be somebody's baby don't ever let them tell you otherwise.

After we were done I wrapped a towel around her wet body and one around my waist. We walked to the bedroom and I dried her off and she did me. I put on my degree deodorant and climbed into my bed ass naked. I grabbed my tray I had in my side dresser drawer and rolled me up a blunt. My eyes went from me rollin' to Kim sexy ass.

She rubbed that berry smellin' lotion all over her body. That lotion had my boo smelling so good. I was hoping she climbed into bed naked like I did. Once she put her hair in a ponytail in the middle of her head she grabbed a tank top. I wasn't too disappointed because it hugged her titties and stopped at her stomach. She stayed bottomless and climbed into bed turning the TV on. It was after 9pm so I knew she was about to put the TV on Everybody Hates Raymond show. My boo loved that white ass show. I lit my fat ass blunt and took a pull.

"Is that stuff good?" she asked looking over at me. I blew the smoke out my mouth.

"Hell yea it's good. Why? You wanna try some?" I asked her. She surprised me when she said yes. My boo and her sisters were squares in a way so I didn't think she would say yes. I passed it to her and she took a pull. Kim started choking as she set up on her feet.

"Boo don't pull so hard you got virgin lungs. Give it to me." I set up next to her and took the blunt out her hand. I pulled on it and held the smoke in my mouth. I brought my lips to hers and kissed her. Kim breathed my smoke in and blew it out her mouth. The shit was so sexy it made me rock up. I put the blunt to her mouth and told her to pull slow, inhale and blow. She did and within minutes her eyes got puffy. I laughed because she looked so cute high. I had another one rolled up and I lit that one too.

"I think I like getting high. I feel really good and I can't stop smiling," she said to me. I laughed at her pretty ass.

"You can only smoke with me, nobody else. This our

thang now, ok?" She nodded her head. We smoked the second blunt. Kim only choked once a then she was good. Watching her smoke was turning me the fuck on.

"Come here boo." I laid down and had her get on top of me. I took her top off freeing those round titties she had. Them chocolate nipples were calling for me. Kim was still holding the blunt in her pretty ass fingers. She took a pull and leaned forward to my mouth. She blew the smoke in my mouth and I blew it out.

"Only smoke with me. Ok?" Her soft ass voice was making me higher then I was. I bit my lip and nodded in agreement. I set up a little and started licking and sucking on her titties. I had both them bitches wet from my mouth. I know I gave her a hickey on both of them. I took the blunt from Kim. Taking a last pull I put it out on my tray. I was horny as fuck and Kim was lookin' like a damn snack. I kissed her soft ass lips and pulled on her bottom lip.

"Get yo' ass on all four," my husky ass voice said to her. She giggled and did what I said. High sex was my favorite. For the first time me and Kim were high together. Her round chocolate ass was in the air looking so good. Before I went in I bent down and ate her out from the back. The weed mixed with her sweet juices was so tasty. Kim started moving back and forth on my face. Before she could come I stopped and slid my dick in. Even though she pushed a whole baby out just five months ago. Her pussy was still tight as a virgin. Her shit fit my dick like jeans fit on her thick ass.

"Ughh Kevin damn boo. Arrghhh." Kim was moaning while I stroked her from the back slow. I was rubbing and massaging her ass cheeks. Her ass was so soft and juicy I sometimes wanted to bite it.

"Yea boo. Give me all that hot pussy." I stopped moving and instantly Kimmora lowered her back more. She started throwing her ass back on my thick 10-inch. Her ass looked like waves in a damn ocean. Seeing that round chocolate ass clap back on my dick was a beautiful sight. I had my teeth gripping my bottom lips so damn hard. The faster she threw it back the more my dick coated with her juices.

"I'm fuckin' cummin' Kevin!" Kim's creamy goodness was all over my dick, balls and thighs. My boo came hard as fuck. She started to slow her pace down with her face deep in the sheets. I pulled her trembling body up and kissed her. With my dick still hard as fuck in her I rubbed her clit. I turned her over and laid her on her back while sliding right back in her.

"You like smokin' with yo' husband? Uh boo?" Kim had her eyes rolled in the back of her head. I knew my dick and the weed had her ass floating in this bitch. I had her legs in the air drillin' her thick ass.

"Oooo yes husband I love smoking with you husband. I love yo' dick more though." That last part she moaned made me show out. I bent down and kissed her pretty ass on the lips. Sitting back put I crossed both her legs. Throwing them over my right shoulder I fucked my wife good as hell all through the night. I don't know how the fuck she was going to go to work in the morning. Yea life was good!

<u>Kimmora</u>

Beep! Beep! Beep! Beep!

I slowly opened my eyes to the annoying ass loud beeping. I realized it was my alarm going off. I was too comfortable too move from my spot but I had to shut that thing up. I rolled off Kevin's chest and hit the snooze button. I had it set for fifteen minutes because that's how long it took me to get up. Laying back down on our comfortable king size pillow top I melted in my pillow. I turned over and looked in the camera at Keion. He was still sound asleep looking like an angel. My snuggles always slept through the night peacefully. Kevin hated that nick name I gave our son. He said it sounded gay, but I didn't care. Keion was mommy's snuggles and always would be.

"Fuck back over here." Kevin's scratchy sleepy voice snapped me out of my thoughts. I loved his sleepy voice. I scooted back over to him and his arms wrapped around my body. I loved our mornings like this. Kevin was such a good husband and father. Every day he made me feel special sometimes without even doing anything.

"Boo I have to get up in another fifteen minutes." My back was pressed up against his chest. He wrapped his arms tighter around me. I smirked and kissed his hand.

"I know boo. I just wanna feel your body a little longer. Last night was fun Kim, we doing that shit again." Kevin kissed my head and my shoulders. His hard ass dick was pressing against my ass. It felt so good and I wanted to grind against it. I had to dismiss that because if I did I never would make it to work.

"If you move that soft ass booty against my dick. Yo' first day of work is going to be tomorrow." What I tell y'all! I know my freak ass husband. Before I could respond I heard Keion on his baby monitor. He was moving around and whining a little.

"Go get ready for work boo. I got my little man," Kevin said before he felt on me some more and kissed me. We both got out of bed. I headed to the bathroom and Kevin headed to Keion's room.

I brushed my teeth and hopped in the shower. After getting my body cleaned I stepped out the shower. Drying my body off I put my robe on and walked out the bath room. I could hear Kevin in Keion's room playing with him. It made my heart smile hearing and seeing how Keion had Kevin. I put on my grey bikini style cotton panties and matching bra. I smiled when I looked down at my animal print scrubs.

Y'all know how much I love my animal print. After putting my uniform on I put my black footies and clogs on. I left my hair in my Kylee bun, what I call it, and put on my white gold stud earrings. I sprayed some Coco Chanel on my risk and walked out the bedroom. Walking down stairs Kevin had Keion in his chair feeding him some baby cereal. My baby boy was so cute and chubby. He had that dip in his top lip like his daddy and them damn light grey eyes. He also had Kevin's nose and that same lightning bolt shape birthmark on his thigh. Keion looked at me when I entered the kitchen and smiled big as hell.

"You look beautiful boo." Kevin smiled at me and said. I kissed him on the lips a few times. If I said anything to Keion he would have wanted me to pick him up.

"Thank you Kevy Kev. What are you and Keion's doing today?" I asked taking a smoothie and yogurt out the refrigerator.

"We chillin' today. I might go see that nigga Karlos and stop at the shop. Why the fuck yo' pants so tight? You tryna have me pull the plug on a few patients?" I couldn't help but laugh.

"Kevin I can't hide my curves boo. But I assure you even if my uniform was baggy my face still would turn heads. And did you forget I work in the labor and delivery floor." I laughed as I put some yogurt in my mouth. I knew he would not laugh at that.

"Kimmora don't make me fuck yo' pretty ass up. And that don't mean shit. It be lesbian bitches up there poppin' out babies. Don't make me have to kill one of them she he's." He got up and put Keion's empty bowl in the sink. That was my queue to show my baby some love.

"Hi my snuggles! Good morning to you." I picked him up and kissed all over him. He giggled and made some baby noises. This little boy has changed my life and I couldn't be more blessed.

"You know I hate that gay ass name Kim." Kevin had wrinkles in his forehead. I smacked my lips and waved him off. Seeing Keion laugh and let me love on him made me sad. I didn't want to leave my baby boy. Even though this was my decision to work I still didn't think it would be this hard. I was so excited about my first day and now I'm sad.

"Kim boo what's wrong?" Kevin stood next to me while I was still holding Keion. I had tears in my eyes.

"I don't want to leave him." I sniffed and Kevin started laughing at me.

"Kevin stop laughing at me it's not funny." I cried harder. That only made him laugh more.

"I'm sorry boo. Come here my beautiful wife, stop crying." Kevin hugged me while I was still holding the baby.

"Kim you know yo' ass don't have to work. You can spend as much time with our baby as you want. Money won't be an issue for Keion's grandkids so you know it's not an issue for us. You the one that wanted to do this. I'm behind whatever you decide." He wiped my tears and kissed my lips. Kevin was right, I did decide this. I always wanted to be a nurse. I at least wanted to try it for a year. I just had to be strong and know I will see Keion when I get off work.

"I know Kev, you are always behind me. I just love Keion so much and will miss him. I'll do better each day. He just so damn cute." Me and Kevin laughed and I wiped my face. I loved on both my guys some more. Then I had to leave to start my first day at the hospital.

*

I cried the whole damn ride to work. Not only did I miss Keion but I missed Kevin as well. My two guys were my heart. Pulling into the employee parking lot I checked my face in the mirror of my Lexus. Satisfied with my appearance I got out my car hitting my alarm. Showing my nurses badge with my picture on it to the security guard.

I took the elevator to the second floor. I worked in the delivery ward. Being around little babies, all day was going to make me miss Keion more. But I have always loved kids. I knew whatever I was going to do with my life would involve children. Clocking in I began to get nervous. I was supposed to shadow someone today to get a fill of the unit.

"Kimmora Royal. Hi, I'm Lynn Hicks but please call me

Lynn. Mrs. Hicks is my mother in-law. You will be shadowing me for the week. I got a little background from HR about you. I think it is impressive for someone your age to go through school without stopping." She smiled at me.

"Thank you so much. I am so excited and nervous," I nervously chuckled. Lynn went and grabbed the blood pressure cart.

"So, we have a total of six patients. The first two I will check their blood pressure and temperature. I want you to observe how I interact with them and the babies. Personality is important in my opinion in any field dealing with people. It's ok to bond with our patients and be friendly. There stay here should be memorable and comfortable." I smiled and nodded my head. I was so nervous my palms were sweating.

The morning went so good. I was in love with being a nurse and it was only day one. I did excellent checking blood pressures and temperatures. The new mommies I met were amazing and had beautiful newborn babies. I missed Keion even more now. One of the mother's child was diagnosed with down syndrome. He was a beautiful 8lb little fella. It made me smile seeing how his mother was still in love with him.

Lynn gave me a phone to carry around with. It was a pager for patients to call us if they needed anything. I learned how to administrate medicine. How important it is to scan every patient's hospital bracelet whenever we came into their room to service them. This career choice was very demanding. And I loved! Thank God we didn't have any deliveries at the moment. I don't think I was ready for that.

Now it was lunch time and I was starving. I went to the cafeteria to look and see what they were serving. I saw there was a fruit and salad bar which was right up my alley. After making a spinach salad with tomatoes and walnuts. I grabbed a bowl and put some strawberries and blueberries in it. Grabbing a cranberry juice, I took a seat and dug in. While eating I took my phone out and decided to FaceTime my guys.

"There goes my sexy ass nurse. How is your first day going?" Kevin handsome face appeared on the screen. My husband was so fine with his sandy brown dreads. They seemed like they grew longer every day. They stopped in the middle of his back now. His long goatee was sandy brown as well. I loved pulling on it when I kissed him. Then those grey eyes that looked at me like I was the center of his world. Whew! Let me stop before I have to change my panties.

"Hey boo, it's going so good. I love the work load and looking at the cute little babies. Speaking of babies, where is my snuggles?" I smiled big as hell whenever I spoke of my guys.

"Damnnn is he the only one you care about? That lil nigga good." Kevin laughed and teased me. I laughed and smacked my lips.

"Let me find out you jealous of a baby! You know I love my Kevy Kev." His sexy yellow skin turned red. I had to laugh because I knew he hated that shit.

"Why you gotta make a nigga do gay shit in front of my employees." I fell out laughing until I realized what he said.

"Kevin, I know you do not have my baby boy at y'all damn warehouse!" I was about to cut my day short and go get my baby. After I kill my husband.

"Kimmora don't make me kick yo' ass! Why the fuck would I have my son at our warehouse! Use yo' head woman. We at the barber shop. I had three heads to cut today and I wanted to bring my lil man. He need to see daddy work so he can pick up some skills." Seeing Kevin smile big talking about our son made me soft up. He turned the camera on Keion. He was sitting in his high chair smiling. He had some toys and those Gerber melt in your mouth candies.

"Hi my snuggles! Mommy misses you and loves you so much.!" I smiled at my baby boy with tears in my eyes. Keion grew excited when he saw my face and tried to eat Kevin's phone. I laughed and wiped my tears.

"Aye lil nigga get my phone out yo' mouth. Let me speak to my wife you done talking." Kevin joked with Keion. He grabbed his phone and kissed Keion on his chubby cheeks. We talked for a few more minutes. I wanted to finish my lunch so I told my guys I love them and said bye.

"Kimmora Tessa Royal is a wife and a mother. And here I thought I would be the lucky man." I turned around when I heard my whole name. When my eyes landed on the man that spoke. My mouth almost hit the floor when I saw Tyler. Y'all remember my ex Tyler? I spoke of him briefly in part 1. If you don't remember go read part one me and Kevin's chapter! Anyways, we were together something tuff. But Tyler went to explore life in other countries. That life just was not for me so we decided to end things. Me and Tyler were friends before anything so we did not have a sour break-up.

"Oh my goodness Tyler! How are you? What are you doing here?" Smiling from ear to ear. I stood up and hugged him.

"After I finished traveling I came back home and went back to medical school. Now here I am starting my residency." He fixed his white doctors coat and smiling. I laughed at his silly ass.

"That's right you did start medical school. I am so happy for you Tyler." I turned to grab my phone off my tray. I didn't want to make a mistake and throw it away.

"Kimmy, I see you still been eatin' yo cornbread girl." I turned back to look at Tyler. He was eyeing my body from head to toe. I knew he was referring to how thick I was. I laughed and rolled my eyes. He never calls me by my name, always Kimmy.

"Stop boy, I'm a married woman and mother now." I held up my 4-karat diamond wedding ring with matching band. Tyler held his hands up in surrender mode.

"No disrespect to you Kimmy. But I am a man and I can't help how beautiful you still are. I am happy to see you have completed your dream. You did it girl! Nurse Kimmora Ricci." He smiled at me and bit his lip.

"It's Royal now. Kimmora Tessa Royal." I smiled back at him and pointed to my badge.

"Damn. I guess I missed my shot huh? Well I won't even bother asking can we exchange numbers. How about we just see each other at lunch tomorrow. I would love to get caught up on your life." He held his hand out towards me. I shook it and said.

"Ok cool. I take my lunch tomorrow at 1pm. See you then, Doctor Tyler McKlain." I walked away and dumped my tray in the garbage.

I could feel Tyler's eyes on me as I walked out the cafeteria. I shook my head and continued to laugh. Tyler had always been a cocky muthafucka. Now I won't lie to y'all, he is fine as hell! He puts you in the mindset of a younger Boris Kodjoe with some deep waves. He was smart and he had money. I never had a cheating problem with Tyler.

When we were together things were good as hell. Him wanting to leave was what broke us up. But who was I to stop him from following his vision. I was sad when we broke up but I had to move on. And boy did I ever! Kevin will always be the best decision I ever made. And now we have my little sniggles and I couldn't be happier. Plus, y'all know how good Kevin dick is. I'd be a fool to fuck my home life up.

After lunch Lynn had me stay an hour after. She wanted my first few days to be short so I can slowly earn everything. Once I was done shadowing I would be on my own. The thought made me nervous but because this was my dream. I pushed those nerves to the side and picked up some confidence. On the drive home, I stopped at Kroger's and picked up some dinner for tonight. Kevin texted me and asked me to make some turkey meatloaf, red cabbage and mash potatoes. I had no problem granting my boo request. I grabbed some bananas and peaches for my snuggles baby food and headed home.

When I opened the door to our home I could hear The Wonder pets on the TV in the living room." All my pearly whites were on display. I loved hearing Keion shows on. That means he was smiling and giggling. I do not know what it is about them Wonder pets. But my baby boy loved them! He makes all kinds of happy baby noises whenever it's on. Kicking my shoes and socks off by the door. I put my keys and purse on the side tables in the hallway.

"Hello my chunky snuggles. Let mommy love on you." I sat next to him on his blanket. Keion was sitting up in his giant donut pillow. I picked him up and kissed him all over. He smelled of baby lotion. Keion's eyes stayed glued on the TV.

"Really Keion? You just gone ignore your mommy?" I smiled at him still. He didn't even look at me. I smacked my lips and put him back in his donut. Giving him another kiss I stood up when Kevin walked in the living room. He had was eating some Ruffle chips which were his favorite.

"Is it anymore love left for me?" His sexy ass smirked at me. I smirked back and bit my lip at my fine guy.

"Always boo." I walked over to him and hugged him. As quickly as his arms wrapped around my waist. They quickly unwrapped and his hands pushed me away.

"Kim why the fuck you smell like Polo cologne? Who the fuck you been hugging?" I looked at Kevin and he was pissed. I didn't even know Tyler's cologne was on me.

"Kevin calm down. I ran into an old friend when I was at work. It's a hospital Kevin I am bound to see someone I know." I tried to make it seem like no big deal but Kevin was not buying that shit.

"I ain't tryna hear that shit Kimmora. I don't give a fuck if the nigga is dying. You don't hug no fucking body if it ain't me. Now, who was it." He remained calm and asked again.

"I was eating lunch and my old friend Tyler showed up. He does his residence there and he surprised me. I gave him a little quick hug because I had not seen him in a minute.

We talked for about five minutes and I went about my business." Kevin looked ten times madder than earlier.

"You talkin' about that ex nigga you were with before me? I thought his ass was in Africa or some shit?" His nostrils flared and before I could answer he started back talking.

"Look, I will keep shit short and sweet. I don't give a fuck if the nigga just cured cancer, aids, diabetes or any other disease. You do not EVER fuckin' touch him again. This is your dream so I will not make you quit. But Kim I'm warning yo' ass. If this nigga is a problem I will pop him one in the dome. Come in this bitch with a different scent or even an extra pep in yo' muthafuckin' step and watch what happens. We clear." He looked me dead in my eyes and I knew he was serious.

"Yes, Kevin I promise we are clear. But just so you know, Tyler has nothing coming from me. No dude will ever have anything coming from me. I am yours and always will be." He tried to hide his smile. I took that as an invite to hug and kiss him. He stepped back quick as hell.

"Don't try to touch me and you smell like that nigga. Yo' and you touched my fuckin' son! Hell no!" Kevin went to Keion and took his onesie and socks he had on off. He picked up the blue blanket Keion was sitting on to. Keion took his attention off the Wonder pets and smiled at Kevin. He laid a green blanket back down and sat Keion down in his donut pillow. He walked over to me and said.

"Strip."

"What!" I said with shock in my voice and on my face.

"I know you speak English. Strip," he said it again. I looked at him for a second to see if he was serious. Those grey eyes didn't budge so I knew he was. I irately took my clothes off.

"Panties, bra and socks to." I squinted my eyes at him but did what he said. He took his beater off and gave it to me. I put the beater on and looked at him.

"Now take this shit along with them ugly ass nursing

shoes to the cellar. Burn all that shit Kimmora. And the next time you touch anybody else I'm burnin' them next." My mouth was dropped so low the devil probably saw it.

I snatched my clothes up off the floor along with Keion's things. Grabbing my nurse shoes, I went down stairs past the basement to our cellar. I cannot believe Kevin is being this childish. Walking back up-stairs I went to the living room and kissed Keion. He still kept his eyes on the TV.

"He don't got shit to say to you right now. He knew his mama was on some bullshit when he smelled you. Get yo' ass up-stairs and shower. I'll be up in a minute to dry you off and lotion you up." I watched Kevin go over to Keion and pick him up. His eyes went to his daddy's and he started laughing. I had seen enough! I marched up-stairs like an angry kid. I was so mad at Kevin and the fact that he turned my son against me. As mad as I was, I looked forward to that rub down. Ha!

Kylee

"I knew cutting the middle section out would make the story flow better. I am so happy she liked it. Now we can move forward, I am so excited." I was in my home office on the phone with my boss. Ink had been so wonderful with me working from home.

My boss was calling to tell me one of our authors approved the changes. Working for Ink publishing company was amazing. All the things I was learning would go great for when I stepped out on my own. I talked to my boss for a few more minutes. She told me I have two new books she was emailing me. I was like a kid in a candy store. Books have been my life since I was young and read Babysitters Club series.

Now I am co-editor for a major publishing company for urban-fiction. After saving the two books my boos emailed me. I downloaded them and saved them to my Mac computer. I was tired and wanted to lay in my bed. Karlos was bringing me some pizza from Pizza Delicious. I had a craving for a large cheese pizza with tomatoes and spinach. I also wanted some Doritos and apple juice.

Before I headed to our bedroom I walked in my baby girl's room. Opening the door, I smiled hard and teared up. I cannot believe I am about to be a mother of a baby girl. I am about to have a mini me. I can already see her beautiful face in my head. I felt bad because I knew Karlos wanted a boy. I told him we could try again when Kaylee turns 3. Yea we have already decided on a name. Kaylee Stelani Royal! Her middle name is my mother Stella and Karlos mother Staci. I looked at her pink sparkly letters on the wall over her crib. Her crib was white and pink and so where the walls. The character I picked out for Kaylee was Marie from the Disney movie The Aristocrats. Now as much as I hated cats I have always loved that movie. It was a little hard finding all the items with Marie on it. But between Amazon and eBay, Kaylee's room was complete. After looking over her full walk-in closet filled with everything a child needs. I turned the light off and closed the door.

I crawled into my bed and laid on my back. I swear this baby was making me tired more and more. Everybody said I was all stomach and I was now starting to see the shit. I loved rubbing on it and feeling her kick. Right now, it was the end of August so I had on some black biker shorts and a pink cami. This whole summer I was either in yoga pants, maxi dresses or biker shorts. November 12th could not get here fast enough. I turned our TV on and went to the firestick to play Look Who's Talking.

While it started I took my phone out to scroll Facebook. I had so many notifications. All of them were congratulating me and Karlos on our baby girl. I can't tell you how many people shared our pictures. After thanking everyone I continued to scroll down. Seeing all the gossip and dirt people would post I laughed at Kelly's best friend Jayla post. Her and her man Ernest had broken up yet again and were on Facebook going at it.

His brother Marques was cussing them out telling them to get off line. Marques was a cute dude and him and Kelly would have looked good together. But Kaylin shut that shit down quick. Scrolling down I liked a couple if pictures. Watched some funny ass videos and shared some crazy ass memes. Karlos was taking so long and my hunger was kicking in. Not to mention I was missing him like crazy.

Walking down stairs I tried to make time pass by. Me and Karlos took some maternity pictures. Karlos favorite ones were the one with me in the tub. I was in a white square vintage tub. It was filled with yellow and pink rose pedals. I had my hair bone straight with a matching rose halo crown on my head. Laying in the tub holding my stomach looking down I looked heavenly. The I loved the one with me and

Karlos.

We both are in all white and he is kissing my stomach and I am smiling so big. The only one we had hanging up was the one where we are both holding a banner that says Kaylee. The other two took a little longer to get back to us. The frames I wanted them in had to be custom made. They arrived today and I was anxious to get them up. The only thing is where I wanted them. I would have to crawl up our latter to get them. Everybody thought I was handicap because I was pregnant. I would never do anything to harm myself or Kaylee but I wasn't incompetent.

Within a few minutes I had all three of the pictures on the wall. It looked so cute and I was smiling. I took some pictures and posted them on my phone. Just as I was posting them on Instagram Karlos turned his key in the door. I smiled big as hell when his fine ass walked through the door.

"Hey baby. Come look at this." I waved him over towards me. He smiled back at me walking towards the living room where I was. I turned and looked at our pictures. Karlos smile left his face and that mug was present.

"Kylee, you gone make me lock yo' ass in a padded room. Why the fuck is you climbing on latter's and shit? Yo' if something happens to you or my baby I'm killing us all." He walked towards the kitchen.

"What!" I yelled in surprise while following him to the kitchen. The pizza smelled so good and the big bag of Doritos did to.

"You heard me. If my two babies die on me ain't nobody gone be happy. I'm offing all of us and then myself. Fuck with it if you want to. We gone be a Dateline special." Now I know I shouldn't be laughing. But I couldn't help it! This nigga was certified crazy. But I love him down to the scum in his nails.

"You laughing but I'm dead ass." His ass even had to laugh at his crazy statement. After I regained myself I stuffed a slice of pizza in my mouth. Opening the chips, I put two in my mouth too. I was in paradise eating this food. Like an orgasm in my mouth. Karlos came and put his arms around my waist. He rubbed on my belly and like always, Kaylee kicked. He smiled big as hell. The moment was cute but I was too busy stuffing my face.

"You know I love you right baby. You and Kaylee my fuckin' air and there is no life for me without y'all." He kissed my neck and ears. I put my pizza down and turned to wrap my arms around his neck. Playing with his curls I just looked in his eyes. As crazy and intense my baby was. I knew he loved the fuck out of me. The feeling was very mutual, him and Kaylee were my world.

"Kiss me baby so I can breathe right." My heart sped up as I put my lips on his. Karlos lips were so big and juicy. He grew a beard a while back and decided to keep it. He had his Drake going on and it was turning me on. His long hair with the beard made him look even more scarier. Not to mention he was more buff. Them light grey eyes didn't help either. My baby no longer looked like the pretty boy with long hair. Still kissing him I finally pulled away and went back to eating. Karlos stood right there in the kitchen holding me from behind. This is how we were 90% of the time we were around each other. No matter who was around we were always all over each other. I never got tired of it and he better not either.

"How did your meeting go? Is everything coming along with the gym?" I asked him as I closed the pizza box. I ate three slices and half bag of Doritos. Karlos put my apple juice in the refrigerator. I walked over to grab it with Karlos big arms still wrapped around my waist. My big ole baby.

"It went well, everything will be ready in the middle of October. You will be reaching nine months so I'm opening after Kaylee comes." He used one of his hands and put some chips in his mouth.

"Karlos I am not a damn patient. You can have the opening baby and I will be there. Kaylee is not due until the

12th of November." We both walked to the living room.

"No, the doctor said that is your due date but Kaylee is low so she could come earlier than that. Yo' I can't wait to meet her, she is going to be so beautiful. I'm buggin' out over having a little girl. My guys coming out here next week to up-grade the war room. I want a lil' nigga to try me over my princess." I looked back at him to see if he was playing.

His face had a serious look on it. I shook my head smirking. This man had a whole room under our basement he called our war room. I say ours because last year he taught me how to shoot. I never have been a fan of guns. I hate them and I hate what people do with them. But the reality we live in today. I thought no harm would come with me learning how to shoot.

"Baby she is going to be a good girl just like her mother and aunties. You won't need any of that extra shit." I laughed at him. Turning the kitchen light off I walked to the living room to watch TV. Karlos was still attached to me from behind and I was drinking the attention up. He sat down first and I sat between his legs. Our extra-large custom made plush couch was big and comfy enough to sleep on. I loved it!

"The war room not for her. It's for niggas who think they got anything coming from my princess. I don't give a damn if he six years old. He better keep his snotty nose ass away from her." We both laughed as I turned on the TV. I went to OnDemand HBO and turned on Insecure. I was a few episodes behind. Karlos low key loved this show to he just tried to front. I knew the next thing I was about to say would annoy him.

"Los at 3'o clock I'm going to run errands with Keira. Ok?" He was rubbing my stomach while I laid my back on his chest.

"I hate when you not with me. Be careful Kylee and do not overdo shit. The minute you get tired sit yo' ass down and call me. You know I will come get you. I know I don't have to tell yo' ass to eat. We all know you got that shit covered." I laughed and hit his arm.

"Shut up! Don't be talking about me. You love me and my extra stomach I got." I stuck my tongue out at him.

"Baby you could have an extra stomach, triple chins and the fat girl lean. I still would love you and feed yo' ass as much as you wanted. Hell, I'm getting fat right with you. As long as this stays the same then we're are good." He pointed to my heart. I smiled and kissed his juicy ass lips.

"Fat girl lean?" I asked him while laughing.

"Yea! You know the ones who are short and really over weight? When they are standing up they have a lean. Almost like that Fat Joe dance Lean Back." I was cracking up at him because I knew exactly what he was talking about.

"Aye some big girls be fine as fuck. I have been with a few and the shit slapped." That made me stopped laughing. Fat, skinny or thick. I did not want to hear about Karlos with another female.

"Now if I get to telling you about the good dick I have had. Yo' ass would be ready to wreak havoc." That stopped his ass from laughing.

"Get a nigga killed Kylee Royal. Give me them fuckin' lips." I did as my baby asked and kissed him sloppy. I knew I should have calmed down because I had to leave in a few.

"Tell me you love me," Karlos said with his deep baritone voice.

"I love you so much my Los." I smiled at him while playing with the back of his curls.

"Not as much as I love you my Ky." We kissed again and watched TV until I had to meet up with Keira.

*

"I can't believe I let you talk me into this shit. If Karlos finds this shit out he is going to flip. I want a nice ass lunch for you making me put my life on the line." Keira looked at me with wrinkles in her forehead. I rolled my eyes.

"Keira your life is not on the line. You know Karlos would never hurt you or any of my sisters. You are being so dramatic." I parked my 2017 Cadillac CTS in an empty space. Grabbing my gym bag, me and Keira got out. We were at L.A. Fitness. The way Keira was acting, you'd think I was cheating on Karlos. All I wanted to do was work out.

"Kylee, you and I both know I am not being dramatic. If this is not that big of a deal then why are you sneaking?" she asked me as she held the door opened for me.

"Ke you know Karlos is overprotective and he wouldn't have even considered letting me come here." Keira laughed and shook her head.

"I love my big brother I swear I do. But he is certified crazy over you Kylee. But he's a sweetheart all in the same breath," Keira laughed as she took her head phones out her bag.

After we checked in me and Keira walked to the locker rooms. I couldn't leave the house in my gym attire. Karlos would have stopped me in my tracks.

"Ky oh my goodness! My niece has made your hips spread like butter. Look at your booty! It looks like you need to be in a porno." Keira was cracking up. I looked in the mirror and I was one fine mama to be. This pregnancy complimented my shape even more. I pulled my biker shorts over my belly. Keira fixed my sports bra in the back and tied my gym shoes. She looked cute too in her PINK yoga set.

Walking out Keira got on the treadmill while I went to the warm-up room. I couldn't wait to get on the jumbo workout ball. Because I was pregnant I was just keeping it light. We only needed to stall for 30 minutes until the class started. I wanted to try the mom to be workout session. Our old trainer John was teaching it.

After working on the ball my stop watch went off. Notifying me that 30 minutes was up. I went and grabbed the Keira off the treadmill. Neither of us had seen John since we started dating the guys. They had an issue with us working out with a male. This is why I didn't want to tell Karlos about this. He would have flipped out even though Keira was with me.

"Welcome ladies! Hope everybody is ready for a nice workout fit for your condition. These workouts I created for my wife. She just gave birth to our twin boys and she wanted to stay active. Her doctor told her the birthing process would go smoother if she stayed active. So, I created some light cardio moves for her. Ok, let's begin." He started us with some stretches and then some leg ups.

The workout had me feeling good. Even the women who were not as far along were feeling it. Me and Keira were laughing because one lady stopped to eat. John was an amazing workout instructor. Had the guys listened to us before, they would have known how professional he was. He didn't just do pregnant workouts. He did individuals, couples with him and his wife. He even did kid workouts and workouts for the elderly.

"Ok let's start the stand in place jumping jacks. Come on ladies in the back don't get tired on me! Let's get it!" We began the next set.

"KYLEE!"

"KYLEE!"

Everyone in the room stopped in place. It took me and Keira a minute to realize what the hell was going on. By the second time I heard my name my eyes grew three sizes wide. Part of me wanted to leave out the back. But I knew that would only make shit worse. I don't even know how he found out where I was.

"KYLEE WHERE THE FUCK YOU AT?!" His deep voice was booming all through the gym. For some reason, my feet were stuck. I could not move. Luckily, no one in the class knew my name. Then Karlos walked his ass in our room.

"Really! This what the fuck you do?" He stood in the entrance looking beyond mad. His hair was all down. With that beard and beater on he looked like a psychotic person.

"Um excuse me you need to leave---" John's words were cut short as Karlos punched him square in his nose. John was not a small man he put you in the mind set of Dwayne The Rock Johnson.

"Say one more fuckin' word to me and I will drop a bar bell on your fuckin' throat. That is MY fuckin' wife nigga!" He kneeled down in John's face and spoke through gritted teeth. Keeping his eyes on John.

"Get yo' shit and let's roll Kylee!" Everyone including me and Keira mouths were on the floor. I was so embarrassed and mad I didn't know what to do.

"I cannot believe you just caused a scene like that Karlos! You broke an innocent person's nose," I yelled at him while we were in the parking lot.

"Why the fuck did you hide this shit from me Kylee? You knew I would not let yo' ass step foot in a fuckin' gym! Not while you pregnant with our baby." He stepped closer to me.

"And if you ever become concerned about another nigga besides me. I promise I will break more than his fuckin' nose. Keira can you take Kylee's car to your house? I will pick it up tomorrow." Keira nodded her head yes. She hugged me and then looked at Karlos like she was scared to hug him.

"Give me some love baby sis. I should kick yo' ass for letting her come here but, I'll leave that to Kalvin." He chuckled while they hugged he kissed her on top of her head and held the driver's door open for her. See, my baby was sweet when he wanted to be. Keira blew the horn as she drove off.

"Get yo' ass in the truck." He opened the passenger's door for me to get in. Then he started with that mumbling shit.

"Up here worried about another nigga. Fat ass booty all on display. And you givin' me some of that as soon as we walk in the house." He waited until I clamped my seat belt and he closed the door. I tried my hardest not to laugh at his annoying ass. I real life was pissed off but Karlos was so fine when he was mad.

"Can I take a shower first please. I'm sweaty and sticky." I put my cute innocent voice on. I knew it made him lighten up. He side eyed me and turned the radio up. I laughed because that was his way of trying not to give in.

Getting home we walked in the house and I went straight up-stairs. I felt so bad for John and I was hoping he didn't call the police. Karlos thought he was getting some ass from me but he was sadly mistaken. I was showering, eating a salad and taking a nap. Then when I woke up I was going to edit one of the books my boss emailed me. I walked in our bedroom and striped out my clothes. I hurried and grabbed some boy shorts and a tank top.

I did not need Karlos coming in and thinking he was about to shower with me. I'm to annoyed with him to be around him right now. Walking in the bathroom I closed and locked the door. I put my hair in a high bun and turned the shower on. The hot water felt so good hitting my body. Kaylee was kicking like crazy.

I put my hands where ever I felt movement which made me smile. After washing my body with Warm vanilla sugar from Bath and Body Works I rinsed off and stepped out. My phone was vibrating on the sink. I looked down and say it was a text from a number I didn't know.

"Hello," I answered it hesitantly because I stored anybody's number who had importance to me.

"So this how we doing Kylee? You block me from Facebook and Instagram like I'm some nothing ass nigga. And you block my number? What happened to us being friends?" That deep scratchy voice spoke through my phone. I knew it was Tony. I blocked his number and him on my social media pages.

"Tony we can't be friends. I am someone's wife and about to be mother. I have told you this. I apologize if you thought it was something more. We just messaged each other a few times that's all. But my husband is not going to let me be friends with an ex. Hell, any nigga for that matter. Please respect that and just chill out." I didn't even give him a chance to respond. I hung up the phone and blocked the number he called me from. I did it just in time too. Karlos came up the stairs and into the bedroom. A few seconds passed, I knew he was taking off his clothes. He turned the knob on the bathroom door.

"Yo' Kylee if you don't open this fuckin' door," he said calmly. I rolled my eyes and put my phone back on the sink.

"Go away Karlos I'm getting dressed!" I yelled at him while rubbing lotion on my arms.

"You think I'm fuckin' playin." He turned the knob again this time making the door knob break all the way off. It hit the floor and the door popped open. I stood their ass naked with my mouth agape.

"KARLOS! You are fucking nuts, look at the door." I was looking down at the lock and wood chips on the floor. When my eyes looked up all my anger and shook was replaced by horny thoughts. Karlos was ass naked dick hangin' like clothes in a closet. He was looking so pissed with his hair all down. I needed some of him.

"Come her Kylee." He kept his eyes locked on mines as I walked towards him. He lifted me up and my legs went around his torso. Our lips smashed together. I always love kissing him nasty with a lot of tongue. He carried me to the bed and set down with me straddling him. He pulled away and looked me in my eyes.

"Can't shit stop me from getting to you. Always remember that shit." He used his perfect teeth and bit his bottom lip. I smiled at him.

"I know baby. Can't shit ever keep me from you Karlos. I love you." Just that fast I was over being angry at him. He smiled big and we went back to kissing. The love me and Karlos had for each other was so dangerous. But so damn addictive.

Tony

'FUCK!" I shouted as I threw my phone across the room. It shattered soon as it hit the wall. I had tried calling Kylee back over and over in denial of her blocking my new number like she did the first one. I went to Sprint and brought a new iPhone 8 and got a new number. I was going to use that phone as my Kylee phone. But as soon as she saw it was me calling her she blocked it. I was so pissed off and in my feelings.

In the morning, I was carrying my ass back up to the store for a new phone and number. I had to talk to her just to explain myself. It had been a year and a little change since I last was in her face. We met up at Starbucks and she looked so beautiful. Kylee was hands down the best thing to ever happen to me.

My stupid ass fucked that up by cheating and getting a THOT pregnant. Kylee was not like these other desperate hoes. She knew her worth. Her ass dumped me and never came back. I tried to fall back and let her have her space. But then she started dating that crazy muthafucka Karlos Royal.

How the fuck that lunatic get my sweet baby was beyond me. Kylee had no idea the nigga she said I do to really was. That man was beyond crazy and a killer in the worst way. It was only a matter of time before he snapped and hurt her.

When my mama called me and told me Kylee was pregnant I almost died. I had to play it cool and act like I already knew. But my mama was no fool. She knew that shit crushed me. A marriage can easily be divorced. But a child means that lunatic ass nigga had been in her raw. One of the things I loved about Kylee was she wasn't a hoe.

I loved having her on my arm. I felt exclusive or some shit. Like every nigga wanted to know my secret on getting a girl like her. Now she was walking around with half of that nigga inside of her. But asked me of that was going to stop me. I still wanted my sweet Kylee back and I was going to get her. As far as the child goes. I would raise baby girl as mines. Even though she has some Royal in her.

Baby girl would have more of her innocent mother in her. I knew Kylee still loved me when we shared a kiss after our Starbucks date. I wanted to take her home and make love to her the rest of the day. But I knew she was still heartbroken over that lunatic breaking her heart. I don't even know how or when they got back together. The last Kylee told me they were done and she was moving on. I felt some type of way.

How the fuck did she forgive him but didn't forgive me? We had a real history. Her dad didn't like me but my parents loved Kylee. My mama always said Kylee was her daughter in-law. My father use to tell me how stupid I was to let Kylee get away.

When I first met Kylee she was coming out Target. I almost hit a pole looking at her beauty. I had to get out my car and approach her. She acted like she was not interested at first and I was just about to give up. But God was on my side, she dropped her phone. I held on to it hoping she would call it and want it back. Just my luck, she did.

I met up with her and her sister Kimmora. When Kylee saw it was me who found her phone she smiled at me so big. I asked her out and she agreed. The rest was history. We were glued to one another from then on. I was talking to other bitches the entire relationship. But no bitch got treated like Kylee. I spent money on her, brought her gifts, took her on dates.

We went on trips out of town and we had a lit ass sex life. As a matter of fact, I still have the little movie we made on my old camera phone. I looked at it every damn day. I kept that phone charged up just so I can watch it and beat my dick to it. No bitch had pussy like Kylee's. I just needed her back and no matter what I had to do I was going to get her.

"Tony what the fuck are you doing? Stop throwing a tantrum and just give her some space for a minute. Look, today is my first day of work so maybe I will see her. What I need you to do is chill out big bro," my baby sister Taylor looked at me and said. She had been staying with me since she came back home.

"T please just stick to the plan. Get in with them and keep me updated on Kylee and that nutty nigga. Tell me every fuckin' thing." I stood up and kissed my sister on the forehead. I gave her a stack and she shoved it in her purse. She grabbed the keys to her Lexus I got her and walked out.

I loved my baby sister so much. We were a year apart and extremely close. When were in 7th grade our parents sent Taylor to live with our grandparents. For some reason, my pops and Taylor just could not get along. Taylor went through a faze when she just didn't talk. My mama thought something happened to her and she was scared to talk.

They sent her to physiologist and self-esteem camps hoping something would help. Taylor just would not talk unless her and my father were arguing. My mama felt she needed to get away so my grandma in D.C. said she would keep her. I cried for three days when my sister left. My parents started working more and my only friend was the nanny.

When I was in high school I joined the football team and became popular. Bitches were endless and my friends changed as well. Taylor was happy in D.C. or so she told me every time we talked. Till this day we still do not know why Taylor just stopped talking. But I didn't press the issue to much.

I was proud of baby girl for graduating high school and going to Barber school. When she told me she wanted to come home I was excited and told her I would cover everything. Money was never an option for our family. Our parents were both surgeons and were very well off. They raised me and Taylor with a silver spoon. Education was very important in our home. Good grades equals hella cash and expensive gifts.

Now that Taylor was back I had the bright idea to get her into the Royals barber shop. I had my two boys work there. I set them up and had them selling dope out of the barber shop. The plan was to get them busted and locked up. But the young niggas I had got caught and the Royals bodied them niggas. Stupid muthafuckas should have listened to me. Taylor was my final shot to getting into the circle.

My next move would be to just kidnap Kylee and expose to her who her husband really was. But I knew Taylor could work her way into the crew. My baby sister was bad and she was talented as hell with the clippers. I knew in a matter of time she would make friends with Kylee and her sisters. All I needed her to do was get everything she can on all of them. All the Royals that is, Kylee sisters were innocent.

All of them needed to be cleansed of them fucked up Royals. I vowed to myself once I get Kylee back I would never lose her again. Fuck all these hoes and they drama. I been knew I fucked up when Kylee left me. I thought once she found out that bitch lost the baby she would come back to me. But Klyee still was not having it.

Truth be told ol'girl didn't lose the baby. I sliced that bitch neck and dumped her body in the swamp. Once I realized Kylee was going to leave me I told that hoe to get an abortion. But she told me no then she threated to tell Kylee all my dirt. All my cheating and lying was going to come out. That's when I knew that bitch and that bastard baby had to go.

All of that shit was now behind me and now I was ready to start over. If Kylee would just hear me out. She will realize me and her are meant to be and I can make her happy like before. Taylor was going to come through for me and we would all be a happy family. All the Royals would be dead and forgotten. Karlos may have been a killer but her still had a conscience. I on the other hand didn't give a fuck who I had to kill to get what I want. I offed the family that were living in this house. I wanted to buy it and the man of the house would not sell it. Karlos and his brothers were not going to roll over easy. The only way to win was to kill the competition.

KNOCK!

KNOCK!

KNOCK!

I got up from my recliner in the living room. Walking to the door I picked up the pieces of the phone and trashed it. I walked passed the full-body hallway mirror and looked myself over. I was shirtless with some blue sweatpants on. My gold diamond chain and my Nike flip-flops. I was a handsome as nigga.

Standing at 6'2 I had brown skin and light brown eyes. I kept my hair cut and my goatee lined up. I played no games about my physical appearance. I worked out every day and ran five miles every morning. My body was hard and muscular body. A lot of bitches says I look like that nigga Ghost from the TV series POWER. When I made sure I looked good I went and opened my front door.

My heart rate sped up when her pretty chocolate ass stood at my door. She had on some ripped leggings and brown sweater dress with gold hoop earrings. Her hair was long and jet black curly and it was in a high bun on top of her head. Those big brown eyes looked at me with lust in them. Her body was so fucking thick. The dress was hugging the fuck out of it making my mouth water.

"I told you to wear pink and white nails." I got annoyed because I paid top dollars for this bitch. I was specific on how I wanted my girl to look. Down to her nails and toes. This bitch had yellow nails.

"I apologize I was told yellow." She held the paper out for me to see. She was right it said yellow. I didn't even stay mad. Fuck it, I had spent $10,000 for this bitch. I couldn't be too picky.

"What are you supposed to say when you greet me and when we fuckin'?" I asked her. I wanted to make sure she at least got that right. If she didn't I was going to slap the fuck out of her and send her on her way.

"I'm supposed to call you my Tony-Wony." She smiled at me just like I said. I swear if you didn't know any better. You would think this bitch was Kylee Ricci. My heart rate sped back up and I got on hard. I paid to have her until 10am tomorrow. I could tell right now I would be spending another 10-grand on this bitch again.

"Get yo' sexy ass in here." I moved out the way and she swayed her thick ass in the house.

"So, where do you want me?" Her sexy soft voice asked me. I licked my lips and pointed.

"In our bedroom." She turned and walked up the stairs. I had my master bedroom ready for her so she knew the one to go in. I followed her and closed the bedroom door behind me. I walked over to her and laid her body on the rose pedal filled bed. I got on top of her sexy body. Looking down at her you couldn't tell me it was not with the real thing.

"I love you Kylee," I said to her. She looked at me with love in her eyes. Smiling lightly, she said.

"I love you too Tony-Wony." I kissed her deeply and began the first of our many fuck sessions that day.

Karlos

"Throw that pregnant pussy back baby." I looked down at Kylee juicy booty slap against my pelvis. The only thing could be heard in the garage was her wet pussy slappin'. One of my favorite fuckin' sounds next to her voice. We had just come back from lunch at Outback, my baby's favorite spot.

All day Kylee had been looking so fucking good with this yellow maxi dress on. She already knows I love bright colors on her chocolate ass skin. He fat ass booty was sitting up right and moving up and down everytime she walked. I wanted to fuck her all through the mall and when we went to go eat. Then she had that pregnant pussy that got extra wet for a nigga. If I could walk around with my dick up her all day I would. I couldn't even make it in the house before I was bending her over in my truck.

Kylee always down for whatever when it came to me. Her doctor told us some bullshit at our last visit. She said I may have picked up some of Kylee's pregnant symptoms. Hormonal was one of them. I dismissed that shit, that damn doctor just didn't know me. I was always addicted to Kylee from day one. Hormonal bullshit symptoms had nothing to do with it. Touching her was a fucking drug and I needed my fix every fuckin' day or I don't breathe right.

"Oh my goodness Karlos I'm gonna cum baby." I pulled out and turned her around. I quickly lifted her up and set her on the passenger's seat. I dropped to my knees and put my head between her legs. Licking and sucking on her clit while she grinded her waist towards my face. Them long chocolate legs were wrapped around my neck for dear life. Fuck! I could eat Kylee's pussy for breakfast, lunch, dinner and midnight snack.

Shit tasted and smelled like sweet vanilla cheesecake.

Swear I'm not making this shit up. I think it's all the cheese cake her as eats and makes. Y'all know that's my baby's favorite dessert. That shit must be in her pores because I swear her pussy tasted like it. I didn't even need to use my fingers. I just let my tongue and lips do all the work. I could here and feel her juices all on my face and on my beard. My dick was about to fall off just thinking of my face smelling like her.

"Ughhhhhh fuck I'm cummin' Karlos." She came hard as fuck in my mouth. I sucked on that clit harder and licked faster. Not stoping when she said she was cummin'. I wanted to drain her pretty ass. I knew I succeeded when her body started jerking. I still didn't stop, just slowed down. I swirled in circles slowly around my clit.

"Sssss what the hell Karlos. Mmm che si sente bene (that feels good)." I laughed to myself when I heard her speak Italian. Yea I fucked her head up. I started kissing her inner thighs as her body still jerked. I kissed her neck markin' that shit up then I got to them lips. I bit and pulled on her lips. She started playing with my curls in the back. That shit calmed me whenever she did that.

"I'm sorry Ky. I just couldn't wait another minute to get inside of you. I got you when tonight though." I went back to kissing her lips.

"No baby I got you later. You didn't even nut I feel bad." She started laughing and covering up her pretty ass face.

"It wasn't about me. I needed to feel and taste you baby. You know I love makin' that body jerk." I smirked at her while biting my lip. She kissed me and rubbed my now wet beard.

"I love this Drake thing you got going on." She laughed and I turned my nose up.

"Yo' fuck that nigga. I'm burning up all shit you got of his Canadian ass." She laughed harder at my ass. But I was dead serious, because of her I now hated Drake. I picked her up bridal style and walked in the house. She been on her feet long enough today.

"Aww baby you know I love you more than Aubrey Graham." I just looked at her ass and kept walking.

"Karlos you do not have to carry me everywhere. You already had the people at Outback staring at me when you did this. I keep telling you Kaylee and I are fine." I ignored her as I walked up the stairs and into our bedroom.

I had some shit to do so I wanted to get my wife right before I left. Kylee pouted the whole time but I didn't give a fuck. She was not about to overdo shit and put herself at risk. I went in her drawer and pulled a yellow tank top out and yellow boy shirts. Putting the clothes on the bed I went to the bathroom and turned the shower on. I grabbed one of her black hair ties and came back to her. Kylee rolled her eyes as I put her hair in a high bun. I smirked at her mean lookin' ass.

"Arms up," I told her as I lifted her dress over her head. I un-did her bra and since I ripped her panties off when we were fucking her in the garage. I took her black sandals off and put them in her closet. I picked her up bridal style and carried her into the bathroom. Pulling the shower curtain back I placed Kylee in the shower.

I grabbed her girly body wash and lathered her sponge up. Once her body was soaked I began washing her up. I love doing this because I get to really see my wife's beautiful body. It was definitely God's best work. I washed her arms, neck and legs. I got to that pretty pussy and that round ass. Once she was all soapy she rinsed her body off getting her hair wet. I looked at the water rinse the soap off her smooth chocolate skin.

"Kylee, you are so fuckin' beautiful girl. I'm a lucky ass nigga to have you baby." She smiled big as hell at me showing them deep ass dimples. Her shit was contagious so I smiled back at her.

After she was done I helped her out and dried her off. Wrapping the towel around her body I carried her back to our bed. Once I had her laid on the bed I opened her towel. I oiled her body up with that vanilla lotion. I went and grabbed her Dove deodorant and put it on her under arms. I kissed all over her stomach and my princess started kicking.

I stood Kylee up and put her boy shorts on and her tank top. I knew she would want her hair to air dry in the bun. I walked downstairs and came back with her cheesecake, apple juice and Doritos. I tucked my baby in and gave her the remote.

"Ok baby I gotta handle some shit but I won't be long." I squatted my tall ass down so I can get in her face.

She looked at me with them sad big eyes. I knew she didn't want me to leave but I had to handle this business. Kylee rubbed the side of my face and played with my curls. Her big brown eyes teared up. I had to fight hard as fuck to keep from laughing at my baby. Kaylee had her emotional as hell. I failed like a muthafucka and started laughing.

"That's not funny Karlos. You always leaving me." She sniffed and cried some more. It low-key made me feel good to see her so thirsty for me. But I didn't want her crying

"Kylee stop crying baby. You know I'm coming back to both of my babies. Tomorrow you will have me all to yourself." I looked my wife in her eyes and rubbed her belly again. "

Tell me you love me so I can breathe right." I wiped her tears and kissed her wet lips.

"I love you Karlos. I swear if you leave me tomorrow I'm divorcing you." That made me laugh hard as fuck. We all know damn well I would never let that shit happen. She gave me my own mug face.

"Word baby. I promise I'm all you tomorrow." Shoving my tongue in her mouth one more time I headed on out. My fucking Ky.

*

"Killz please listen to me man. I'm begging you please! I had no idea my debt would roll over to y'all. I'm used to dealing with my debt with your uncles. R-R-Ricky told me if I kept paying him five grand a month everything would be settled. I didn't know he never settled shit." Nook was crying bad as fuck as he pleaded his case to me.

About a month ago I got a visit at our club Royalty. My security guy tells me some niggas in black and white were outside for me. I turned the cameras on and saw six big niggas and one skinny nigga. Of course, my crew stays ready so we strapped up and went to get at them. They tell me they lookin' for a nigga named Nook. He set them up back in L.A. a year ago. Nook made them lose a lot of money and product.

Not to mention a few of his crew members were killed. Nook has been working for us going on four years. I don't know him personally but like all our crew members. I had all the facts and details on his life. My pops brothers put us in him they told us he needed to make some quick cash. So we made him a seller in L.A. with five of or trusted sellers. Well Nook fled L.A. after he set them up. He told my pops brothers what happened.

Apparently, they contacted the niggas from L.A. and settled the debt. In exchange Nook had to pay Ricky five grand a month. Ricky and Charles sour asses never made such a deal. The niggas from L.A. let me know he told them I would cover the ten million worth of shit that was lost in the set up. He told them to give me a year and I would have their money. Now, imagine my surprise when I was told this shit. I kept it real with the L.A. niggas. I told them about my pops dirty ass brothers and that I bodied them.

They showed respect and understood. But they wanted me to give up Nook. Since pussy don't run in my veins I told them Nook split. And I told them to suck my nut sack on the payment. No man walking this earth out fear in me. Them niggas didn't take to lightly to being played out of ten million. Even though my pops brothers were dead they still were short ten million. My crew and their crew had a stare down in the lot of my club. They ended up leaving but when you in the game. You know that does not mean shit is over.

"Why the fuck would you even set them niggas up? You eatin' good as fuck Nook. I feed you and your family enough that you own three houses. Then you ran yo' ass to my pops brothers who fucked you over." I walked circles around him while he was tied up in a chair. I stopped in his face.

"Now your fuck up is my fuck up. I don't play about the Royal name. Because of yo' ass now the is a little dirt on my name. I cannot have that shit nigga," I said through gritted teeth. I felt my eyes get black and veins grow in my neck.

"K-K-Killz pleaseeee. Y-Y-You said they left man. If they wanted beef you would have heard something." I punched him right in his stomach with full force. The nigga threw up all on my shoes. I smiled big as hell.

"You can't do this. I have a family and they will come looking for me!" he yelled when I pulled my black duffle bag from under the table.

"Oh, you mean your fine ass wife and baby boy right?" I walked over to the darkroom in our warehouse. When I stepped back out I had his wife by the arm with a black sack over her head. I snatched it off and she was crying hard as hell. I removed her duct tape off her mouth and hands.

"Please don't kill me or my family Mr. Royal," she cried and looked at me.

"I am not going to hurt you or your baby boy." I signaled for my boy to come over here with her baby. She smiled when she saw he was fine and smiling. Royals don't hurt women or children unless we had to. Children were always off limits no exception. Zena's ass was an exception.

"However, your husband is not so lucky. But I want to show you something to help ease your mind. If you want to walk out of here with your entire family I will let you. If you want to walk out if here with just your son. And let me handle your husband then I will let you. We clear?" She nodded her head yes. I pulled out a manila folder out my black bag. I gave it to her shaking hands. She looked from her husband with tears and down at the folder.

"You can open it," I told her. When she did her sadness turned into shock. She flipped through all the 8x10 pictures. All the pages of text messages and receipts to expensive stores, hotels, trips and clothes. Tears fell from her eyes uncontrollably.

"OH MY GOD NICHOLAS! YOU TOLD ME YOU STOPPED THIS! HOW COULD YOU!" She screamed at him while dropping the folder on the floor. She sobbed bad as hell. Her sobbing and her baby cooing was all you could here. Then she calmed herself down and started taking deep breaths. She wiped her face and looked at her son then at me.

"Kill that sick ass faggot." She went over to her son and took him from my boy arms. I had my boy take her home with a suitcase with two million dollars in it.

"CLARA! CLARAAAA! DON'T DO THIS TO ME!" Nook yelled after her. She didn't even look back. I smiled big as hell as I pulled my 16" heavy steel chain out my black bag. He started crying so loud.

"A killhis ass he is shittin' and peeing on his self! Nasty ass nigga!" One of my crew members pointed out. The asses fell out laughing. I was to until that nigga started to stink.

"Dick in the booty ass nigga. Stop shittin' on yo' self and man up to this shit." I walked behind him. In one swift move, I wrapped the chain in moth my hands and put it over his neck. I squeezed hard as fuck. Nook squirmed and jerked his body. I only squeezed tighter until his eyes popped hanging from the socket. I squeezed harder and before I knew it his entire head snapped from his neck. When I finally let the chain go it along with his head fell on the floor.

"Dirty dick ass fag," I said as I spit on his dead body.

"Give his head to the dogs." I walked towards the basement to shower and burned my clothes.

Stepping outside the summer night heat hit my face making me put my hair up. It was hot and humid as fuck outside. I hopped in my truck and turned the A.C. on and headed to my next stop. I was ready to get back home to my baby and be up under her all night. Inside of her too. Ha!

I swear my wife pumps blood from my veins to my heart. And now she was having my princess and I couldn't be happier. Kylee thought I was hurt about not having a son. I kept telling her I didn't give a fuck. Yea I did want a boy because a girl would have me on edge. But we had a lot of good years ahead of us so trying again was always an option.

I pulled up to Royal Trim and hit the alarm on my car. I needed to pick up the books for this month. Plus, this was me and my brother's hangout spot besides our club. The shit was like no other barber shop. After I popped those fools for selling in my brother's shop I knew they would hire new help. When I walked in everybody spoke to me and showed love.

"Bro-Bro what up!" Kalvin and Kevin yelled out to me. I dabbed my baby brother's up and kissed them on the head. My brothers were my heart next to Kylee and Kaylee. Them, my sister in-laws and my nieces and nephew were all mines. And I'd kill anybody if they fucked with them.

"What's good niggas. I gotta get them books so Marvin and handle that shit. I'm swinging by Brandon's carwash to get his too." I set down in an empty barber chair.

"Killz this is Ron and Wayne. We hired them two weeks ago. Taylor will be here and you can meet her," Kevin said. I nodded towards the two niggas he introduced me too. My brothers knew I didn't do well with new people. I'll to trust them like they asked me to do so I didn't have my P.I. guys investigate them.

"Y'all hired a girl? Damn she must ne the shit with the clippers." Just as I said that the door chimed alerting is someone walked in. We all looked up and this bad ass thick bitch walked in. Not being blind to the fact she had it going on.

"Hey everybody. I got six heads to cut today as requested." She smiled at us and walked to the break room.

"Damn! She bad as fuck, how the hell can y'all work?" I

asked them. They fell out laughing but I was dead ass. O'l girl was lit. But let me shut my happily married ass up. While we talked and laugh Taylor came back out. She had her coat off showing her curvy body in tight jeans.

"Hey Kalvin." She looked at my brother and spoke to him.

"Sup Taylor." This nigga smiled and bit his lip. She blushed and started setting herself up for her client. Me and Kevin exchanged looks. I know damn well goody to shoes Kalvin is not playing with fire like this. Hell naw! I had to chop it up with this nigga on another day. The way him and ol'girl looked at each other. His ass is asking for shit he don't want.

"A'ight I'm outta her niggas. Gotta get to my wife." I looked at Kalvin when I made that last statement. I dabbed them up and headed out.

I stopped at the liquor store to get me some rellos and get Kylee some apple juice. While I was in the liquor this nigga walked in. He had a bitch on his arm that made me do a double take. This bitch looked so much like Kylee that I thought it was her.

Like no bullshit I was about to yank her ass up. I didn't know if I wanted to fuck her or kick her ass for being with a nigga. Even her style was like my wife. She had black curly hair in a bun. She had on tight jeans, a sweater and tall heel boots.

This bitch even had the dimples and brown eyes. But, no matter how identical she was. My heart was not racing. My breathing didn't change and my dick was not hard. That's how I knew for sure she wasn't my baby. The nigga she was with kept her close. That was smart because his bitch kept side eyeing me. I chuckled, paid for my shit and bounced.

Pulling up to our house I parked my car in the garage. Walking in I put her juice in the refrigerator and put my rellos in my man cave. I planned on smoking tomorrow while Kylee worked in her office.

"Where my Ky at?" I smiled when I walked in the bedroom. My baby was sitting in her exercise ball watching that cartoon she loves. Rockos Modern Life. I laughed and shook my head at her.

"Hey my Los. I missed you baby." Her face always beamed whenever she saw me. That shit made me feel so damn good. I went over to her after I took off my shoes and jacket. I picked her up off her excerise ball. I kissed her long and deep.

"You didn't miss me as much as I missed you. I'm about to take a shower and it's me and you. Ok?" She giggled and said ok.

"Aye, I saw this girl today in the liquor store. Baby she looked just like you. I mean she could have been your twin or some shit. I wish you were with me so you could have seen it." I still held her in my arms as I talked to her.

"You were about to fall in love all over again?" Kylee laughed and teased me. I shook my head.

"Naw. She looked like you but you can tell she wasn't you. Only you make a nigga's heart rate change. Fuck that clone bitch." We laughed and I kissed her some more. I put Kylee down and went to the bathroom. I took another quick ass shower and hurried to my baby in the bed.

"You not leaving me tomorrow Karlos. I don't care who calls or who needs Killz to come through. The answer is no," Kylee said to me as I held her in my arms. Her back was to my chest. I was rubbing her stomach. It was late so I knew Kaylee was sleep because I felt no kicking.

"I got you baby. Me and you tomorrow I promise. Anybody call me who is not family I'm fuckin' them up." Kylee laughed and so did I. She turned over and kissed me while my hand went down her boy shorts.

"I love you my Los," she said against her lips.

"Nowhere near as much as I love you my Ky." I started putting soft kisses on her neck.

*

I woke up to my baby in my arms sleeping so peacefully. I kissed the top of her head and slid out of bed, careful not to wake her. Walking to the bathroom naked as the day I was born. I lifted the toilet seat up and drained the anaconda. After I was done I handled my hygiene and walked back to our bed. Not even bothering to put my boxers on, I climbed back in with my wife. I turned the TV on NFL Network and watched some highlights of the past season.

Kylee was still knocked the fuck out. I knew it was my princess and this dick that had her sleeping that hard. After watching TV for a minute, I got up to fix me and my baby something to eat. I grabbed my boxers and walked downstairs. All I wanted was a bowl of Cinnamon Toast Crunce. But I knew if I brought my wife a bowl of cereal she would throw it at my ass.

After about fifteen minutes I had some pancakes, hashbrowns with onions cooked in them. Some scrambled eggs with cheese and a slice of vanilla cheesecake. Don't fucking laugh at my wife's breakfast! She eatin' for two. I put all the food on a tray and walked upstairs with my bowl of cereal in my other hand. When I walked in the room Kylee was sitting on the side of the bed with her phone crying.

"Baby 'what's the matter, who gotta fuckin' die?" I asked her as I set the tray of food and my cereal on the couch in our room. I walked over to her and kneeled down in front of her face. She sniffed as I wiped her tears away.

"I thought you was gone. I sent you a nasty ass text." She looked at me with sad eyes. I looked at her pretty ass and kissed her deep with some tongue. After I pulled on her lip a little I looked at her beautiful face.

"Kylee, this baby got you losing it." I laughed and she did to. I could tell she took care of her hygiene because her breath smelled like Crest Mint toothpaste. She had some peach boy shorts on and a peach PINK sports bra. Her pretty ass hair was on top of her head in a bun matching mines.

I brought her over to the couch so we could sit down

and eat. After saying grace, we both murdered our food. I pulled my phone out my pocket and turned in on silent. I didn't want any interruptions. I opened the text she sent me and I laughed as I read it. This crazy girl said when I get back home she would have divorce papers waiting for me.

"Kylee, why you so quick to leave yo' husband? Why would you fuck up Louisiana like that? You already know what I would do if you not with me." I laughed but it was nothing funny about what I said. Y'all know I ain't lying.

"I'm sorry baby, I thought you left me here by myself." She leaned over and kissed me. All my annoyance went out the window.

"Thank you my Los. That food looks so good." Kylee smiled at me with them deep dimples showing. I nodded and kissed her forehead.   We set down on the couch in our bedroom and ate our food. After I took the tray and dishes back downstairs I came back to her picking up her Kindle. My baby loved reading that urban-fiction shit. Before I met her, I had never read any of those books. Now, her ass had me interested and that's when she started reading them to me.

Don't mistake it, a nigga wasn't dumb I could read. I just loved doing shit like this with my wife. I craved intimate shit with her and not just us fucking. Books made my baby happy and I wanted to be apart of it. I liked when she read to me especially the sex scenes. My freaky ass be picturing the shit be me and her.

"Baby, what was the series called we finished last week?" I asked her as I climbed back in the bed.

"Oh, that was My Baby Is A West Coast King by Shvonne Latrice. We can read another one of her series after we finish this new I got for us." She turned her Kindle on and I turned the TV off and laid my head in her lap. I just looked at my pretty ass wife while she got her Kindle set up for us.

I loved this girl so much the shit was crazy. Only her ass could take this crazy savage and have him laid up getting read to. She had changed me for the better and I don't ever think she would know how grateful I was to have her. I would die being a ruthless killer but I was blessed to find love and have it returned to me. God was that nigga for hooking me up like this. I kissed her belly and my princess kicked. Kylee looked down at me and smiled.

"Ok, so this series is called Then There Was Us by Miss Candice. Her shit be lit baby so I know you are gonna love it." Her eyes beamed at me and I leaned up and kissed her lips a few times.

"Anything you read to me I'm gonna love. Come on wit it." Kylee started reading and I started listening. I loved our bond.

Keira

Three weeks later

"So, has Kalvin come around with to us opening the braid shop?" Kelly asked me while biting into her sandwich. We had just got out of class and were at Panera Bread eating. I was loving the hair braiding class. Even though we had the shit on lock. It still was so much we learned.

"I'm assuming he is. We really haven't talked about it much. Lately he has been working a lot." I wiped my mouth and tool a sip of my chai tea.

"What about when he comes home and y'all do that pillow talk shit you always bragging about." Kelly chuckled and so did I. I loved me an Kalvin pillow talks. We have been having them ever since the night we met. We would talk about everything under the sun but we had one rule. We always had to be honest and not hold back. It was a judgement free zone.

"Um well Kyra has been up at night so we have not had any time to talk." I looked everywhere but at my sister. Sometimes I hated that we were twins. I could get away with some lies with everybody else. But Kelly could see right through the bullshit.

"Keira what's going on? You won't look at me and you look like your about to cry." She pushed her food aside and waited for me to answer. I pushed my tears back and cleared my throat.

"It's really nothing, Kelly and I'm probably being dramatic. But it's like Kalvin is always busy and when he is home. He is either in his man cave or in the living room. We sleep in the same bed and he holds me the same. We even still have good sex. It just feels like something is off. He still bonds with Kyra and we have dinner and breakfast together. But I feel like some shit is out of place with him." I shook my head and drunk some of my tea. I wrapped my sandwich up because I had lost my appetite.

"Keira, you have to talk to Kalvin. He is not just your baby daddy or boyfriend any more. He is your husband. You should never walk around your home feeling uncomfortable. We all love you and Kalvin's relationship. Why do you think we call y'all asses the Hallmark couple?" We both laughed.

"You guys are in sync in a different kind of way, a pure way. You know Kalvin better then all of us do. You just have to talk to him and get to the bottom of it. If you want I can keep Kyra for you tonight so y'all can have some privacy." I smiled at my twin.

"You're right, I have to talk to him. Thank you twin." She came on my side of the booth and hugged me. Tonight, I was taking Kelly's advice and talking to Kalvin.

*

I put the lid over the pineapple upside down cake. That was Kalvin's favorite dessert so I knew he would love it. I cooked all his favorites tonight and set our dining room table for two. I cooked jumbo shells stuffed with lump crab and a béchamel sauce over it. With garlic bread and asparagus salad.

When I heard his car pull up in the garage I went to our hallway mirror. I gave myself the once over and smiled at my pretty self. I had my short white silk robe on with a white bra and panties lace set on. Kalvin loved white on me so I stopped at Lover's Lane after I dropped Kelly off. I heard Kalvin turn the knob to the front door and I greeted him.

"Hey bae love, welcome home." I smiled big at his sexy self. He looked at me from head to toe and smiled. After taking his jacket and shoes off I hung it up for him and took him by the hand.

"What's all this love?" He looked at the set up in the dining room. I went all out and used the Italian crest table cloth and matching china set. My dad gave it to us as one of the many wedding presents. I pulled his chair out and ushered him to sit down.

"I just wanted to do something special for my husband. I let Kyra spend the night at Kelly and Kaylin's house. Your brother was happy as hell, he is really ready for a baby." Once Kalvin sat down I was about to do the same but he grabbed my wrist.

"Give me a kiss." I bent down and pecked his lips. I didn't want to do too much. I wanted us to eat and talk. I needed to get some stuff off my chest that I let sit for too long.

"This food looks good as hell Keira. I see you made all a nigga's favorites." We smiled at each other. After we said grace we began to eat. I gave us a few minutes to enjoy the meal. Halfway through I started talking.

"Kalvin, I wanted to talk to you about something." He looked up at me with a mouth full of food. After swallowing he drunk some wine.

"What's on your mind wife." He looked at me and for a moment I wondered if what I was about to say even need to be said.

Maybe I was being extra and over thinking shit. Then I saw him take his phone out his pocket. He looked at it and sit it face down. That was something I didn't tell Kelly. Kalvin started hanging on to his phone like a life line these day. If he ever did put it down it was always face down. Usually Kalvin would leave his phone all over the house and didn't care.

Now it was glued to his hand. Reminded me of a teen who was waiting on her crush to call. This was my bae love, he was the sweetest of all his brothers. His own mom used to call him her baby cakes because he smiled so much. I know as soon as I tell him my thoughts he would fix it.

"Keira, love talk to me. What's wrong?" He snapped me out of thoughts. I cleared my throat and took a sip of wine.

"Kalvin what has been going on with you lately? For the past two-weeks you have been off a little. We don't pillow talk at night anymore and you are always working. I'm happy the shop is doing good. But you don't even ask me how my braid program is going. You don't even be in the same room with me anymore unless we are sleep. What is going on and please don't lie to me." I looked him in his eyes the entire time I talked. I felt like a weight was lifted off me like I could exhale now. Kalvin looked shocked with his eyebrows furrowed.

"Wow. I was not expecting you to say all of that. Love, nothing is wrong with me or you. I'm 100% fine I promise you that. I apologize if I seem off and if I have been working so much. But that's all I have been doing is working----"

"Kalvin, I asked you not to lie to me! I know something is going on. You keep your phone glued to your hand. You like to be alone now more than before. Just tell me the truth or don't talk at all!" I yelled the last part because I was getting annoyed by his lying. He got mad and hit the table hard making me jump.

"Keira, I don't know who the hell you are raising your voice at. But you better chill out! Now, I told you nothing----" I didn't even listen to the rest I got up from the table while he talked.

"The fuck!" Kalvin jumped up and roughly grabbed my arm. I turned around and looked at him mad as hell.

"The fuck you walkin' away from me for Keira? I don't take kindly to disrespect you know that shit. You are my wife and I would never hurt you but don't EVER walk way when I'm talking to you." I was not trying to hear that shit. I snatched my arm away hard as fuck so I could go up the stairs. That only pissed him off even more. This time he used both his hands and grabbed me by my arms turning me around.

"Keira what the fuck is wrong with you?! I just told you don't walk away from me." I still tried to squirm and get out of his hold but he held tighter and started shaking me.

"Listen to me! Listen to me! I ain't on new shit and never will be! It's only you Keira! You are the only woman that I'm on." I stopped moving and tears fell from my face. I had been holding this cry in for weeks.

"Keira look at me love, please." After a few seconds, I did as he asked.

"I apologize if I made you feel like some shit is wrong. Believe me when I tell you I'm good. We are good Keira. Stop fuckin' crying, the shit is fucking me up." Those light grey eyes were filled with sadness. I softened up a lot.

"Kalvin, I love you so much and I became scared. When we stopped connecting I felt empty. Just promise me we will always be Kalvin and Keira. Promise me your not playing with my heart." My tears were falling uncontrollably. I loved Kalvin with all my heart and I loved our family.

"Keira, I promise you we will always be ok and I am not playing with your heart. I love you girl so damn much. Your my wife, mother of my child I would never hurt you." He tried to kiss me but I turned my head. I was confused and all in my feelings. I had no real reason to be upset but then again, I can't shake this feeling. To go from being us to this strange behavior he was showing just was not normal.

"Keira kiss yo' husband, please. I didn't do anything wrong I promise love. Kiss me Ke. Kiss me now." Kalvin was holding my face with both of his hands. His breath smelled so good mixed with his cologne. I could not deny that I love this man and I wanted us to be ok. I needed us to be ok. Him and Kyra were my world and I needed them. I looked in his eyes a little longer. I saw so much love so I kissed his lips. Kalvin kissed me with so much force and passion. Like he was talking to me through this kiss.

He pulled my robe down and cupped my ass with his big hands. I loved that Kalvin was so much taller than me. I ran my fingers through his sexy mini curly fro. He moaned against my lips making wetness gush between my legs. I was so ready. I pulled away for a second so I could pull his blue Nike shirt over his head. His hard-muscular body made my mouth water as I eyed his sexy ass. I loved his tattoo of a dream catcher with my name in the center of it.

I had a matching on with his name on the back of my shoulder blade. Kalvin pulled the string on his Nike sweatpants and pulled them down. I watched him get undress as I took off my bra and lace panties. Once we were naked we went back to kissing. He lifted me up holding my legs around his waist and carried me up-stairs. Once we were in our room he laid me down on our couch. Our tongues were still dancing together.

He moved to my neck and my ears making me moan out loud. Those were my spots and he knew it. He bit down a little on my neck and my back arched up. I was scratching up his back. My body was grinding and hot as hell and I had not even had the dick yet. Kalvin hand went down my stomach until it reached my pussy.

The TV was off so when his fingers opened my pussy lips. You could hear my wetness soak up his fingers. He put his index and middle finger in my tight pussy hole. Moving them in and out real slow I felt like I was losing my mind. His fingers plus him biting and pulling on my nipples had me cumming in no time.

Kalvin replaced his fingers with his thick long dick. He brought his wet hand to my mouth and I licked my own juices off his fingers. Not only did I enjoy my own taste but I loved Kalvin's face when I did that. He would bite his lip and grunt like he was so turned on he wanted to scream. Kalvin set up with his dick still in me. He had me straddle him while he set up on the couch. I got up and turned around to reverse cowgirl him. When I slowly slid down on his dick I took a deep breath.

Even though his dick fit me like a missing puzzle piece I still was not use to his girth. I put my hand on each knee and started bouncing up and down. Kalvin legs were bouncing under me. His dick felt so damn good as I bounced like a crazy person. My body was sweating and my curly hair was sticking on my back.

"Fuck Ke! This view is the most beautiful thing I ever seen. Ride that muthafucka bae." He had his hand going up and down my back. When his hand went around my waist and he started playing with my clit. I could no longer hold it anymore.

"Arrghhhh Kalvin shit I'm cummin'!" I creamed all on his dick. Not having no more energy Kalvin took a hold of my waist. He started bouncing me up and down until he came all in me.

"FUCK!" He hugged my wet body from the back tight as hell. We both was out of breath but we just held on to each other. Kalvin started kissing my back all over.

"I love you so fuckin' much Keira. I would never fuck us up bae love, I promise." I set there with his dick still hard inside of me. Tears fell from my face as we set in silence. I don't know why I was crying but I couldn't stop it.

I felt Kalvin answered my questions and concerns. Maybe my gut was wrong and things were fine all along. Or maybe I wanted things to be fine so bad that I'm forcing it. I just feel confused and I hated this feeling. All I could do was trust my husband. Until I had any real proof I just need to be happy with our family.

Kalvin

The neighbor loud ass lawn mower woke me up out my good ass sleep. I was wrapped around Keira like some damn rope. I felt like a true bitch at that moment. Moving out from under her I looked down at my beautiful wife. She always looked so peaceful when she slept. Her hair had that just been fucked frizz. Them soft ass lips she had always puffed up in the morning. I bent down and kissed them a few times.

I kissed her like she was going to break. I didn't want to wake her from her sweet dreams. After loving on her for a few minutes I went in the bathroom washed my face and brushed my teeth. Turning on the shower I stepped in once I took my diamond Rolex off. The hot water hit my body hard as fuck but the shit felt good as hell. I closed my eyes and rested my hands on the wall.

Dropping my head under the water I went into deep thought. Last night scared the hell out of me. When Keira hit me with what's been on her mind I was lost for words. I didn't know she was feeling any type of way. What hurt me the most is when she started crying. That shit broke me and I knew I had to stop her from crying.

I don't know what the fuck was wrong with me these past few weeks. Ever since Taylor came and worked for us I have been on some other shit. I thought the shit would have worn off by now but working with her every day was not helping.

We have been closing together the past three nights and the shit been cool. Here is the crazy shit. I get along with her the same way I do with Keira. At first, I was not trying to talk to her at all. I was only working with her and keeping it hi and bye. But she is so sweet and cool. It started with us liking the same type of music that came on in the shop. Then it went from sports. When we would have the TV in the shop on ESPN.

All of us would be talking shit about the games. While talking we found out we liked some of the same teams. Last week I was in the break room eating and she came in. I tried to just keep watching TV and eat my food. She came and set across from me on the other couch. We exchanged looks then we started talking. The next thing I knew we swapped numbers. She knew all about me being married with a daughter.

We didn't talk sex, hooking up or even going out. We only talked about sports, TV shows, music and movies. The only thing is our texting would be hours and hours. I always had my phone with me in case she texted me and I was at home.

We never called each other we only texted. But lately I would find myself missing her or hitting her up seeing what she was doing. I knew damn well I never should have got myself in this. But who said I couldn't have female friends?

I love Keira and Kyra more than life itself. I would never leave my wife for anybody. I don't know how I found myself neglecting her. I swear it was not on purpose. I would be texting Taylor and before I knew it Keira was sleep. I can't tell you the last time me and Keira had a pillow talk session. I just found myself wanting to text Taylor instead of talking about the same stuff. Naw, I'm lying like a muthafucka.

Me and Keira talked about all kinds of shit. That's why I'm so fucked up. I don't understand why I can't shake Taylor's ass. Her honey color skin, pouty lips and pretty eyes. Her hair was always in a long weave but the shit looked nice. Her thick ass body was so fuckin' bad. Her booty was sick as shit and I bet it was soft. Then she had this laugh that was contagious as hell. She was fucking my damn dome up big time. All I know is I still wanted to be married to Keira and nobody could change that.

As I stood under the water I jumped when I felt hands

wrap around my body. Damn! I was in that deep of a thought about Taylor. I didn't even hear Keira step in the shower with me.

"Why you so jumpy? Did I scare you?" She had her hands around my waist kissing my back.

I turned around and faced her. That damn face was so beautiful it should have been a crime. Hands down Keira looked better then Taylor. The only thing Taylor had over my wife was her thickness. Rubbing the side of Keira's face, I traced her lips and her ears down to her neck. I brought my lips to hers. My wife sucked and pulled on her lips making my dick stand at attention like a soldier.

"I love you so much bae love. Please don't ever feel otherwise. I will fuckin' kill for you and die for you." I didn't even need her to respond. I kissed her and turned her around. I wanted to fuck the shit out of her doggy style.

*

"Nigga what the fuck you doing for your birthday this year?" Kevin asked Kaylin as he passed him the blunt.

We were in Brandon's man cave smoking, listening to music and playing the game. It had been a minute since all of us were in the same room together. Our parents didn't play that shit. No matter how busy we were she made sure we stayed close. After Karlos nutty ass sent us a threating text saying we need to hang. We decided to meet at Brandon's spot. The girls and the kids went to my father in-law house.

"Shit I don't even know. I was going to have a dinner then I said I wanted to go to Disney World." We looked at each other and bust out laughing.

"Nigga do you have a pussy down there now? What happened to turn up Kaylin? You be having the best parties out of all of us. You on some Nick Jr. type of shit now! Gay ass nigga!" Karlos said making us all fall out laughing.

"This nigga said Disney World! You ridin' the tea cups Kaylin?" I teased his ass cracking up.

"Fuck you small dick ass niggas. So, let me ask y'all

this. If we party like we use to on my birthday will we still have our girls after?" As soon as he said that shit we all got quiet as fuck. You could hear cotton drop.

"Kylee a member of that Groupon shit. She may can get us some cheap ass tickets to all the parks," Karlos big ass said breaking the silence.

"Yea, that's what the fuck I thought smart asses. Now, I was also thinking a tattoo party at Royalty." He threw that idea at us while he threw darts at the dart board.

"That's what the fuck I'm talking about! That shit will be lit as fuck and the girls can turn up with us," Brandon said from his game chair. Him and Karlos were playing Madden on his 65-inch TV.

"Yea me and Kelly want to get some matching tattoos anyways. Two birds with one stone ya' feel me." Kaylin put the darts down and went to grab a sub sandwich. We had Jimmy Johns cater our get together.

"Yea Kylee will have had Kaylee by then so she can come and get tatted up." Kalros passed me the controller because it was my turn.

"Nigga I know yo' ass bet not be getting shit else on you of your wife. This looney ass got Kylee all over his body!" Kevin laughed pointing to Karlos. I didn't want to laugh at my love-sick ass bro. But the shit was true.

"Fuck you bitch!" Karlos roared over the music. We didn't have the shit blasting just up enough so we can all hear it. The TV was on mute.

"Nigga you got her name on your neck, your inner arm, you got her fuckin' face on your right outter calf my nigga! Yo' ass a fucking walking shrine." Kevin continued teasing. He was flammin' our big bro. We was cracking the fuck up!

"Fuck you Kevin. Ok, fuck you bitch. Kim had yo' ass listening to B2K and you liked that shit" Karlos said and I think we all died from laughing. I rolled out my chair laughing so hard. Brandon jumped up pointing laughing at

Kevin. Karlos was hitting his closed fist in his hand cracking up.

"A-A-Aye they music is not that bad," Kevin said with an embarrassing look on his face. We laughed even harder. While I was laughing my phone went off alerting me I had a text.

Taylor: Hey big head. Wyd?

I got up and walked in the kitchen. I don't know why anytime she texted me I felt more comfortable being alone when I responded.

Me: Naw, you the one with the big head lol. But I ain't doing shit. Chillin' with my brothers. Wyd?

She responded instantly.

Taylor: Oh ok that's cool. I'm just leaving the nail shop. So do I have the honors of closing with you tonight?

I smiled at her text.

Me: Yea we close up shop tonight. Aye tonight we playin' all trap music. No girly ass music tonight.

Taylor: ☹ Aw please Kalvin. Just a little bit.

That shit made me bit my lip. I can picture her sticking that lip out looking all cute. We texted for a few minutes.

"Damn nigga, Keira be having you smiling that hard." Karlos walked in the kitchen snapping me out of my trance. I tried to play it off.

"Yea she on some cute shit." I gave him a half smile and put my phone down. I

was leaning on the kitchen isle in front of the refrigerator. Karlos opened it and grabbed a beer. My phone went off and we both looked down at it. Taylor's name popped up making my stomach drop. He looked from my phone and back up at me.

"Don't do that shit nigga. Come on Kalvin, don't do this shit to Keira. To your family that I know you want." He put his beer down and stood in front of me. I felt like a child in trouble with their father. Karlos looked so much like our pops the shit was scary. We all looked had features that made you know we were related. But Karlos looked identical to our pops.

"Listen to me bro on some real shit. You don't want to go down this road man. Trust me that shit will fuck you all up. I saw the way you and that bitch looked at each other. And judging on how you are looking at me when I called her bitch. Let's me know you like this girl. I don't know what you on or what is going on in yo' dome. But don't do Keira this way man, she doesn't deserve this shit right here. That bitch may look, smell and walk good as fuck. But she will not be worth half of what the fuck you got at home. The shit is all fun and orgasms until someone gets hurt nigga." He picked his beer back up and walked out the kitchen.

"Stupid ass nigga. Keira look better than that bitch anyways." He mumbled his smart-ass remark but loud enough for me to hear it. I stood there feeling dumb as hell. I needed to get my shit together fast.

<u>Kelly</u>

"Kelly get yo' ass out the bathroom I'm trying to shit!" Kaylin yelled at me.

I was sitting on the bathroom sink trying to show him these buildings. Me and Keira narrowed our choices down to three. We both were beyond excited about this braid shop. The Braid Factory is what we decided to call it.

Kaylin had been busy all day with business with Karlos and business at their club. He was off these next few days. We were leaving out in a few to go eat with Karlos and Kylee. But I really wanted Kaylin to see these buildings before we go.

"Pleaseee Kay just look at this last one. I promise this is the last building." I waved my iPhone 8 in his face.

"Bae, I will look at the damn building when I'm done in here. A nigga just trying to shit in peace." I started pouting and he dropped his head.

"Give me the fuckin' phone wit'cho crybaby ass." I smiled big and gave him my phone.

"Now really look at them Kaylin don't just-----" my sentence was cut short when a foul odor hit my nostrils.

"UGH KAYLIN OH MY GOD YOU STANK!" I jumped up off the sink and hauled ass out of that bathroom.

"Naw, bring yo' ass back in here and get my feedback," he yelled and I could hear him cracking up. Stanky ass lil boy.

*

Pulling up at IHOP Kaylin grabbed my hand as we walked to the entrance. He opened the door for and lightly slapped my booty when I walked past him. I smirked at his sexy ass. I love my King Kay.

"Hi welcome to IHOP. Two adults?" The hostess asked. She was smiling hard as hell but not because she had good customer service. This trick was looking at Kaylin like he was some fucking dessert.

"Naw, we got two other adults joining us. We will take a booth and to for you to stop fuckin' smiling all in my face like you don't see my woman right here." Kaylin looked at her with his nose turned up. The hostess quickly wiped that smile off her face and looked away. I chuckled as Kaylin grabbed my hand and we followed her to our both.

"Your waiter will be with you in a few." She lightly smiled and nodded her head still not looking at me or Kaylin. I laughed harder and so did Kaylin.

"Stupid ass bitch," he mumbled loud enough for me to hear it. We picked up our menus and looked them over.

"Bae try some chocolate pancakes with me. You get the same shit every time we come here." I looked up at Kaylin. Like a kid refusing to eat some vegetables he shook his head no.

"Nope. Stick to what'chu know, that's how you'll never fail." I smacked my lips at his dumb theory.

The waiter came to our table but we told him to come back when the rest of our party gets here. While me and Kaylin talked we saw Kylee and Karlos walk through the door. My big sister was so beautiful pregnant. She was all stomach but the rest of her body looked like a video chick. Now, all my sisters, including myself, had a bomb shape but for some reason my niece was making my sisters body look better than it already did. Kaylin signaled for them and they walked had in had towards us.

"Wazzam bro, hey baby sis." Karlos greeted us as he helped Kylee take her jacket off. After we spoke to each other and they set down. Kylee's greedy ass hurried up and grabbed the menu looking at it with a glow in her eyes.

"Oh my goodness I am so hungry," she said making us all laugh on the low.

Karlos put his arm around her and kissed her cheek. I just loved them together. I looked over at Kaylin and he winked at me. I wanted what my sisters had with their guys but I was just scared. Scared of getting pregnant, scared of giving birth and scared of being a wife. I never talked about this with Kaylin because out of fear of him leaving me. But I knew sooner or later I would have to open up about this.

"Hi folks! Are we ready to order?" Our happy ass waiter came back with his pen and pad. We all knew what we wanted to order. He had to be around our age and I almost asked for his autograph. He looked like Quavo from the rap group Migos.

"Let me get the waffles with scrambled eggs and cheese and some fried chicked strips. And get my girl the chocolate chip pancakes and scrambled eggs with cheese. Her weird ass wants a chocolate milk shake with that too. Knowin' damn well she will be shittin' all day." Him, Karlos and Kylee cracked up. I laughed and hit him in the arm. The waiter tried not to laugh but he ended up letting it out.

"And what can I get you beautiful?" He smiled and looked at Kylee. Lord if I had a camera to capture my brother in-law face.

"You wanna die nigga?" He looked at the poor waiter with the coldest stare. Kylee put the menu in front of her face getting embarrassed.

"Um no, I meant no dis---"

"Shut the fuck up and take our order. Give my baby some hash browns with onions, them cheesecake pancakes and some grits mixed with scrambled eggs. And get me a big steak omelet and that appetizer sampler." Karlos gathered our menus and shoved them in the waiter's chest.

"Get'cho goofy ass on." The poor waiter took off with the quickness. Kaylin ass was cracking up while me and Kylee just shook out head at him.

"Fuck that nigga. Gone try to get at my wife in front of me." Karlos put his arm back around Kylee and kissed her cheek again. Her ass loved that shit because she smiled and blushed.

"Aye sis you ready to pop out that baby?" Kaylin asked just as the waiter brought our drinks to the table.

"Oh my goodness yes I am. I'm so over her, she about to get an eviction notice," she said as she rubbed on her stomach.

"I can't wait to meet my other niecey pooh. She is going to be beautiful and drive you crazy." I laughed and pointed to Karlos. He shook his head while drinking his Pepsi.

"Just wait until you get knocked up. The shit is not as fun as it looks especially when *somebody*"- Kylee tilted her head at Karlos. "Won't let you do shit." I lightly laughed as Kaylin cleared his throat.

"She don't want to give me a baby. Hell, she don't even want to be my wife. But little does she know she don't have a choice. It's me or nobody," Kaylin said calmly as the waiter came and set our food in front of us.

"That's right bro. Tame that shit." Karlos dabbed his brother up.

I mugged both of them and smacked my lips. Kylee chuckled as she put syrup all over her food. We were eating and talking when the hostess walked past us and seated a customer in the booth directly behind us. He was an older black guy probably in his late 30's. The dude was alone but he carried a heavy scent with him. Almost like he soaked in a bottle of musk. Nobody noticed it but me and then I looked at Kylee. She was blinking fast then she took a sip of her apple juice. When she tried to continue eating she made a sour face and put her fork down.

"Kylee are you ok?" Before I could get an answer Karlos was on it.

"Baby, what's wrong? You good?" he asked putting his fork down and turning towards her. "I'm ok." She gave a weak smile.

"No the fuck you not, now what's wrong?" Karlos was getting pissed but his face had concern all over it.

I swear if she was about to give birth I was going to scream. I missed all my other nieces and my nephew being born. Me and Kaylin were out the country but I was blessed to be here now that Kylee is pregnant. There was no way I was missing Kaylee's birth. Karlos already agreed I could be in the delivery room. After Kylee persuaded him to say yes.

"His Old Spice musk. It's really making me nauseous giving me a headache." I was digging in my purse looking for a Tylenol. I kept Tylenol and Aleve on me because I had the worst cramps in the world. Karlos got up and I thought maybe he was going to tell the waiter os something but he shocked me with what he did next.

"Aye nigga! You gotta get the fuck up outta here." Karlos stood in front of the guy in his booth.

"Excuse me?" The guy looked up at Karlos and said. Kaylin jumped up and stood next to his brother. "Yo' musty ass cologne is making my wife and daughter sick. She can't even enjoy her meal without smellin' yo' stank ass." I looked at Karlos face and this nigga looked evil as fuck. Kaylin was standing next to him looking like his twin. I was so scared for the guy, I just wanted him to get up so these two psychos could calm down.

"I'm sorry I can move—"

"Naw you need to roll up out of here." The guy didn't even have time to say anything Karlos had the man buy the collar of his shirt. The man's feet never even touched the ground.

"Karlos it's ok baby! I was full anyways." Kylee tried to get him to stop ruff handling this full-grown man. He ignored her and dragged the man all the way to the door and threw him out. When he walked back in he set down with his eye brows furrowed.

"Smelly ass nigga. You good baby?" He looked at Kylee and asked. She nodded yes and she kissed his lips. Swear my sister low-key loved all the nutty shit he did.

"Big brother you are insane. That poor man didn't even get to eat his food." Now that it was over I was able to laugh about the shit.

Karlos crazy ass actually kicked a whole nigga out a

restaurant. Gotta love my brother in-law. We laughed and went back to eating. After we were done Karlos crazy ass had the manager handle our bill. This fool said it was for emotional distress towards his wife. After witnessing him toss a nigga, the manager didn't even hesitate to give us our food on the house.

After we left IHOP Kylee and Karlos decided to go back home so Kylee could put her feet up. Me and Kaylin needed to go to the mall to get me something to wear for Karlos gym opening. He didn't want a black-tie event. He wanted more of a turn up for his grand-opening. While Kaylin drove, and played J. Cole 4 Your Eyez Only album his hand was in mines.

He used his left hand to stir the wheel. My mind was on something else. I thought about his comment he said about me not wanting his child or wanting to be his wife. Even though I was afraid in me it bothered me that Kaylin would say the shit in front of everybody. Not being able to hold it in any longer I turned the radio down to talk to him.

"Kaylin why did you make that comment about me not wanting to have your child or be your wife?" He kept his eyes on the road and arched his eye brow.

"I said that shit because it's the truth. You have not done shit to plan our wedding. When I try to talk to you about it you just brush it off. As if I'm some lame ass nigga. And if I even think of talking to you about getting pregnant you act like your fuckin' jaw is wired shut."

"But why would you feel the need to say something like that in front of people? How do you know I want everybody in my business? And I never said I wouldn't marry you or have your child. Your putting words in my mouth." He did a low laugh.

"You ain't gotta say those words for me to feel the shit is true. Listen, I know some shit is up and when you are ready to talk about it I'm here. But Kelly I do want a wife and kids someday and you will be the person to give it to me." We came to a red light and he looked at me.

"I meant what I said also. It's me or nobody, word bond." He kissed my hand that he was still holding. This nigga really is a mini Karlos.

*

"Ughhhh fuck Kaylinnn." I was riding Kaylin's while he laid on his weight bench. Kaylin turned one of the three bedrooms into his workout area. I don't even know how we started fucking. I came and brought him his plate and he looked so good all sweaty and buff. His light skin was wet and his scruffy thin beard was glistening.

The next thing I knew he was pushing his basketball shorts down. And my ass was coming up out of my pajama shorts. We went to the mall and I found a nice outfit and shoes for Karlos party. When we came home I started cooking and Kaylin went to work out. Now we are here.

"Yea bounce on this big dick Kelly."

Slap!

"Bounce on that shit bae." He slapped my ass and squeezed my ass cheeks. That turned me on even more. I leaned forward and bounced like my life depended on it. I started twerking on his dick just he liked it.

"Damn bae," he whispered in my ear with his husky voice. I loved Kaylin's sex voice. It made me wetter when he moaned or talked shit.

"Stay on the dick and turn backwards." I stopped and did what he said. Kaylin ruff ass grabbed both my arms and held then behind me. He lifted his pelvis up and started fucking the shit out of me. His dick was thick it felt like it was massaging my insides. I started bouncing on my own while he still held my arms.

He used his other one and rubbed my clit. I felt like I was going to go crazy. My long hair had to be all in his face. But I don't think he gave a shit. My titties were bouncing everywhere and I felt sweat develop on my body. Kaylin was showing no mercy.

"You never fuckin' leavin' me Kelly."

"Say it Kelly. Say you never leavin' me. Say you having my baby and marrying me."

"Ahh Kay! I'm having your baby and I'm marrying me I mean you!" Kaylin's dick had me talking retarded. I felt me juicing up all on his dick. My body felt like it was about to explode with a strong orgasm.

"What about you never leavin' me? SAY IT KELLY! "

"Ughh! I-I-I never l-l-leaving you King Kay. Fuck I'm cummin'." I came for what felt like forever. Kay still was pumping inside of me taking me higher and higher. My body felt like a deflated balloon.

"SHIT!" Kaylin released all in me. Didn't matter because I was on the pill. Finally, he slowed down. I fell on top of his chest with my hair sprawled all on his face. He hugged my body tight as hell. Sitting up with me still in his arms he kissed my wet shoulder a few times. Both of our bodies were drenched.

"I love you Kelly. It's me or nobody." I closed my eyes because his voice and soft kissed had me still high.

"I love you too Kay. It's always you." I meant every word. It will always be Kaylin for me. With that being said, it was time to talk to him.

Kimmora

"Ti amo papà (I love you daddy)," I said to my daddy. He had put a plate of roast and potatoes in front of me with some roasted carrots. Of course Ella cooked it like always. Ella has been with our family before I was born. She is the one who taught us and our mother how to make Italian dishes. He and our nonna(grandmother) were the best in the kitchen.

My daddy took Keion out my arms so I could eat. I had to be to work in an hour so I dont even know why I was eating all thus food. Anytime I hate a lot all I wanted to do was sleep. But when I came in my daddy's house and smelled Ella's cooking I knew I had to make me a plate.

"Kimmora he is so beautiful. He has you and your mother pretty skin color and big eyes. The first Ricci male from my blood line. I'm one proud papa," my dad said as he smiled and kisses Keion on his chubby cheeks. It was such a joy to see out father with his grandchildren.

He looked like he was 100% happy. Not saying we never made him happy, but he looked complete. For him to have girls, and no woman in the house he was such an amazing father. We put our poor father through everything. From tea parties, dress-up, cupcake making and concerts when eachbof us were obsessed over a celebrity. He never missed one dance recital, play, girl scout meeting or contest. Kenny Ricci is just the worlds greatest father and now he will be the greatest grandfather.

"He favors a lot of my baby pictures. But daddy you have to see when he makes his serious face. Or when he is taking a dump. He looks just like Kevin." Me and my daddy started laughing.

"Granddaughter!" My nonna came downstairs smiling hard. Our nonna was beautiful with her round face and long white hair. Yes, her hair was pure white and touching her ass. She always kept it in one big braid. Unless she was brushing it before she went to sleep. Me and my sisters loved playing in her hair when we were little. Our daddy told us that nonna and our mom were very close.

"Kenny, why you not tell me my sweet grand baby was here." She hit the back of my dad's head as she walked passed him. My grandma had a thick Italian accent so whenever she yelled or cussed it was funny.

Nonna went straight and grabbed Keion out my dads hands, after she kissed and hugged on me. Keion was staying with them today while me and Kevin worked. While I sat there laughing at my dad and nonna yell and cuss in English and Italian my Facebook notifacation went off. I pulled my phone out to see it was Tyler sending me yet another friends request. I shook my head and laughed. Tyler was harmless but still I did not need Kevin bringing out his inner Karlos and acting a fool. I rejected the request and went back to eating. I'm sure when I get to work his ass will be there to annoy me some more.

*

"Hi Mrs. Jones, how are you doing today?" I walked into one of my patients room rolling my cart in.

"I'm doing good Kimmora. Ready to get up out of here and home with my baby girl." She responded to me as she took her daughter off her breast. I smiled back while scanning her bracelet.

"I will talk to the doctor today and see what we can do about that. You had a c-section so normally you would stay admitted for 3-days. We just dont want you doing to much and you start hurting. Because once you start hurting it's hard to get you to stop hurting." I talked to her while I checked her blood pressure and took her tempature.

I filled her baby drawer up with diapers and more formula. I knew she would be taking alot of it home. Hell me and Tiff ghetto butts did it when we had our babies. Keira and Kalvin goody asses said it was stealing which was wrong. I love my Hallmark sister and brother in-law they were perfect for each other.

"You are such a cool ass nurse. The nurse on schedule last night was so rude and mean. She kept saying smart shit about me being only 19 with a baby." I shook my head because I knew exactly who she was talking about.

"That's Mrs. Ritz, she is so old school and set in her ways. She thinks I'm an aboomination because I work. She says I need to be home taking care of my man and my child." I waved my hand.

"Listen, don't let anyone make you feel bad for your decisions. As long as you have a plan and see it through then that's all that matters. Enjoy your baby girl and ignore what the rest say. You graduated high school, your in college and you have a lot of family supporting you. And the child's father is supportive. Your blessed, forget what the rest say." I smiled at her and rolled my cart out her room. She declined my offer on needing anything else so I went to check on the rest of my patients.

Like always my shift went pretty smoothly. I did have a patient of mines mother get smart with me.

She didn't understand how I was a nurse and not even in my 30's. The bitch tried to tell me I look like I dont know what I'm doing. She had the shit face when her daughter's doctor came in and said I was one of his favorite nurses.

Stupid hoe! The time for me to take my break came rather quickly. This time I packed me a lunch. Well, Ella packed me a lunch with a slice of her caramel cake. I set in the cafeteria eating my food and on Snapchat watching Brandon and Tiff silly asses.

"I see you started eating without me." I didn't even look from my phone. I just smirked and rolled my eyes. I knew it was Tyler annoying ass behind me talking shit.

"Um I do not wait on you to eat. We not friends Tyler I keep telling you that." I guess he took that as an invitation to sit next to me. He put his salad and fried chicken down then he took a seat.

"Damn Kimmy, you don't have to be so mean. Look, I respect your married and a mother. Hell the type of girl you and your sisters are I expect you to be locked down. But Kimmy you gotta admit we were good friends before anything. That's all I want is a friendship with you. How you expect us to work in the same space and not talk to each other?" He took a bite of his salad licking the dressing off his lips slow. This nigga is too funny.

"Tyler I don't want my husband having female friends so I would never turn around and have male friends. Married couples should have the same friends in my opinion. Would you go shoot hoops with my husband? Would you hang with him and his brother's? No because you know damn well your interests in me is not in that way. I know you Tyler and you have always been a smooth talker and spoiled. We won't make good friends anymore." I went back to eating my food.

"I see Ella is still throwing down in the kitchen. I miss that woman's cooking. How about this, since you don't want to be my friend. Why don't we just be lunch associates. We only talk and chill in here with our food. No messing with you when your on the clock, no poking you on Facebook and no number exchanging. Just this nice cafeteria will be the only time we talk. Deal?" He held his hand out and I looked at him laughing.

"Ok Tyler. We will be lunch buddies. Now if you'll excuse me, I need to get back to work. Enjoy your food." I walked away trashing my empty water bottle.

Tyler was all games and talk. It's true, we were good friends. But the attraction between us used to be so strong we would always end up fucking. But not this time, my heart was all Kevin's. Not to mention this pussy between my legs had his name written all over it. Tyler could try all he wanted but he was always gonna come up dry. He better get his rocks off with one of these interns in the supply room like all the other doctors did.

I finished the rest of my 8 hour day and was gathering my things so I could head home. I had not heard from Kevin all day which was weird. We always texted, facetimed or called each other. I texted him I love you earlier and he did not respond but it says he read it. You can best believe when I get home I have a mouthful for his ass.

I got on the elevator and took it to the ground to the parking garage. Getting off I took my keys out so I could just hit my alarm and get in. I watched to many scary movies which is why I hateparking garages. Usually security is here but he must be on break or something. It was nearing 8pm so it was dark outside with only the lights in the garage to guide me. Seeing my car I hit the alarm ready to open my door.

"Excuse me." I jumped when a voice startled me. I turned and saw a woman standing behind me. She had on a red zipped up hoodie and black leggings with some army boots.

"Your name is Kimmora, right?" She asked me with both her hands in her hoodie pocket. Lord please do not let me die tonight. Please let me make it home safely to my family and protect me. In Jesus Name amen. I said a quick silent prayer.

"Um yes that's my name. Do I know you?" She took her hood off and her face looked like she was missing about a years worth of sleep. She was a light skin woman so the dark circles under her eyes stuck out. Her hair were in these raggedy ass braids and she had an odar to her.

"No you don't know me but your husband does. He knows my daughter also as a matter of fact he knew her very well. Until your black ass came along." She turned her nose up at me. I looked around and then back at her.

"I'm sorry I don't OK now what your talking about or------"

"I'm Chrissy's mother." My eyes almost popped out of my head. Why the fuck was she approaching me. Kevin has not talked to that lying bitch in over a year.

"Her and Kevin were together and things were going good for them. And then you came and brought your nasty ass around and stole him from my baby. Him being a nigga and thinking with his dick, he dumped my baby girl. AFTER he knocked her ass up, I'm guessing he wanted to hide it from you. So, now my baby girl is missing. Now let me ask you this, how the FUCK does a healthy pregnant girl just up and disappear? Hm? Tell me HOW?!" She raised her voice and steppes closer to me.

"Let me answer that for you. I think you and that nigga killed my baby and my grandchild. Y'all needed her out the way so you wouldn't have to play step mama." Her voice started to crack and her bottom lip started to shake.

"I'm here to tell you and I want you to tell your husband this as well. When I prove y'all muthafuckas killed my Chrissy. Jail will be the least of y'all worries."

"Kimmy is everything all right?" Tyler came from the stairs of the hospital. He looked concerned as he looked at me then at Chrissy's mother. I stood there frozen with tears in my eyes.

"Whoever the hell you are, you need to leave before I call the police." He looked at Chrissy's mom and said. She threw her hands up in a surrender mode and bagged away.

"I'll be seeing you, Mrs. Royal." She smiled at me with her fucked up brown teeth. Once she was out of sight I was able to breathe.

"Kimmy who the hell was that and why was she bothering you?" I couldn't even answer Tyler. All I could think about was getting to my husband and my child. I knew some shit was not right when I didn't hear from Kevin since this morning.

"I gotta go Tyler. Thank you for helping me." I hurries and opened my door. He stood there looking confused but I didn't give a fuck.

Pulling off in a hurry I wiped my tears and reached for my phone. Zooming through traffic I called my daddy to see if Keion was still there. He told me Kylee took him to her house. I asked had he talked to Kevin he said yea. Kevin facetimed him to see what Keion was doing. Confused I hung up from my dad and called Kylee.

She said Kevin just hung up with Karlos. Now I'm annoyed as fuck. I called Kalvin's phone to see if Kevin was at the shop. He told me no, Kevin just left. Before I got pissed I called Kevin one more time, this nigga sent me to voicemail. So, he was fine but he was just ignoring me?! What the fuck for? I have not done shit.

When I left this morning we were on good terms. Hell, we were on great fucking terms. Why the hell was he avoiding me and only me? I called Kylee back to let her know I was coming to pick up Keion. I wanted to feed him and get him in the bed. I wanted him sound asleep when I dig in his daddy's ass.

Kevin

Instead of being home with my wife and son I'm in Lake Charles on Jacob's street waiting for this nigga Tyler to pull up at his crib. Him and Kimmora had the game fucked up. I got word from my homegirl who works in the hospital cafeteria that Kim were having lunch together. At first I took it as some bullshit because I warned her ass to stay the fuck away from him.

But when Nina dyke ass sent me a picture of them laughing it up over some nasty ass hospital food. I hit the fucking roof. I called Karlos to get the niggas address. He wanted to roll with me but I told him hell no. I didnt want to kill the nigga, just scare his ass. I don't know why these fucking girls like pushing me and my brothers to the edge.

Knowing how we all are, especially Karlos ass. But leave it to my wife to test me. He probably told her some shit like we can be work buddies type of shit. And Kimmora ol' gullible ass ate that shit up.

Well, he gone learn today about fucking with mines. Hell, I fucked a nigga up for dancing with her in Mexico. So you know I'm kicking his ass for sharing lunch with her. I purposely have not talked to her all damn day. No text or anything but I made sure to talk to everyone else so she can know I was only avoiding her.

I'm sure when I get home she was gonna go off but I didnt give a fuck. *Fuck this nigga at?* I said to myself sitting in my black no license plate magnum. I had my black gloves on and trap clothes. Just as I was about to turn my radio on I saw his ass pull up. He was driving a 2017 Equinox, fucking pussy ass car.

Once he parked in his driveway and turned the car off I got out my car. It was dark as hell and the only lights were on porches or windows. He opened his back seat and grabbed a black brief case. I approached just as he was about to step on his first porch step.

"Aye Tyler." His scary ass jumped at the sound of my deep voice.

"Who wants to know?" He set his suit case on the first porch step. Turning towards me with his hands in his white doctors coat. Nigga better not say the wrong shit or he will be buried in that muthafucka.

"Check this out nigga. You been mighty fuckin' friendly with my wife and I don't even have to say her name because you know who the fuck I'm talking about. Listen to this shit cause I'm only going to say this once. Stay the fuck away from my wife. Don't speak to her, don't joke with her don't even be in the same room with her. If you see her giving the wrong medicine to a patient you *still* bet not say shit to her. Just let the nigga die." I walked all in his fucking space and spoke through gritted teeth. This nigga started laughing.

"You know she is a good girl. The life she has always wanted could not possibly come from you. You think I don't know who you and your brother's are? All you going to do is bring her down. She can't see it yet because she loves with an innocence. But trust me she will see it soon enough. I have always been right for her." He wiped his smirk off his face and looked me dead in my eyes and said.

"She will always be *My Kimmy.*" That alone made me snap like a fuckin' twig on a tree. I hit that nigga hard a fuck in his jaw. Not giving him a chance to think about defending himself I kept the hits coming. I hit his ass with so much strength in his nose making blood gush out. Then I hit him in his ribs and his stomach making him fall over on his grass.

I was so hot by him calling her *My Kimmy.* I kneeled down and grabbed him by his now bloody white collar. With a closed fist I hit him twice in the face. Out of breath and blood all over my gloves I lifted him by his collar again.

"Say it again nigga. Call her yours again." I was in his face talking calmly. He struggled to talk through the blood and his fucked up face.

"M-My K-K-Kimmy," he said right before he spit in my face.

This nigga had a death wish. I let his head hit the concrete and stood up. Taking my shirt and wiping my face I took my foot to his face. One good ass kick sent his head back and a few teeth flying out. I know his ass was not dead. But I'm sure this will be an ass whopping he will never forget. Now to go home and deal with my hard headed ass wife.

*

After going to our warehouse I dropped off the magnum for my boy to pick up. I grabbed the trash bag with the bloody gloves, clothes and shoes and threw that shit in the furnace of the warehouse. I got in my Bentley and drove home ready to deal with my wife.

Driving on the freeway I had 10 misses calls from Kimmora and 8 text messages of her cussing me out. She accused me of fucking around on her. I laughed because one text she sent said she hope I get burnt and my dick falls off. I cracked up at her crazy ass.

Pulling up to out home I got out and hit the alarm on my car. Looking at my house I noticed all the lights were out. I didn't even see any light from a TV on. See, Kimmora is going to make me catch a fuckin' case if I walk into this house and her and my son are not there.

Tall enough to look in the window of our garage I saw her car was in there. That calmed me down all the way thinking maybe there just asleep. I put my key in the front door and turned the knob. Closing the screen door and big door I turned to walk down the hallway.

BAM!

I'm telling y'all God was on a niggas side tonight! I ducked just in time before Kimmora could fuck my head up with a steel bat. She hit the wall clock instead shattering that bitch in pieces.

"Kimmora what the fuck-----"

BAM!

She swung again making me duck once more and her hitting the wall putting a big hole in it.

"KIMMORA! STOP SWINGING THE FUCKING BAT BEFORE YOU FUCK ME UP!" Now her ass had me scared as fuck. My pops didn't raise us to be scared of shit but at this moment I was.

"WHERE THE FUCK WERE YOU"?! For the first time since I have known my boo she had a face I never seen her have. She looked like a fucking lunatic holding that bat. Her hair was in a low ponytail with a bun. She had on some black sweat pants and an oversized black T-shirt with some black Nike gym shoes. She didn't have on no jewelry, not even her wedding ring. She looked like a fucking stud bitch.

"Kimmora listen, calm---"

"I DON'T WANT TO HEAR SHIT IF IT'S NOT YOU TELLING ME WHERE YOU WERE! AND WHY THE FUCK DO YOU HAVE ON DIFFERENT CLOTHES AND SHOES FROM THIS MORNING!" She took another swing and was an inch away from missing the side of my head. I heard the wind leave the bat when she swung. She had me feeling straight pussy. My heart was beating and I just knew one of these swings would have ya' boy retarded for the rest of my life.

"Boo if you just stop swinging the bat I can tell you everything you wanna know. I wasn't with a bitch." I had my hands up like she was the fucking law. I talked calm and looked in her eyes. Even though she was looking like a butch bitch you still couldn't deny my boo's beauty.

"Ok, I won't swing. Talk!" I made sure I chose my next words carefully.

"I was at work when I got a call from---" I stopped mid-sentence because of her stance she was giving me.

"Kim I can't talk to you with you standing there in yo' Jackie Robinson pose. Please lower the fuckin' bat boo." She looked at me for a second then lowered the bat down by her legs.

"Thank you. Like I was saying I was at work and a friend of mine hit me up telling me you was having lunch with yo' fucking ex at work. The same muthafucka I told yo' ass to not talk to. After hearing that shit I ignored yo' ass the rest of the day and went and found out where that nigga stay. I paid his busta ass a visit." I looked at her waiting for her to sound concerned about his ass. I'm telling y'all caution tape is going to be around our house.

"Kevin what the fuck did you do? I don't even work with him on the same floor. And for your information I don't even talk to him. I was having lunch by myself and he came and sat down. I can't stop him from sitting where he wants to sit." I looked at her like she was fucking stupid.

"Kimmora miss me with that bullshit. You know how to tell a nigga to leave you the fuck alone. Yo' ass like that shit and probably told that fool y'all can be just work friends. Well I hope you can do without your buddy for a few weeks because I fucked his ass up after that bitch looked me in the face and called you his!" I walked close to her and snatched that bat out her hand. I tossed in on the floor and pulled her to me. Just repeating when that nigga called her his had my eyes fill up with black. I could tell I was scaring her because her breathing changed.

"Ain't no nigga gone look me in the face and claim my fuckin' wife. Kimmora I promise you, if you don't stay away from him I'm killing him and fucking you up." Knowing damn well I would never hurt my boo. But I wanted her to know how serious I was. Oh but you can best believe I would kill ol'boy and his whole fucking family.

"Ok Kevin, I apologize for even entertaining him. I do not want him in any way nor do I feel anything for him. It will always be you Kevin, always you." She fucked me up by speaking in that soft pretty voice. I felt my eyes go back to normal and she gave me a smile. Those damn dimples.

"Kim I love you so much, just don't fucking test how far I'll go for you because shit will get out of hand and the body count will pile up. You love me?"

"Yes I do love you. I love you so so much my Kevy-Kev." I hate when she calls me that shit but this was boo so I let it slide.

I pulled her closer and kisses her. Grabbing on that big soft ass booty she has I was squeezing that big muthafucka like a lemon. Kim was moaning all in my mouth making my dick hard. We stood there kissing deep with our tongues getting tangled up.

"I missed you so much Kevin. I really thought you were out cheating on me." She pulled away from our kiss and said to me. Looking sad with puppy dog eyes.

"Kim I would never ever fuck up our family boo. You and Keion are my whole fuckin' being. No hoe walking this earth can get me to fuck that up. Not even Gabrielle Union fine ass." She rolled her eyes making me laugh.

"Aye look how you fucked up our house." I laughed while we both looked at the broken clock and two holes in the wall. I'd have that shit fixed tomorrow.

"I'm sorry, I just snapped the more you ignored me." She shrugged her shoulders like it was nothing. I think these Ricci sisters are just as fucking looney as me and my brother's were. They just cute as fuck and can hide it well.

"Come take a shower with me and take my damn clothes off. Lookin' like a she he and shit." We walked up stairs while I squeezed her booty the entire way.

We stopped in Keion's room to check on him. I didn't know how the fuck he slept through our loud asses but he did. Lil nigga slept like he had a job. When we closed his door my hand went right back on my wife' booty. Kimmora' ass was so big even the sweatpants couldn't hide it. When we walked into our bedroom we both started undressing each other. I was stealing kisses from her pretty chocolate ass.

"Kim put your ring back the fuck on and don't take it off no more." I towered over her short thick ass looking pissed off.

"I only took it off because I was mad at you. I thought you were cheating on me. I was going to divorce your ass." She joked as she put her ring on but I didn't find shit funny.

"You thought you was going to divorce me and be with that nerd nigga? Have his mark ass around my son? Naw Kim, you know me better than that. I would kill him, beat yo' ass, bring you home and shove my dick up you." I grabbed her arm and pulled her now naked ass over to me. I took that rubber band off her hair releasing her long curly hair. I love when that shit would fall all down her back. I looked down at her with my teeth gripping my bottom lip.

"Kevin something happened to me while I was at work today." I dont know why when she said that I immediately thought the worse. My mind started to think all these things involving her and that nigga.

"Speak on it," I said calmly to her, I wanted to maintain my cool.

"When I was leaving work Chrissy's mom approached me. She said Chrissy is missing and she thinks you and me have harmed her. Kevin she was saying all this crazy shit about jail being the least of our worries if she found out we harmed Chrissy. What is she talking about Kevin? You told me Chrissy lied about her pregnancy and skipped town. Why would her mama think we hurt her if she moved? What are you not telling me?" She looked up at me. All I could do was look deep in her eyes and not say shit. She slowly started to back away from me.

"Kevin what the fuck did you do to that girl?" Her backing away from me and asking me that question made me feel some type of way. The comment her corny ex said about me not being able to give her the life she wanted popped in my head.

"You moving away from me like you scared of me or some shit. Kim you knew the type of nigga I was from the beginning. So it's cool when Karlos shows his ass but when I do it you get fearful of me." I walked towards her and she took some steps back. I stopped and squinted my eyes at her with my head tilted. That shit broke my heart to see my wife scared of me.

"Kim I have never raised my hand to you and never will. You wanna hear me say I killed Chrissy? Cool, I killed that bitch and if I could dig her up and do it again I would. That day I left to go see her about the baby she supposedly was pregnant with. I got to her crib she set me up for 2 niggas to rob and kill me. Turns out all three of them were working with my uncles. They were supposed to kill me and have Karlos and my brothers start a war. But I ended up slicing one of the niggas in the throat. When I went to the back of Chrissy's apartment to get the other nigga she was sucking his dick. She had the fake pregnant belly and pump shit on the floor. So I put a bullet in between both of there eyes." Kim's mouth fell open and she started to get tears in her eyes.

"Oh my God Kevin I'm---" I cut her off when she started moving close wanting to console me.

"Naw, get the fuck back. You look at me like you don't know me or some shit. Like in that short amount of time you regretted ever being with me. Like you wouldn't have to worry about shit like this if you were with a nigga like your ex." That shit as making me madder and madder.

"No Kevin it's not that at all. I just got scared that you would go to jail or her mom would do something to you." She started crying. I stepped closed to her and hugged her. Both of us were naked in the middle if our bedroom.

"Kevin I would never regret our life together. Not even for one second, I love you and Keion so much. I'm sorry if I got a little scared but no one else can give me what you give me. I'm all yours Kevin and always will be." I smiled at my beautiful ass wife and kissed her lips.

Lifting her up so they could wrap around me. Her hands ran all through my long light brown dreads I loved when she did that shit and when she would tug on them while I eat that pussy. Shit does something to ya boy! I carried her to our bed and laid her soft ass body down. Fuck the shower for right now. We can can fuck now and shower after, then fuck some more, then shower some more and fu---you get the picture.

Kalvin

" So you telling me Kevin Hart is funnier than Kat Williams? Get the fuck outta here!" I laughed hard as fuck at the bullshit Taylor was telling me.

"He is funnier! And he has more movies than Kevin Hart does," she said to me while sweeping up hair. Both of our last clients just left. Kevin was in the back eating the rest of his Jets pizza he ordered.

"That don't mean shit because he has more movies. Kevin kisses ass more than Kat does so of course he has more movies. Hollywood ain't shit but a popularity contest. Just like how you think Rihanna is a singer. She a lot if things but a singer is not one of them." I laughed while I was cleaning up my work station. I knew that shit would irritate Taylor because she was a die hard Rihanna fan.

"Don't come for my girl. She is a bomb ass singer better then Beyonce washed up ass."

"Now I know you talking shit if you think Beyonce is washed up. You and I both know Rihanna can't sing better than Beyonce. I would fuck Rihanna faster then I would Bey but that's only out of respect for my nigga Jay." I looked up at her when I was emptying the trash because she got so quiet. When I looked at her she had a scowl look on her face.

"I do not want to hear about you fucking other girl's." She must have caught herself because she tried to recover her statement.

"You like a brother to me so I don't want to hear about you fucking." That shit made me laugh when she hit me with the little brother shit. I grabbed my squirt bottle of water and walked towards her.

"Little brother huh?" I aimed the bottle at her. She gave me that pretty smile and started bagging up.

"Kalvin stop playing! If you wet my hair I'm kicking your ass!" Taylor tries to run but I grabbed her from behind making her squeal. Kevin couldn't hear us because the radio was still on playing Migos album.

"You gone kick my ass! I wanna see that shit, say it again and watch I wet all this horse hair." Me and her was cracking up while I was tickling her.

While we were playing we didn't hear the front door open until the bell chimmed. We both looked up and Kimmora walked in. I hurried up and let Taylor go but by then Kimmora was already looking at us like we were kids caught humping each other.

"Hey brother in-law, who's your little friend?" Kimmora asked me but kept her eyes on Taylor. Before I could answer Taylor smiled and held her hand out.

"Hi, I'm Taylor the new barber. You must be Kevin's wife, he keeps you and your son picture in his station. Your son is so cute." Kimmora looked at Taylor and her hand like it was infected.

"Charmed to meet you. I'm also Kalvin's *wife* big sister. Who I'm sure you'll meet very soon." Thank God Kevin walked in from out the break room. Him and Kimmora hugged and kissed each other. I was happy Kimmora's attention was off of me and Taylor. We wasn't doing shit anyways but playing around.

"Bro you good to lock up right?" Kevin asked me as he put his coat on. I threw him the duesces and hugged my mean ass sister in-law.

"I love you brother in-law and please remember to think with your big head, not you little one," se whispered and said to me. I laughed and kissed her on top of her head.

"Nice to meet you Tawayna." Taylor looked like she wanted to say something but Kimmora was out that door along with Kevin. I closed the door and locked it.

"I don't think your sister in-law likes me. You know Kalvin, I would never disrespect your marriage. But I can't lie and say I don't think about you when we are apart. The way we bond and have fun with no effort intrigues me." Taylor walked in front of me.

I had never been this close to her unless we were playing around. She smelled like that perfume I brought Keira a few months back. I can't think of the name all I remember is she didn't like it. Taylor caught me off guard with her confession. We never talked about feeling each other, even when we texted. All we did was joke around about nothing. I can't say I'm surprised at the shit she was saying.

"Taylor I do think you are beautiful and I like how we vibe. But I have a whole wife and baby girl at home ma. I can't even imagine fucking around on her." She ran her hand through my mini curly fro and rubbed the side of my face. On reflex I bit my bottom lip.

"Kalvin tell me you don't think about me. Tell me you don't miss me or daydream about me. Go on one date with me. Let's see what this really is. We both are very young and no one can blame you if you caught feelings for someone else." She moved closer to me and like a dumb ass I put my hand around her waist and kisses her lips.

Bringing her closer to me she wrapped her hands around my neck. We were deep in our kiss until my phone ringned Usher-There Goes My Baby played which was Keira's ringtone. I pulled my phone out and looked down at it. Taylor stepped away wiping the sides of her mouth. I couldn't even answer the phone with fear Keira would sense some shit on the phone.

"You all set? I need to lock up and get home." We avoided eye contact as we finished cleaning. Once we were done we both walked out and I locked the door. Me being a gentlemen and it being dark I walked Taylor to her car.

"I'm sorry for kissing you Kalvin. I hope shit does not get weird between us because I really like our friendship." She smiled at me and kissed me on the cheek. When she opened her door I started walking towards my Land Rover.

It was October but in Louisiana the weather still was pretty nice. I rolled my windows down and let the night air hit me while I drove on the freeway. I had so much shit on my mind, mainly my wife and Taylor. Keira was the entire package and I could not be more happy to have her. But I can't even deny the attraction I felt towards Taylor. She is so fucking sexy and cool as hell to be with. Ever since Keira told me she felt I was a little off. I had been making sure to be on my game with her. I didn't need her even thinking I was fucking around on her.

Pulling into the driveway of me and Keira's house I turned my car off. Sitting there I pulled my phone out and went to the text message icon. I looked at Taylor's name and just stared at it. I knew damn well I had no business doing this shit but fuck it. YOLO!

Me: Dinner tomorrow?

Taylor: I would love to Kalvin

Me: Meet me at Upperline restaurant at 7

Taylor: I cant't wait 😊

I put my phone in my pocket and headed in the house. Now that I have a date with Taylor there was not point in feeling bad about it. Shit it's not like we are fucking or anything. I'm not even

picking her up from her house. I just wanted to sit down, eat some food and pick her brain. All we ever talk about besides sports is TV shows, movies and food. I wanted to see if there was someting else there besides fun.

The shit was stressing me out so this dinner was needed. Walking into the house I put my keys on the hook by the door. I took my shoes off and walked in the kitchen. Washing my hands I went in the microwave and saw my plate in there. Keira cooked some fried chicken, macoroni and cheese and greens. I warmed it up and went to smash mode. Once I was done I downed it with a blue Powerade drink.

After going into Kyra's room and kissing on her sleeping beauty self I went into our bedroom. Keira was sound asleep as I stripped and went to take a shower. I came out the bathroom drying off and put my boxers on. After I put my deodorant on I dried my fro off some more. I threw the towel on the floor and climbed in the bed. I gave Keira a few kisses and turned over to catch up on some much needed sleep.

Karlos

Tonight was the night of the grand-opening for my gym. I was geeked as hell about this shit. I decided a few weeks ago to let my sis Tiff become a partner. She's a workout nut so I hired her to be a yoga fitness instructor. Brandon was cool about the shit because he knew I wouldn't let niggas get at her. My bros talked about me being ghetto not wanting a black-tie event. I felt like fuck all of that!

This was not your typical gym. I had pole dancing classes, yoga classes, dance classes, and the basic workout machines. I also had masseuses, tanning beds, massages chairs and a huge lounging area with TV's, smoothie bar and a five star chef. This gym was going to be the shit. My plan was to open one in Miami in the next two years.

Putting my platinum chain around my neck I sprayed the only cologne my wife would let me wear. That new Sean Jonn in the black bottle was the only thing Kylee wanted to smell on me. I could not wait for her to have my princess and have my wife go back to normal. I put on my crushed diamonds studs and my matching platinum link bracelet. I had my hair in a low ponytail and my beard freashley trimed by Kevin. I was looking fly as hell in my Armani Exchange fadded jeans and black matching t-shirt.

I wore black my new black Mauri shoes that I ordered from on-line. After I made sure I was straight I walked out of my walk-in closet. I went to the bathroom where Kylee was at and I watched her put her earrings on. We were three weeks away from meeting our daughter and my ass was ready. Watching Kylee's body go through this for our daughter made me love my baby even more. If that's even possible. Tonight my wife looked just as fly as me. She was rocking some black ripped leggings with her new Versace black and silver button-up on.

My Ky was all belly but that body was still bomb as fuck. Her peach shape juicy booty was looking good as fuck. She tried to wear some fuck me stilettos but I deaded that shit. No heels until Kaylee gets here. She had on her fitted over the knee black cowgirl boots. It had that fat ass little heel which was cool with me. When she saw me in the door way her face lit up like always. I walked over to her and put my arms around her waist. Inhaling her perfume, I knew she had her favorite Flower Bomb shit on.

"You look so handsome my Los. You better be lucky I'm your date because I'd definitely try to take you home." We looked at each other through the mirror.

"Oh is that right? Well I would let yo' fine ass take me home too. But you would never be able to get rid of me." I bit my lip looking at her sexy ass. I was alread ready to get this party over with so I could get my wife back home and dig in her sweet pussy.

"Lossss stop kissing on my neck baby. We gotta get ready to leave out." She started giggling when I didn't stop kissing and licking on her neck. I pulled away from her neck because I wanted to ask her something.

"Kylee, are you sure you are up for this? I told you we can say fuck this party and stay in baby. My gym will make money with or without a grand-opening." I turned her around so she could look at me. I was serious as hell, her and Kaylee comes before anything. So if she was to tired or wasn't feeling it, I would trash this party in a minute.

"Karlos for the 100th time I am ok. I want to be here with you on your big night. I wanna see people congratulate you and see there reaction to the gym. I'm fine, I promise. I won't over do it. Now come on so we can go." She smiled at me and gave me a punk ass peck on the lips. I just stood there looking at her ass like she was crazy. Kylee laughed at gave me a real kiss while playing with my curls on the back of my neck.

"Come on let's roll before you make my dick fall off." We both started laughing as we walked out the bathroom.

*

My turn up was packed. I held it at the gym and had workers come and move all the equitment out for the night. I had a D.J. a full catered soul food buffet, drinks and weed was welcomed. Like I said, this was no black-tie event the only thing is smoking was in the back. My baby was pregnant and I didn't want her inhaling any smoke. My driver pulled up with us in our royal blue Rose Royce and opened the door for us. Once we were out people from everwhere started calling my name.

This party was invitation only because I didn't want to many muthafuckas fuckin' up my gym. If you really wanted to see it either sign up for the tour or come buy a membership. No invite then yo' ass was not gettin' in. After me and Kylee took pictures for some local on-line magazine, I walked my pretty ass wife inside. I couldn't keep my hands off my Ky she was the finest bitch in here. Don't get ya' panties in a bunch you know what I mean.

"Aye bro! This shit is lit, congratulations man." My brother's walked up and greeted me and Kylee. I thanked them and dabbed them up after hugging my sister in-laws. All of them looked like money with there wives on there arm.

"Appreciate that y'all. See how everybody chillin' and comfortable. Told y'all assess a black tie theme wasn't necessary." Pointing around to everybody.

"Yeah you was right. This shit is way more lit and I ain't gotta be all uncomfortable in a damn suit," Brandon said while putting his arm around his wife." All my baby sister's were looking good as usual and we was the luckiest niggas in here.

"Baby I'm going to go eat. Mingle with some guest and I'll be over there." Kylee said to me as she pointed to the buffet. Keira pulled her hand but I had her other hand in mines.

"Oh my goodness Karlos let hand go we got her you are only a few feet away." Keira was laughing pulling Kylee's hand. My baby looked at me with her pretty face and kissed my lips a few times. I let her hand go and watched her fine ass walk away.

"Yo' clingy ass," Kevin said making the rest of them laugh. I shot that nigga the finger and laughed to. I never gave a fuck what nobody thought about me being a thirst bucket for my wife. Hell, I was proud of that shit.

I talked to a few of the guest that was starting to arrive. I had a couple of on-line bloggers and reviewers interview me about the gym. They asked questions about why I wanted to open a gym. What makes my gym different then the rest. And how do I stay so fit. Truth be told I am not on the best diet and I don't always work out.

I lift more dead bodies then I do weights. But when I do workout I gets the shit in. Of course I didn't say all of that in my interview though.

I kept my eyes on my wife while she sat down and ate her third plate. My baby was so damn greedy the shit was funny as hell to watch.

"You good baby?" I said to Kylee while sitting down next to her. I slide my chair close as hell to hers so I could rub on her stomach. I was a little tipsy from some champange and high from going in the back to smoke. She looked at me and bit her lip. My wife loved

when I was high because she said it reminded her of when we first met. The day that changed my life for the better.

"Keep looking at me like that and watch I bend yo' pregnant ass over and fuck you in one of these back rooms." I looked at her with a serious face. I was dead ass, Kylee in heat face always turned me on. Either she would bite her lip looking at me or she would cross them chocolate legs and look at me. Her ass wouldn't stop so I squeezed her sexy thigh lightly. I leaned forward and whispered in her ear.

"Get yo' ass up and follow me." She smirked and did what I said. I had her thick ass body in front of me to shield my hard ass dick. It was poking her in the crack of her ass as we walked. Kylee was giggling while I kissed on her neck and whispered nasty shit in her ear. I couldn't wait to open them thick ass legs and taste that warm sweet pussy.

Fifteen-minutes later we were walking out of the yoga room. I had my arms around her waist while she buttoned up her last button on her blouse. I fucked her good and licked that pussy good. I didn't get in it like I wanted to but it was enough to get me through the rest of this party.

I be on some real life thirsty shit when it comes to my wife. I needed to touch, kiss and look at her everyday. I was obsessed, the shit was not normal but it was *my* norm and I dare a muthafucka to tell me different.

"Baby let me go holla at these people real quick. I'll be right back and then we can leave." Kylee nodded at me and went over there with her sisters after she gave me a kiss. I had to go talk to these bloggers and local news people.

"OH MY GOD!" Even though Bruno Mars- That's What I Like was booming through the speakers I still heard my wife's voice.

Like a fucking bull I went through the crowd knocking nigga and bitch out my way to get to her. When I did she had her head down looking at some water spill between her legs. My eyes bucked out my fucking head when I realized her water had broke. I thought my baby needed some adult diapers at first. Ha! Snapping out of it I rushed over to her a picked her up bridal style.

"Oh my God! Our bags are in the Escalade!" Kylee cried and screamed out. Fuck! I forgot all about that shit.

"Bro don't worry about that. I can go to your crib and get it for you. Just get sis to the hospital." Brandon yelled out to me. I made it outside to the Rolls Royce.

"Don't worry baby I got you ok?" Kylee was breathing hard and she nodded ok. I grabbed the keys from the driver so I could drive to the hospital.

"NO! Sit back here with me Karlos don't leave me!" Kylee yelled from the back seat. That was all she needed to say.

"Get us there fast and safely or I'm killin' yo' ass." I tossed him the keys and got in the back with my wife.

"We following you bro and Kimmora is calling the family," Kevin said as him and Kimmora ran to there truck with Kalvin and Tiff following. The driver took off into the street towards the hospital. Kylee was breathing hard and tears rolling down her face.

"It's ok baby just breath----"

"Shut the fuck up Karlos this is your fault! If you would have kept your dick in your pants I wouldn't be---- OH MY GOD IT HURTS!" Kylee shouted so loud I know the windows on the car wanted to shatter. I was still stuck on her outburst.

"Baby you wanted the dick just as much as I-----."

"SHUT UP!" She sounded like a fucking man when she said that making me look at her in question. We pulled in the emergency zone and I hopped out before the car came to a complete stop.

I picked Kylee up and carried her into the hospital with our family right behind me. After I had to damn near pull a gun on the nurse for hounding me about some fucking forms. We checked in and Kylee had her room. She was hooked up to these machines that tracked when a contraction was coming and one for her and the babies heart rate. Kelly was in the room with me like I promised she could.

She was nervous and happy as hell. The whole waiting room was filled with our family and friends. Our entire crew was out there and that was like forty people alone. Then my in-laws were out there which was like another thirty. Brandon came back with our bags. I changed into some sweat pants and t-shirt after Kylee got settled into her bed. My poor baby was in so much pain. The doctor put in a order for her to get an epidural to stop her pain.

"Oh my Jesus this is unreal! Ughhhhh!" Kylee had her eyes in the back of her head looking possessed. I walked up to her and tried to give her some ice chips.

"Karlos get that shit out my FACE!" I tried not to laugh at her ass. I have been cussed out for about two hours now. I didn't pay the shit no mind because I knew it was the pain talking. Every I hate you was an I love you. I looked at her contraction machine and saw another one was coming.

"Brace yo' self baby here come another one and that shit looks big." Once it passed Kelly got up and gave her some ice chips. I laughed because she easily ate it coming from Kelly. Looking back at the machine I saw another one on it's way.

"Ooo baby here comes-----"

"Karlos shut the fuck up! Stop looking at the fucking— OUCH! OUCH! OUCH!" Kelly came and punched my arm.

"Ok I'm sorry baby I won't read it again." I smiled at her but she looked at me like she was the devil. I was turned on like a muthafucka!

The doctor came in and gave Kylee her epidural. The next four hours were just waiting for her to dilate. Going on the sixth hour it was time for Kylee to push. Two nurses had Kylee's legs holding them up and her doctor was sitting right in front of Kylee's pussy waiting to grab my princess.

I looked at Kylee's tiny pussy hole and wondered how the fuck a whole baby was going to come out of that. Kelly was wiping Kylee's head with a cold rag. I was on the side of Kylee letting her squeeze my hand however hard she needed to.

"Come on mommy! Give me a strong push!" Her doctor said. Kylee held her breath and pushed hard as fuck.

I looked down by her pussy and saw her shit on herself. Then I saw Kaylee's head come out Kylee's push itself out. Now, I'm a man but I almost threw up. Kylee pushed two more times and Kaylee came sliding out with blood and boogers all over her body. She had a head full of jet black hair.

Kylee fell back on the pillow and was breathing hard as hell. The doctor let me cut her cord and they began cleaning Kylee and Kaylee up. I was fucking amazed at what the fuck I just witness. I went over to Kylee and kissed her all over her face.

"You did real good baby. Thank you Kylee this is the realest shit anybody has ever done for me. I love you my Ky" She looked up at me with her gorgeous ass face and smiled with them deep ass dimples.

"Your welcome my Los. I love you more." The nurse yelled out time of birth 6:15am Kaylee Stelani Royal was 8lbs, 7oz. My Princess was a chucky thing. After they stiched Kylee up they brought Kaylee to her. Kylee looked at our daughter like she strucked gold. I was happy as hell I had my camera phone out recording it. I was going to post that all over social media.

"Go see daddy baby." Kylee kissed her on the cheek and handed her to me. I took her out of Kylee's arms like she was going to break.

When I had her secured in my arms I looked down at her and she opened her eyes at me. My heart skipped several beats. Her eyes were big and beautiful like her mama's but they were light grey like mines. When Kaylee moved her mouth you saw those beautiful deep dimples. That shit had a thug about to cry but I held my nuts together. Kelly held her next and took a million pictures of her.

I picked her back up and carried her out to the waiting room. Everybody looked at her from a distance and congradulated me and Kylee. Once I came back in the room Kylee was going to sleep. I set in the rocking chair and just held my daughter taking her all in. Wow! I was a fucking father now.

Kylee

Six weeks later

"Hey my Kaylee baby. What you in making a fuss for?" I picked my sweet baby girl up from her crib. I knew she was hungry and ready for a diaper change. This little girl had me and her daddy wrapped around her finger and, she was only three-weeks.

My baby was so chuncky with some big grey eyes and a head full of black curly hair. I was in love with looking at her especially when she showes her dimples. It reminded me of myself, my mother and my sisters.

Seeing what me and Karlos created made me feel blessed beyond measure. It also made me love and apprecitae my husband even more. That's why I wanted to trade places with him tonight. Instead of him taking me out and treating I wanted to spoil him. I haven't exactly told him that I wanted to do this. Convinceing him to let me wine and dine him is going to be hard. Ever since he messed up that one time he feels he has something to prove. I just want to reassure him we are fine and always will be fine. I couldn't live without that man and I just wanted him to know that tonight.

Kaylee was going to spend her first night out with my nonna. I trust that woman with my life so I knew she would care for Kaylee as I would. I really wish my mother and Karlos parent's were here. I would have loved for them to see us all has parents and living our married lives. As sad as the thought was I took comfort in knowing their legacies would live on.

"Do you feel better baby girl? Now you are all changed and looking pretty. Let's go feed you some breakfast and get our day started."

She had just got her little ears pierced three days ago. After I cleaned them up I put a receiving blanket over my shoulder and placed her over it. I held her back and rubbed on her litte head. Walking down the stairs I was always careful taking my time on these stairs. My sisters told me I was having new mommy mindset, whatever that means. I warmed my baby some formula on the stove and walked into the living room. It was a little chilly in the house so I turned the air down.

August was showing it's ass in Louisiana this year so Kaylee had on some furry baby socks and a onesie. Sitting on the couch I put her bib on and started feeding her. This little girl was so greedy she took the breast and formula. I guess that's why she had me eating so much when I was pregnant. Speaking of eating, my body after giving birth Kaylee had my body looking amazing. Don't get me wrong I still had a little stomach but my hips and thighs looked amazing.

My ass looked like I did squats in my sleep and it was extra soft. Hell, I wanted to make love to my damn self. Karlos definitley took notice. After Kaylee ate and I burped her she was wide awake. I was told most newborns slept all day and up all night. Well not this little girl, she was up all day. Wide eyed and looking around being nosey. I loved every minute of it. While we sat on the couch I turned Nick Jr. On and set Kaylee up in her swing. Something about the colors had my baby infatuated. I set her in her swing while I went to the kitchen to grab some cofee and a bagel.

While sitting back on the couch I heard the front door open. I smirked to myself and shook my head. Ever since I found out I was pregnant Karlos would not have a full work day. Rather street work or business work. His has would be gone for three hours - four tops and that's pushing it. When I heard him in the kitchen watching his hands I knew he was coming right in to pick Kaylee up. I soaked up watching him love on her. It was a similar feeling to when he loved on me. Minus being turned on.

"Good morning my Ky." He kneeled down and kissed me with tongue taking my words away. After pulling on his lip I pulled away remembering Kaylee was in her swing.

"Good morning my Los." I smiled at him kissing him one more time before her went and picked up Kaylee.

He had on a blue and white Nike basketball shorts and a muscle tank to. I could tell he was at his gym. He took his jacket off showing his big tattooed arms. Sitting down on the couch with Kaylee in his arms I watched his face glow. He smiled and kissed all on her. She have him a dimpled half smile looking at him with her eyes matching his.

"Los baby you know you can work a full day right? I can hold shit down here without feeling overwhelmed. Ink has been amazing and know I won't be able to turn in as many books as before. That's why they let me hire a co-editor." I told him while finishing up my bagel.

"I know you got this baby. I just be missing y'all and don't want to be away from y'all long." While he talked Kaylee squirmed in his arms. I knew that meant she was about to throw up and fall asleep. I grabbed her throw up rag on top of her play pen. I loved this play pen Tiff brought. It had a changing table on top of it. As soon as I grabbed the rag she threw up all on Karlos beater. I laughed and so did he.

"Damn Kaylee baby, why you gotta do daddy this way. You lucky you so pretty and have my heart. Anybody else would be knee deep in the ground." I hit him in his arm laughing. Karlos cleaned up Kaylee and took his shirt off.

My mouth became wet looking at his sexy ass chest. His hair was in that high bun, which everyone said was my signature bun. He looked so good with his hair and his full beard. I never could get enough of my Los. We watched some Nick Jr with Kaylee until she fell asleep on his chest. Karlos got up and put her back in her swing. Turning it on he kissed her some more and came back over to me.

"Come here Kylee." Damn I loved whenever her told me to come here.

His voice was so deep and he just looked so demanding whenever he said it. I scooted over to him on the layout part on our sectional. We immediately started kissing like some horny ass sixteen year olds. My hands were in his curls and his big hands were all over my body. I knew where this was leading but I wanted to save all of that for tonight. I pulled away and he looked at me annoyed making me laugh.

"Fuck back over here Kylee." He pulled me back over to him with really no force at all.

"Karlos I need to ask you something." I whined while trying to make some space between us. He was getting more annoyed.

"Well ask me while you on this dick." I started cracking up while trying to scoot over away from him. He was getting madder and madder making me laugh even more.

"Stop playing Kylee and take care of this baby. I was a good nigga and waited the whole six weeks for you to heal. Now I'm ready to explode if I don't feel you. I don't want no fuckin' head I need that pussy." He squeezed his now hard dick.

It took everything in me not to put that big fucka in my mouth. But I was trying to save it for tonight. Shit I wanted to suck and fuck the shit out of my husband. He ain't been the only horny one for six weeks.

"Karlos listen to me ok. Tonight I want take you out and wine and dine you. But you gotta let me drive and pick up the tab. Deal?" He looked at me like I had spiders coming out my head. I tried not to laugh because I needed him to see how serious I was.

"Before you say no just hear me out." I locked our fingers together and used my other hand to play with the back of his curls.

"I know ever since you messed up in the past you feel you have to make it up to me every day. But baby you have made it up to me beyond measure. I was a little insecure about us when we first got back together. But baby I'm am over all of that now. I know you love me and Kaylee and I trust you. You are always showing and telling me how much you love me and need me. Now I just want to show you how much I love and need you as well. Ok?" I looked at his fine ass face and he nodded his head. I kissed him hungerily then pulled away.

"What the fuck Kylee!" He was mad and I bust out laughing.

"I wanna save sex for tonight ok?" He let out a long breath and agreed.

"Ok baby. Well can you at least touch on me then." I smiled and laid on him with my hands in his hair." We watched TV and chilled the rest of the day until tonight. My Los was going to be so surprised tonight. My Los baby.

*

"So did you enjoy your steak baby?" I asked Karlos as we pulled out of Ruth's Chris Steakhouse. We had just had a great dinner with some good wine. Karlos was really enjoying himself. It was hard for him to let me handle shit but overall he did good. I had to stop him from picking up the check though.

"Yea that dinner was lit as fuck. Thank you baby for fillin' yo' nigga stomach up. I'm ready to head to the house and have you fill my mouth and dick up." I could fill him looking at me biting his lip. I looked at him when we stopped at a red light. He was so fine and I was so blessed to have him. My sisters set shit up for me while we were eating dinner. Karlos face is going to be priceless when he sees it.

"It feels weird looking at you on this side of the truck. You look relaxed and laid back. I might have to play this role more often." I laughed because I knew Karlos would be annoyed.

"Kylee don't make me fuck you up. This ain't no Usher tradin' places type of shit." He reached over and squeezed my thigh.

When we pulled up to the house I got excited on the inside and outside. I parked the truck in the garage and got out. Karlos grabbed our leftovers from the back seat and closed the door. He looked good as hell tonight he had on black, red and green Gucci from head to toe. With some black Yeezy's and his sexy hair sitting on top of his head.

I wore the same Gucci from head to toe with some heel boots. It felt so good to wear my five-inch heels again. Karlos grabbed me by my waist with one hand as we walked into the house from the door in the garage. Turning our alarm off, he placed the food on the counter.

"Thank you so much for tonight baby. You made a nigga feel more love then a person like me deserves. I appreciate this Kylee and I appreciate you too baby." He pulled me towards him by my harm while he leaned his back against the kitchen counter. I smiled and we shared a kiss. I felt his dick get hard so I pulled away.

"Kylee I swear to God, if you don't stop pulling away from me imma rape yo' ass." We both had to laugh at that shit.

"Ok baby I promise I won't do it no more. I just want to give you the rest of your surprise." I grabbed his hand and we walked up stairs.

When we stopped at our bedroom door I opened it slowly and turned the light on. All around the room was shopping bags from Karlos favorite stores. Nike, Footlocker, Jersey store, Northstom's, Gucci, Lids, Express and on the bed was boxes from Zales and Jaraed. Karlos had his hand over his mouth laughing. His face was so surprised and he was trying not to blush with his yellow ass.

"Real smooth Kylee. Yo' this shit is bomb baby. Besides my mama no woman has ever brought anything for me. Thank you so much baby, but don't do this shit no more. You got a nigga blushin' and shit." He pulled me over to him and gave me the sweetest hug ever. I looked up and him and kissed his bug juicy lips. Those lips takes care of all problems in my life. They were so soft, full and I could not get enough of them.

*

Now I had our room dimley lit with soft light bulbs. My Alexa speaker was playing my sex playlist I made. Karlos was siting on the bed waiting for me to come out of the bathroom. I had on a red thong and red pumps, my stripper pumps I like to call them. My hair was bone straight like Karlos liked it. Stepping out the bathroom Karlos looked up at me like I was a main course.

Since my hair was long as hell I had it cover my breast. He had his juicy bottom lip in his mouth biting it. When I got in front of him I rubbed the side of his face and ran my fingers through his long hair. It was big and curly all down because we were fresh out the shower. Him being the aggressive man he is, he yanked me on top of him. We looked at each other for a while his hands rubbing all over my booty and back.

"You my baby?" He asked me while still looking me in my eyes.

"I will always be your baby. You my baby?" I asked him.

"Always. I am never leaving you I put my life on that. Kiss me so I can breath right." I did what he asked and this by far was the best kiss we ever shared. It was so much love and passion in this kiss.

"Let me handcuff you to the bed rail. I wanna please you over and over without you stopping me." I looked at him and said.

"You can do whatever you want to to me. As long as you don't fuck with my ass." Leave it to this silly ass man to say some shit like that.

We both started laughing. Karlos set up on the bed and I grabbed the handcuffs out the side drawer. I brought two pairs of handcuffs from Lovers Lane. I handcuffed each of his wrist to the rail of our bed. He looked good as hell naked in the center of our bed while I straddled him. His dick was so hard it made me wet my thong up.

Once he was cuffed I started kissing him nasty and good like we always do. I licked and kissed on his neck bitting and putting hickeys on it. Karlos was lightly moaning under me sounding so fucking good. I kissed and licked his chest, nipples and his hard ass abs. I got to his pelvis and kissed and licked it as well.

His yellow dick was bouncing up and down looking good and strong. I stroked it with my hand and squeezed it. He was biting his lip watching my every move. The lust in Karlos eyes was making my mouth water. I took the tip of his dick in my mouth and played with the head of it. Then I took his dick in my mouth as much as I could.

I never gagged but I could not fit his thick ass dick down my throst. I would die trying though. Ha! I was sucking the life out of Karlos dick wetting it up. While I massaged his balls, my saliva was coating his dick and sliding to his balls.

"Fuck Kylee baby. Look at me while you suck my dick." I did what he asked and kept eye contact with him. He was biting his lip so hard I felt that shit like it was my lip.

"Imma nut Ky. SHIT!" He spilled his cum all down my throat. I kept sucking and stroking until he was empty. Once I was done I licked my lips and went to massaging his balls again. Karlos loved that shit. His dick sprung back up like a check point. Now it was my turn to cum all over my husband dick. I straddled him backwards, moved my thong to the side and slide down slowly on his pole.

"Uhhhhh Karlos babyyyyy. You feel so damn good." I started moving slowly up and down.

"Gotdamn girl! I gotta touch you Ky uncuff me baby." I heard him talk but the dick was so good I was not listening. I grabbed Karlos ankles and started slow stroking on his dick. I felt my pussy juice up as I rubbed my clit. The next thing I knew I heard a loud ass pop and snap. Almost like bending metal. Looking back my crazy ass husband has broke our bed rail completely in half freeing him self. He still had each set of handcuffs on his wrist hanging.

"I told you I needed to touch you. He grabbed me from behind making me squeal and laugh.

"Karlos you gotta stop fucking up our furniture. I would have uncuffed you after I came." I was cracking up at my crazy ass baby. He had me on my back looking serious as hell. After kissing me hard he slid back in me making me shutter.

"Tell me you never leaving me Kylee. Say it baby." He was fucking me so good I couldn't talk. I had to find my words because he was going deeper and faster.

"Ughh non ti lascerò mai Karlos (I'm never leaving you Karlos)." His dick was feeling so good the shit came out in Italian.

"Say it again," he said deep voice roaring in my ear.

"I'm never leaving y-y-you. I promise." We fucked good all night and then two more times in the morning. The love and obsession I had for Karlos was out of the normal. But it was my norm and I dare anybody try to tell me different.

Keira

"I hate all men. I swear I am so done with dudes! I might just bat for the other team." Jayla said while putting a spoonful of ice cream in her mouth.

Jayla was Kelly's best friend. Her and her boyfriend Ernest had yet another big fall out. She claimed this time it was over for real but if you knew Jayla and Ernest then you knew that was not true. Jayla became all of our friend and she was a cool chick.

"I tried the whole girl thing. Not for me, our menstrual cycles kept coming on at the same time every month. Nothing worse then two moody bitches., Tiff said making all of us laugh. We were having a girls night at her house since she lived the closeses to the mall and restaurant we went to earlier. We went to eat then decided to have a sleepover.

"Bitch you never told us you messed with girls. How was it? Did y'all use a strap and dildos?" Kelly ass asked. She was making her a root bear float.

"Naw we didn't do the strap but we did do dildo's and alot of pussy eatin'." Tiff bit down on her tongue and started twerking. We were cracking up. I loved when we did shit like this. All of us were in relationships, had children and had careers. I loved how we could still make time and hang out.

"So did you date a stud or a femm?" Kimmora asked. This girl loved freak as stories. She was the one who introduced me to porn. Freak ass.

"I had a femm girl. I ain't down with them she he's! I never understood girl's dating bitches that looked like niggas. Shit defeats the purpose in a full girl on girl experience. I like a soft ass girly girl like myself. Plus the shit looks sexier when we fuck!" Tiff said while cutting bananas up in her ice cream. We were in her kitchen making all kinds of ice cream desserts.

"Well stud or femm I might try that shit. These niggas don't know how to act right." Jayla was eating out of the cookie dough ice cream carton.

"Damn bitch I was looking for that." Kelly pointed to the cookie dough ice cream. We finished making desserts and went into the living room.

"How cool is y'all family for kepping all of our babies for the night." Tiff turned the TV on so we could bend watch Power.

"Girl our whole family loves kids. They been waitin' since we all started having periods to pop out some." Kylee spoke the truth. Our family was so old school and believed once a woman hits a certain age. We need to be married and have some babies. Sometimes I would love to see how our mother's side was. But she was an only child and her parents died a year before she did.

"I'm just grateful y'all came together for me. I have not been out or had a girl's night in months. I work, go to school and be with Ernest every day." We looked at her crazy.

"What! Girl why the fuck you ain't been called us? Look boo, it's ok to handle yo' business and be with your man. But you gotta make time for yourself and have some time without work, school and your man." I looked at her and said. My sisters nodded in agreement.

"Yea Jayla we are always down to hang all you gotta do is call us. Let's do someting tonight. It's still early as well and it's Friday night. Let's get out the house and have fun," Kimmora suggested.

"Hell yea! Let's go to XO night club!" Tiff jumped up and said. Hollered and agreed.

"Yea the guys go to there club all the time to *work*. So why can't we have some fun. Besides we not about to be in nigga's faces. We just gone have some good ol'fun." I jumped up egging us on. We high fived each other and laughed.

"I say what they don't know won't hurt'em. All we gotta do is go out, have fun and they never have to know." Tiff said.

"Tiff, Brandon seems cool as hell. He doesn't seem like Kaylin's crazy ass puttin' red dots on peoples head." Sarcasm and humor was in Jayla's voice We all started laughing except Kelly.

"Y'all better leave my King Kay alone. He was in his feelings that day. He wouldn't harm a fly."

"Girl yea right! Kaylin told yo' ass either you be with him or nobody. Sounds crazy to me," Kylee said cracking up. We all stopped and just looked at her with a serious face. She stopped laughing and looked at us confused.

"What?" she asked.

"Kylee I know damn well you not calling somebody's man crazy. We have a list a mile long of the crazy shit Karlos has done!" Kelly jumped and we fell out laughing. Kylee looked at us with her nose turned up.

"Forget y'all bitches." She pouted and y'all know how I am about my big sister so I went to hug her while still laughing.

*

Two hours later

Tonight was definitely meant to happen. The clothes we brought from the mall earlier was club appropiate. Tiff helped us out with some accessories and make-up. It almost September but it was still hot outside. Getting to the club there was a line but Jayla knew the bouncer so we got in with no problem. We looked good as fuck and the niggas was watching. They had nothing coming from either of us though. Even Jayla wasn't tryna talk. We were simply just having fun enjoying each other.

Said little bitch, you can't fuck with me
If you wanted to
These expensive, these is red bottoms

These is bloody shoes
Hit the store, I can get 'em both
I don't wanna choose
And I'm quick, cut a nigga hustle
Don't get comfortable
Look, I don't dance now
I make money moves
Say I don't gotta dance
I make money move
If I see you and I don't speak
That means I don't fuck with you
I'm a boss, you a worker bitch
I make bloody moves

All of us were rapping Cardi B-Bodak Yellow song with our drinks in our hand. The club was packed and we were able to get a section with some chairs and two tables.

"Ayeeeeeee!" We were all hollering while having so much fun. We got off the floor and went back to our little section. We had been here for an hour now and we were a little tipsy. We called an Uber with my app so it was all good. I didn't want any of us worrying about driving. We got back to our section and ordered more drinks. The bartender liked Kelly so he kept our drinks coming free all night.

"Thanks y'all for this shit I am having a fucking blast. We gotta do this shit again!" Jayla talked over the music. Cardi B song went off and the ass shakin' anthem of the summer came on next. The whole crowd got hype as fuck. You could see the dance floor good as hell from where we were sitting. Every girl in here was twerking their asses off like niggas was throwin' money.

"Get the fuck up Kylee, I want a dance with that fat ass booty you got." Tiff tipsy ass yelled over the music. Kylee started laughing shaking her head. We egged her on.

"Come on Kylee!" I shouted over the music. My sister could dance her ass off so I don't know why she was acting shy.

"Bitch you doing it with me!" Kylee pointed to me. I took a shot and stood up. We all had on the right outfit to dance in so I figured why not. I told Jayla to sit next to Tiff in a chair. The both of them gay hoes were so ready. Kylee and I began shaking our asses like we were pros.

I tell all my hoes - rake it up
Break it down, back it up
Fuck it up, fuck it up, back it up, back it up
Rake it up, rake it up, back it up, back it up
I tell all my hoes - rake it up
Break it down, back it up
Fuck it up, fuck it up, fuck it up, fuck it up
Fuck it up, fuck it up, rake it up, rake it up

"Get that shit Ky and Keira!" Kimmora yelled. I was dancing on Jayla like she was a paying customer. I looked over and Kylee and my sis was killin' it. After the song went off Tiff and Jayla was fanning themselves. We made a toast and took another shot. Tonight was so fun! While we were chilling talking about people who walked past us two girls were making their way over to us. Both of them were very pretty with some long ass weave in their hair. One of the girls were very thick with some full lips.

"Hi, I'm Taylor. I work with Kevin and Kalvin at the barber shop. I recognized you from the other night," she said pointing to Kimmora. Kim gave her a fake ass smile and a wave. Which was weird because Kim likes everybody. Kelly's ass was the mean one.

"Well thank you for the announcement but we are kind of in the middle of something," Kelly said to Taylor and her friend. See what I mean. Taylor and her friend looked at each other.

"Excuse my sister she is a little tipsy. I'm Kylee and this is Jayla and Keira. You know Kimmora and the rude one is Kelly," Kylee said pointing to all of us. Kelly and Kim rolled their eyes. Taylor and her friend set down with there drinks.

"Your Kalvin's wife, right?" Taylor looked at me and asked.

"Yup. For almost a year now." I smiled at her. She gave me a weird smile almost like it was forced. I blew it off and took a sip of my drink.

"So, all of y'all are married to the Royal brother's?" Taylor's friend asked.

"All accept me. I'm the single one the rest of these chicks on locked down., Jayla laughed making me laugh.

"I used to have such a crush on the one with the long hair. He so fuckin' fine to me with his mean ass." We looked at Kylee and her face was twisted up in a mug.

"Karlos. His name is Karlos or better know as my husband. Also known as you will get yo' ass dragged if you speak of crushin' on my husband again." Kylee stood up and walked torwards the girl with her wine cooler in her hand. I jumped up before she cracks that girl's face open.

"Um ok look we are gonna get out of here. I apologize for the interruption I just wanted to come over and introduce myself." Taylor stood up pulling her friend away from us.

"Damn Kylee, you been around Karlos to long. You were about to knock her ass out with the wine cooler bottle. Have the bitch seein' stars," Kelly said. We started laughing and went back to having fun.

It was almost midnight and the club was still jumpin'. We went back to dancing and having fun. Some dudes tried to sit with us and buy drinks but we shot their asses down. Jayla got some fine nigga's number. He had some long black dreads and was tall as fuck. Everyone went to the bathroom but me and Kim. I wanted to ask her why did she give Taylor that fake ass smile.

"Kim what was that about with Taylor? You are usually the mice one out of all of us." She took a sip of her drink and turned torwards me.

"The other night I met Kevin at the shop so I could pick him up. When I came in there Taylor and Kalvin were playing. He was holding her trying to squirt her with a water bottle. They were playing but I just didn't like it and I don't like that bitch. I know I'm trippin' because it's Kalivn. He is so sweet and he would never do anything like that. I just don't like that bitch. I'm sorry I didn't tell you sooner boo I just didn't want you to freak out over nothing." I looked at my sister and could not believe what she was saying. She was right what she saw wasn't nothing.

It was everything. Everything I needed to know as far as why Kalvin had started acting funny. Why Taylor gave me that forced ass smile. He has feelings for someone else. I thought I would break down at the thought of it being another woman. Instead I felt calm and like I know what my next move needs to be.

"Thank you Kim. Your right, it's not nothing. I will bring it up to Kalvin and let him know don't be horse playing with co-workers." I put on my best preformance and she brought it. We hugged just as our sisters showed back up.

"Oh my God!" Jayla said making us all look at her. She pointed to the entrance and all the Royal brothers were walking in including Brandon. Karlos was in front with his hair down and big looking like a fucking wolf ready to attack.

"Has anybody checked their phones?" I asked pulling mines out.

"I have seven missed calls!" Tiff said holding her phone up

"Me to," myself and Kelly said in unison. We all looked at Kylee.

"I have fifteen." She held her phone up and we all busted out laughing.

"I'm happy y'all think this shit is funny!" Karlos deep as voice was louder then the music. He looked at Kylee like he wanted to kill her. A normal person would have run in the opposite direction. Kylee's ass walked to him with no fear and grabbed his hand. Karlos reminded me of King Kong and Kylee was his Ann Darrow!

"You and you! Y'all all over fuckin' Instagram!" Kalvin shouthed holding his phone up pointing to me and Kylee. We looked at him in confusion.

"Doing what?" I stood up and snatched his phone. Someone recorded me and Kylee giving Tiff and Jayla lap dances. We had a shit load of hashtags behind it. #BadBitches #LookatDatAss #LightBrightAndChocolate #Sexy. Kylee stood next to me watching it as well. She walked over to Karlos and he was mugging her like he had true beef with her.

"Kalivn we were just having fun. How was we supposed to know someone was recording us? Plus, we didn't entertain any niggas. All we wanted to do was have a girl's night out." Kalvin snatched his phone from me still mad.

"Kim, you a fuckin' wife and mama now! Look how you dressing with them short ass shorts! I want some good ass sloppy head when we get home. Y'alls little sleepover, lady's night or whatever the fuck y'all call it, ain't including you tonight." He pulled her over to her and squeezed her ass.

"Keira, I should kick yo' ass for real girl. But you do look good as fuck wife." He walked over to me and kissed me. I kissed him back and put my arms around his neck.

"Next time you don't answer yo' phone Keira you gone see a different side of me." He whispered in my ear. As much as I wanted to kick his ass I played along. My pussy had a mind of its own anyways.

"I'm sorry bae love." I looked up at him and kissed him again.

"KARLOS!" Kylee screamed snapping us out of the trance our guys had us in. Karlos punched some nigga and had the guy by his shirt.

"GET MY WIFE OFF YOUR PAGE NIGGA! NOW!!" He barked at the guy with the loudest deepest voice that made the club shake. With a bloody nose the trembling guy pulled his phone out his pocket and erased the video. Karlos stood over him and made sure he did it. He threw the guy on the floor and walked back over to us. Our mouths were on the floor.

"Y'all hungry? Let's go to Denny's." Karlos looked at us and said while sitting down. His brothers were cracking up. Kylee looked at him and bit her lip and sat down on his lap. The started making out as if we were not all in a night club. Her ass loved that crazy shit.

"Oh I met you and Kevin's new co-worker Taylor." I looked at Kalvin when I said that to him. It was something I was looking for in his face and eyes when I said that.

"Is that right?" he asked. There it was, the face and look in his eyes I was looking for. I nodded my head and took a sip of my drink. I knew just what I needed to do.

Kalvin

It was almost 7pm and I was outside of the restaraunt I was meeting Taylor at. Part of me wanted to go in and part of me wanted to leave. After Keira told me she met Taylor at the club the other night. I was scared as hell. I thought she was going to tell me they fought or some shit. If that would have went down I most definitely would have stood Taylor up. But then I would have to face Taylor tomorrow at work. I told Keira I had some street shit to handle after work. She told me her and Kyra were going over her father's house to eat. This shit I was doing was not me at all. I had ever been the player type.

Now don't get me wrong I have had my share of pussy and three-somes. But when it came to me having a girl I was always faithful. My brother's use to clown me about how easily whipped I would get. No bitch would walk over me but once I made you my girl it was me and you. I guess I got more of my mama ways in me then my pops.

He use to tell me it's good that I am so loyal just don't give my loyalty to every piece of pussy I climb into. *Fuck it.* I said to myself as I got out my Lexux truck. Hitting the alarm I walked into the spot to get this shit done.

Upperline was a nice joint with some good ass gumbo and pecan pie. I haven't had a chance to come here with Keira and now I probably never will. After the hostess gretted me she showed me where Taylor was sitting. I walked over to her with her back facing me.

"What's up girl." I spoke to her while taking my Saints fitted hat off. I didn't want to dress to fresh and have Keira notice. I kept it simple with some black True Religion jeans, a crispy white Polo shirt, and my Bvlgari iced out watch with diamond stud earrings. I had Kevin line my hair up today not because of this date but because it was just time.

"I was just about to leave. I thought you stood me up." Taylor looked at me and smiled. I smiled back and looked at what she had on.

She had on some fitted ass skinny jeans on with a black see through button up. She had a black bra like top with some sparkle shit under it. Her hair was the same straight long weave and she had some red lipstick on. Taylor was thick and bad as fuck. Like, she looked feminine but I like my woman to wear dresses sometimes. I liked for her to show her pretty feet off or wear those long heel boots. You know the one's y'all wear with them tight jeans and shirt stop right above y'all asses. Yea, that shit be lit as fuck.

Taylor always wore chucks or heels but I never seen her feet. And she never wore her real hair, always weave with those long ass eye lashes and a pound of makeup. I never noticed that shit until now. Keira rarely wore makeup because her fine ass didn't need it. And weave was out the fucking question. Not because of me but because Keira's hair looked like the shit bitches pay hundreds of dollars to have.

"Yo' ass was not about to go no fucking where. Stop lying to yo'self girl." She blushed and picked up her menu. We both looked it over in silence as if we didn't know what the fuck to say.

"I know what I'm getting already. I want to try the dumplings and shrimp," she said as she put her menu down.

"Let me ask you a question. What exactly do you expect to come out of this. You know I wouldn't leave my wife and child for anybody. So what do you think will happen after this date," I asked cutting right to the chase. I had already knew I wanted the gumbo and peacan pie anyways.

"Well Kalvin honestly I don't know. I am fully aware you won't leave your family and I respect that. All I would want after this is for us to still be cool and hang out from time to time." I nodded my head just as our waiter came. We placed out orders and gave her the menus.

Me and Taylor did some small talk and I realized she is

spoiled and lazy. Yea she cut hair and shit but that was only becuase she felt it was fun. She wanted to live off her parents and brother for the rest of her life. And she did not like kids. She said they get in the way. That right there had me over this bitch like a fucked up bridge.

I had a daughter who was my heart and any hoe who didn't like that could kick rocks after I beat they ass. I made sure to not let the conversation go to sports or any other shit we talked about before. Outside of that shit I just did not find her intresting. After dinner I was ready to go home to my wife and baby. And put this fucked up night behind me.

Taylor excused herself and went to the ladies room. I pulled my phone out while she was gone and looked at my screen saver of Keira and Kyra. My beauties were my whole life and all I needed. I couldn't wait for Taylor to come back from the bathroom so I can end this shit. I wasn't even trippin' about being at work with her from here on out.

Either she maintained being prefessional or she would be fired. I felt Taylor walk pass me and sit down. I hit the button to black out my screen on my phone and looked up at her. Only to see Keira sitting across from me, not Taylor. I could feel my face freeze and my heart rate speed the fuck up. *How the fuck? What the fuck?* Was all I kept saying to myself.

"Surprise to see me? Well, I'm sure you are. You look just like your little girlfriend did when I popped up in the bathroom on her ass. Dont worry about her, she needs a little more time powdering up her nose." Keira put her hands on the table and they had some blood and hair on them.

I looked at her white Nike gym shoes she had on and they had blood stains on them to. My wife has never scared me more then she did right now. A nigga couldn't even say shit. She sat across from me smirking with her hair in a high Kylee bun with no earrings on or anything. She still had on her wedding ring so I guess that was a good thing.

"Why are you so quiet Kalvin. Oh wait let me guess, you didn't think I knew about your date?" She chuckled and continued. "I bet you also didn't think Kimmora would not tell me about y'all playing grabby ass at work. *And* I bet your stupid ass also didn't think I could go into T-mobile and ask for a print out of your text messages." She clasped both of her hands together.

"Well I went through all 100 pages and I must say you have found quite the little boyfriend. Because that's all she is right, a nigga with breast. She can talk to you about sports teams and which player is better. You know, shit you talk about with your brothers. Well now you have the whole package. A homeboy that you can fuck." Keira slid her ring off and sat it on the table in front of me. My wife had no emotion on her face, no tears or sadness not even anger.

"Listen to my words Kalvin." She leaned forward with a cold stare and a tight mouth.

"Don't bring your ass home or I swear I will shoot you." With that my wife got up from the table and walked out.

"Fuck!" I said out loud not caring who the fuck heard me. Some people turned and looked at me like I was crazy.

"Finish yo' nasty ass fish and stop lookin' at me nigga." I yelled at this fat ass white guy with his fat ass whale of a wife.

I can not believe my life right now. I went from being happily married to having the shit ripped from under me. I should have just took Karlos advice and let this stupid ass fantasy alone. I in no way shape or form want Taylor------ Oh shit! I forgot about this bitch being beat up in the bathroom. Ugh! Fuck my life!

Kaylin

Today was a good a fucking day. Not only was it my birtday but Kelly had been spoiling a nigga all day. I woke up to some bomb ass head, pussy in the shower and some bomb ass breakfast. Then she gave me my presents which was a pair of Yeezy's and a Rolex. Then we went to the movies to see Daddy's Home 2.

I was a big Will Ferrell fan so I was like a big ass kid when we went to see it. Then my bae gave me some lit ass fucking head in the movie theather. Shit had my knees buckling and wiggling in my chair like a bitch. Now I was downstairs in the living room of me and Kelly's condo waiting for her to come down.

We were on our way to our club Royalty. I was having my tattoo party tonight and I was ready to turn up. I had ten of the best tattoo artist in town coming. D.J. Calvin Harris was hosting my party tonight. I also had the same caterer that did Karlos grand opening since I loved the food so much. Tonight I was killin' the game with my Dolce & Gabbana jeans on and matching shirt with the logo all over it. Kalvin hooked my hair and goatee up so I was looing like a Zaddy tonight.

I wanted the rest of my sleeve done from my tattoo artist so I was bringing another shirt with me. Looking at the TV on ESPN Kelly came walking down the stairs. Her sexy slim thick ass looked so good tonight. She had this fitted red t-shirt dress that had her whole back out with theses black Giuseppe heels.

Her little feet matched her hands and her skin looked sexy in red. We both had on red and black. Her hair was straight but in a ponytail so I could see her beautiful face. Kelly's and myself jewelry was blinding just the way I wanted tonight. Standing up I walked over to her.

"Damn Kelly. You look so fuckin' good bae. When we get back home I wanna fuck you in this dress and heels." I kissed her before she could answer.

Her sweet scent mixed with my hard scent went perfect together. Shit between me and Kelly been bumpy lately. She still was on that no baby tip. And we still have not made any steps towards getting married. Tonight I didn't even want to think about all of that. I just wanted to have a good night.

"Come on bae so we can get our party on." I grabbed her leather bomber jacket and mines to and we walked out. Kevin and Kimmora got me a luxury party bus as a gift. They had it filled with my favorite liquor, weed and it was red and black. I was happy they did this so all of us could turn up and not worry about driving.

*

Pulling up to Royalty the line was wrapped around the block. No VIP section was offered tonight. I wanted the whole section clear for only for myself, Kelly, my brothers and their wives. I looked at all of us while the bus parked and we all looked like fuckin' money. We got out and helped our ladies off the bus and made our way inside. I just wish Keira was here. She still was not ready to be around Kalvin so she sent her gift through Kylee.

"Shit is lit bro! This a nice ass turn out!" Brandon said to me over the loud music. We made our way up to VIP and took a seat on the round suede couch. We had our employees set it up with a giant birthday banner. Food, drinks, and weed was at our disposal.

She's a very freaky gurl
Don't bring her to mama
First you get her name
Then you get her number
Then you get some brain in the front seat of the Hummer
Then you get some brain in the front seat of the Hummer

Gucci Mane- Freaky Gurl blasted through the speakers. I had some dancers on stage makin' it clap. Kelly was in my lap dancing like she should be on stage with that ass. I took me a shot and enjoyed the show. Looking up at my brothers, I noticed Kalvin was already drunk. His ass had been in a funk since Keira put him out.

It had been two months and she still was curving that nigga. I had to push that shit out my mind too. Kelly was makin' my dick grow. Kylee must have taught Kelly this shit because she was dancing on Karlos too like a pro. Karlos nasty ass dragged Kylee upstairs to his office. That fool had his shit re-done from the ceiling to the floors. The nigga said he didn't want no part of Zena's dirty ass.

After dancing with our girls, drinking and smokin' we were all feeling good as hell. Kimmora and Kevin were in the corner smoking and shoving their tongues in each others mouths. I didn't even know she smoked but I guess he must have turned her out.

The tattoo artist came and set up shop. Karlos gave me the idea to have invitation only tonight which made shit more mellow. We turnt-up and partied like it was our last night alive. All of us got tattoos. Me and Kylee got the most ink done. I was so fucked up I don't even remember what anybody else got. All I know was I got my sleeve finished and I fucked the shit out of my woman. 26 was going to be a good ass year.

*

Two weeks later

"Kaylin would you stop being annoying before I slap you." Kelly laughed when I put my hand over her phone.

She was on her Instagram putting up pictures of the heads her and Keira did. They were almost done with there braid program and getting ready to take there state test. We both didn't have shit to do today so I was annoying her cute ass.

"I dare you slap me. Watch I slap this dick on yo' ass cheeks while I fuck you silly." We both started laughing. We was both looking bummy laying in bed being lazy. Me and Brandon had been talking about opening a Car Wash so for the next few weeks I would be busy. I wanted to spend all my free days with my bae.

"Kay you are so nasty bae. We both know when I throw this pussy back at you yo' ass be ready to tip over." I set all the way up and looked at her with a look of dismay on my face.

"Now you know you bettas stop lying Kel. This dick be makin' you cry out like a lone wolf at the moon. King Kayyy that's my spot bae, nobody fucks me like you." I moaned and tried to sound like her. Kelly fell over laughing. I loved her pretty smile with them deep dimples.

"Give me a kiss bae." I told her. She bit her lip and leaned over to kiss me. That quick I was ready to fuck. She was to because she straddled me and pulled my dick out.

KNOCK!
KNOCK!
KNOCK!

"Damn, which one of these niggas poppin' up at my shit. Hold on bae keep that pussy ready." I pulled my boxers back up and slipped my sweatpants on. Kelly's hard headed ass slipped her pants on and followed. I got to the door and opened it thinking it was one of my brother's. It was some black old guy holding a box.

"Who are you?" I looked at him with a mug. My heat was on the table next to my door so he bet not be on no stupid shit.

"Hi my name is William Grant. I am your grandmother's husband, your mom is her daughter." I looked at him unimpressed.

"Listen, she died last week and she left this box for you. I got your address from her sister who has always kept tabs on you. I have no idea what is in this box all I know is your name is on it. She told me on her death bed to give it to you." He handed me the box and looked at me like I owed him something.

"Good lookin' nigga. You can step on now homie." I closed the door in his face. Kelly smacked her lips.

"Bae that was rude," she said to me. I chuckled as we both walked into the living room.

"Bae do you want me to give you some privacy?" I shook my head no and she set next to me.

Opening the box I saw a bunch of pictures of what looked like my mother. She was beautiful with long black hair. Her skin was brown and her eyes were small and brown. There were a bunch of pictures of her when she was a baby and when she was in middle school. There was one picture with her and my so-called grandmother. I didn't know how the fuck to feel. If my grandmother and her sister was still around why the fuck haven't they ever tried to reach out.

There was two envelopes one labled open first and the other labled open second. The first enevelope was a letter from my grandmother to me. She basically was saying she loved me and always have but looking at me and being around me reminded her of her only child she lost. She told me my mama loved me and was happy when I was born. She said my mother had a drug problem and couldn't shake it.

She left me her sister, my auntie, number and address. I folded the letter up and picked up the second envelope. I opened it and saw it was a birth certificate. I had never had anything except my social security card. I read it with Kelly sitting next to me. I saw my mother's name Pamela Nina Williams and the father's name said Kaine Lamar Royal.

"Wait, does that say-----" Kelly said squeezing my arm.

"WHAT THE FUCK!" I jumped up still looking at my birth certificate. I stood in place and read it over and over. I couldn't focus on shit else. I didn't even here Kelly calling me.

"Kaylin, bae your crying." Her soft voice said snapping me out of it. She was right, my ass was crying.

I stuffed the paper in my pocket and slipped on my Jordan's. Grabbing my keys I walked out our condo slamming the door. I can't even describe to you how I fuckin' felt. Confusion, anger, hurt and a shit load of questions ran through me. All I knew was I needed to get to my brothers. In my Lexus I texted them 911 and told them to go to Brandon's house. I knew no matter what they were doing they would come at a 911 text.

Pulling up to Brandon's crib I saw all my brothers cars outside. I got out and the November wind hit me. It was 8 day until Thanksgiving which was my favorite holiday. Now I was out the holiday mood and ready to kill somebody. I walked up to the door and knocked. Tiff answered the door holding my niece Brandy pretty self. Look like they were about to leave. No matter what, a pretty baby will soften anybody up.

"Hey brother, you ok? You look pissed off .All of your brothers flew over here." I kissed her on top of her head and kissed my niece on her chubby chocolate cheek.

"I'm good sis, let me go holla at these fools." Tiff nodded and as I walked in she and Brandy walked out.

I went down the basement where I knew my brothers were. As soon as I got down there Karlos walked up to me.

"What's good bro? What happened?" All of them stood up waiting for me to talk. I grabbed my birth certificate out my pocket and gave it to Karlos. He read it and his face changed quickly. I stood there as he read it over and over like I did when I first saw it.

"Will somebody please fuckin' talk! What the hell is on the paper?" Brandon stood up and said. He snatched the paper from Karlos and read it. Just like me and Karlos his face changed. Kalvin stood next to him and read it as well.

"My grandmother died and left me a box of pictures of my mama. There was two envelopes one with a letter from her to me and the other had that in it." I pointed to the birth certificate.

"Her husband said my auntie has been keeping tabs on me that's how he knew where I lived. This whole fuckin' time they been fuckin' lying to me. They let me call them auntie and uncle knowing damn well I was his son. They told me my last name was Royal because legally they adopted me. They told me my mama was auntie Staci's sister. All that shit has been a fucking lie." I stood there in the middle of the floor. They all looked shocked and speechless.

"Kaylin nigga I know shit seems fucked up man but its more to this story. Pops would nev-----"

"THAT AIN'T MY FUCKIN' POPS! THE NIGGA DIDN'T WANT ME! HE PLAYED MY UNCLE FOR YEARS! Y'ALL DON'T WANT TO SEE THE SHIT BECAUSE TO Y'ALL HE WALKED ON WATER! HE WAS JUST AS FUCKED UP AS HIS BROTHERS"

WHAM!

Karlos came charging at me like a bull hitting me in my face making my lip split. I jumped up ready to charge him but Kalvin had me and Brandon had Karlos.

"DON'T YOU EVER TALK ABOUT OUR POP'S LIKE THAT! SHIT IS FUCKED UP I'LL GIVE YOU THAT! BUT NIGGA YOU ATE AND REEPED THE BENEFITS JUST LIKE US!" Karlos yelled at me while Brandon held him back. Karlos is a big nigga. If he wanted to he could have got to me. I knew he didn't want to fight me forreal he was just mad. Shit I was to!

"Fuck this shit and fuck all of y'all!" I pushed Kalvin up off of me and stormed out. I needed to get some air and get some liquor in me. This shit just can't be life right now.

Kelly

Five days later

These past three days with Kaylin have been awful. I have never seen him so down and out of it. All my bae does is get drunk and pass out. He does not talk to his brothers even though they have reached out everyday. Karlos pops up every day a few times a day to check on him. One night he passed out in his car in our garage with the engine still on. I know what your thinking but it was not on purpose. Thank God I left the top windows on our garage open. Karlos came and got his heavy ass out for me and brought him in the house.

Yesterday I couldn't take it anymore, I had to try and fix this. Or at least get him to get some type of understanding. I was able to catch him before he started drinking and convince him to see his grandmother's sister. I told him he needs to do this for himself. All the questions he has may not be able to get answered. But at least his she can shed some light for him.

Well the visit went awful. We get over to her house and she looked just like the pictures of his grandmother and mama. When we got there she seemed please to see us. Kaylin just had so much anger in him that he made the visit dreadful. She had snacks and lemonade out for us. But Kayin declined everything and wanted to cut straight to the chase. His aunt told us that his mother met Kaine working for him. She worked for him in his trap house. He paid her five-hundred dollars a day to cut and package drugs for him. He had had her work with his other workers as well.

She was not hooked on drugs at the time she was trying to make some money for her and her mother. Well I guess Kaine became attracted to her because they developed a sexual relationship. But the only problem was, Kaine was married with two boys at the time. When Kaylin's mom became pregnant and wanted Kaine to leave his wife Kaine let her go. He paid all Kaylin's mom medical bills and moved her and her mom out the hood. When Kaylin was born Kaine's wife became pregnant with Kalvin.

Well Kaylin's mom couldn't take it and started using drugs and hanging with pimps. Kaine tried to get her some help when Kaylin was six-months old. But she refused and ran off leaving Kaylin with his grandmother. When he was ten-month's old she was found dead in a motel in Slidell, Louisiana. When Kaine found out from her mom he went straight to get Kaylin. Him and Staci didn't want to confuse the boys so they told him he was there nephew. But Staci and Kaine legally adopted Kaylin when he turned one.

Kaylin and myself sat there and let his aunt tell use the whole story. I honestly thought Kaylin would feel some type of relief. But he grew more angry and claimed they didn't love him. He said if his mom wouldn't have died Kaine and his brothers never would have been in his life. I tried to calm him down and tell him not to think like that but he was not trying to hear that.

Even his aunt told him Kaine use to visit him everyday and let Kaylin fall asleep on his chest. Kaylin still was closed minded on hearing anything. After we left his aunt's house Kaylin dropped me off at home and I have not seen him since. I called and called but his phone just kept ringing. He had his find my iPhone app off so I could not track him. Now here it is a full 24-hours later and still no Kaylin.

I was at home laying in the bed watching Good Times reruns. I heard the door downstairs open. I jumped up out the bed and went downstairs. Kaylin was yanking his key out the door stumbling in.

"Kaylin where the fuck have you been?" He looked up at me with red and low eyes. He was high and drunk.

"Kellyyyyy I was in the zone mann."

Hiccup!

Hiccup!

He fell over and I hurried and helped him to the couch. Once I slammed his body down I took his shoes and socks off. Covering him up Kaylin started snoring. I looked down at him and shook my head. I did not want to walk away from Kaylin at this time in his life. I couldn't imagine how he felt finding out Kaine is his father. I went back to our bed room and got in the bed to catch some sleep. At least he was home and safe now.

Feeling a hand touch me I opened my eyes and saw the clock on the night stand said 3am. I turned over and Kaylin was in bed with me smelling like Hennessy and weed. He was rubbing on my breast and trying to get between my closed legs.

"Kaylin go take a shower you stink. I just put these covers on the bed." He ignored me and started kissing on my shoulders. I pushed him away which was hard with his solid ass.

"Damn Kelly I can't get none of my pussy? Why you doin' me like I'm a stranger." He sat up looking mad as hell.

"It's not that Kaylin, you just smell and you have not been home in almost two days. Sex is really not on my mind." He looked more angry by my words.

"Oh so I'm no good for you? Is that what the fuck you been saying? Who you been fuckin' Kelly? Open yo' legs so I can see if that pussy still the same. " He got on top of me before I could get out the bed. Being stronger then me Kaylin dug aggressively between my legs.

"KAYLIN STOP! I HAVE NOT BEEN FUCKING ANYBODY!" I yelled for him to stop and get off me. Once he slid his fingers out he smelled them and got off me. Once I set up in his face I slapped the fuck out of him.

"Get the fuck out Kaylin!" I yelled at him and pointed to the door. He smirked and nodded his head up and down.

"Wow. So just like everybody else you don't want me either. I come in here to make love to you and you put me out." He stumbled out the bed and put his pants back on.

"Fuck you Kelly." He walked out. When I heard the front door closed I broke down. I just wanted my King Kay back. He was letting this tear him down.

It is two days before Thanksgiving and here I was throwing up yet again. I think this shit between me and Kaylin was making me sick. I have not seen or talked to him in two days. I have given up on calling blowing his phone up. I even stopped inboxing him on social media. I was all out of ideas on what to do. His brothers told me to give him some space to sort his head out.

All that would be good if I was not sitting in Tiff's bathroom looking at a positive pregnancy test. At first, I was not going to take one but my breast had been sore. My cravings for certain foods have changed and I find myself sleeping more. I just wanted to cross everything off the list in seeing what was wrong with me. Well now I know, me and Kaylin were about to be parents. A knock came at the door making me jump.

"Come in," I said still sitting there looking at the test. Tiff walked in and closed the door. Brandon was downstairs with Brandy and she didn't want him to know what I was doing.

"So what does it say boo." I looked at her with tears and held it up. She covered her mouth and walked closer to me. Tiff kneeled down and hugged me and I just broke down.

"Kelly it's going to be ok boo. You know we got you and so does Kaylin. Things may not look like it Kelly but everything will be ok. You guys are going to be great parents." Tiff looked at me, wiped my tears and smiled at me.

"Thank you Tiff. I just wish me and Kaylin were on better terms. I don't even know if he wantes kids anymore." I wiped my face and put the test inside the box. I placed the box in my purse and stood up to wash my hands.

I chilled at Tiff house for a while. Me and her played with Brandy, aggravated Brandon in his man cave and cooked some food. Being around them was really making me feel better. Tomorrow I was going to tell my sisters I was expecting. Me and Tiff were in the living room when Brandon came in talking on his phone. When he hung up he looked at us shaking his head.

"Aye my boy called and said Kaylin's car is parked in the parking lot of his bar. He wants us to come get him. Bae I called your mama she said we can bring Brandy to her." Tiff nodded and we both got up to get ready.

I was so sick of this shit. And I was sick of Kaylin inconveniencing other people. I apologized for Brandon and Tiff having to do this but they both told me we are family. It wasn't that late only 10pm but it was too late for Brandy to be out. While we drove I just said a prayer. I wanted this to be over with Kaylin and I wanted him to see all the love around him. I understand this was a hard pill for him to swallow but he was spiraling out of control.

We pulled up to the bar Brandon said he was at. There were a lot of cars parked but I knew he was in his blue Mercedes Benz. We all got out and started walking around the big parking lot. I was starting to thing we arrived to late and he left. Which made me worry more because taht means he was drunk driving again. Tiff spotted his car parked at the end. The closer we got to the car the more I was able to see some shit that seemed off.

"Aw fuck." Brandon said because he noticed what I did. Kaylin was fucking in his car.

I felt like I was having an out of boby experience. For a minute I stood there with shock running through my body. Then anger and fire felt me up from the top of my head to the tip of my toes. For a while no one else or nothing else was around me. Just Kaylin foggy ass car. Looking to the side of me I saw bricks lined up seperating the parking spaces. I picked one up and before Tiff and Brandon could stop me I walked closer to Kaylin's Benz and slammed the brink in his windshield.

The car started shaking and I yanked the passengers door opened. The bitch was trying to crawl of of Kaylin but I grabbed her by her legs and yanked her out. Once she hit the ground I looked at her and saw it was Emily. I snapped further and started beating her ass. Just the fact that she knew about me and Kaylin made me beat the fuck out of her. I felt my nails break with each punch I gave her. Emily was screaming begging me to stop. Then I felt my body lift in the air.

"Ok sis, you done beat her ass enough! Come on lets go home!" While Brandon had me in the air I looked at Kaylin standing by his car with his head in his hands.

"FUCK YOU KAYLIN WIT'CHO NASTY DICK ASS! NO WAY I'M KEEPING THIS BABY!" I yelled at him as Brandon carried me to the car. Tiff was kicking Emily while she was on the ground.

"TIFF BRING YO' ASS!" Brandon yelled at her. Kaylin started running torwards Brandon's Bentely.

"What the fuck you mean! You pregnant Kelly? Bae, please ok! Please don't kill my baby! I'm sorry bae for real for real." Brandon placed me in the back seat while Kaylin pleaded at my window.

"Kaylin bro, go sober up and chill out. Both of y'all are fucked up and need to relax. Kelly will be at my house, go home bro and talk to her tomorrow," Brandon said to Kaylin outside the car. I had my mouth scrunched up and looking straight ahead. I did not want to see Kaylin's face today or any other day. Brandon pulled off leaving Kaylin standing outside looking stupid.

Kimmora

I had just arrived at work feeling a little tired. For the past two nights me and my sisters had been staying nights at our dads house. Tiff was right with us. We had our babies there as well. Our nonna and dad was loving having us and our children in the house all together. You could not tell nonna and dad that Brandy was not there grandchild also. Kelly wanted all of us together ever since she found out she was pregnant and Kaylin cheated on her. I felt so bad for her and Keira going through that bullshit. Thanksgiving had just passed. We had a good holiday at Kylee and Karlos house. We did a pot luck and everyone was there accept Kaylin.

He had been staying at Brandon and Tiff house while Kelly went back home. The shit was just a mess for them. Kalvin and Keira kept staring at each other on Thanksgiving but still would not say anything. Kevin told me Kalvin and Taylor do not speak to each other at all when they are at work. I was happy because this time I was going to beat her ass. Kevin said the ass whopping Keira put on her scared her straight.

My patients must have sensed I was tired because the first half of my shift went by smoothly as hell. Now I was in the cafeteria eating my fruit salad. I had a million things on my mind. While reading on my Kindle one of these new author's Kylee out me up on.

"Damn Kimmy I have missed you." I looked up from my phone and saw Tyler standing in front of me. He didn't have his uniform on so I knew he was not on the clock. I had not seen Tyler in three weeks.

"Tyler what are you doing here? I was told you were not coming back until next week." I put my phone down when he sat down. I loooked around to make sure no one was watching us. I didn't need anybody reporting back to Kevin.

"I don't come back until next week but I wanted to see you. Listen, I don't blame you for you husband hoodish ways. I didn't tell the police shit either Kimmy on behalf of you and your son. But Kimmy you do not need a man like that. He is not going to get you anywhere but down." Tyler tried to grab my hand but I snatched away.

"Look Tyler, you don't know shit about my husband. You know me and you should know I don't just choose anybody to be with. Now before you get another ass whoopin' by my thug of a husband. Please stay the fuck away from me and never try to tell me what I need." I got up and walked away from his ass.

*

I stepped off the elevator of the parking garage. I was tired as hell and my feet were hurting me. I was off tomorrow and excited as hell because I planned to spend the day with my two guys. It was dark out and the only light was the light bulbs in the parking garage. I took my keys out my purse ready to hit the unlock button. I saw the security booth empty so I really started speed walking to my Lexus.

Hitting the alarm when I got closer I place my phone in the pocket of my scrubs. Right when I was about to open my door I was pushed to the ground. My purse fell to the ground spilling out all my shit. When I looked up I saw Chrissy's mom with two other ladies standing over me. They didn't talk they just started kicking me all over. I felt like a bag of rocks was hitting my body over and over. I was about to scream but Chrissy's mama kneeled down, grabbed me by my hair and punched me in the nose.

I felt my nose gush blood. She turned me over to my stomach. One woman grabbed my legs and held the down and the other woman grabbed my arms and held them down. She pulled my pants and panties down to my ankles. I tried to wiggle out there hold but the grips got tighter. I was so scared and opened my mouth to scream but I choked on my blood.

Chrissy's mom sstood on the side of me with a thick black belt.

She started coming down hard on my ass with the belt. I screamed over the blood in my mouth. I was wiggling and trying to break free. She kept hitting over and over again until I could not scream any more. My ass and back of my thighs burned so bad. Once she felt she had enough she kneeled down in my face and said.

"That was for Chrissy." Then she hawked and spit in my face. Her and her friends took off down the garage. I tried to move but my head was pounding and my legs felt numb. Finally I felt my eyes get weak when I saw a security guard step off the elevator and run over to me. He was saying something but I couldn't hear anything. Then my eyes closed and I heard and saw nothing.

Kevin

"Y'all nigga's crazy as hell! How the fuck you think Cam Newton a better quaterback then Drew Brees?!" I was at the barber shop cutting my last customer head.

All my employees worked today. With it being the holiday season, everybody and they mama was having Christmas parties. It was almost time for us to close and tonight was me and my brother turn to close. Since that shit with him and Taylor I made sure to never let them close together.

"Nigga shut yo's die hard as fan up! You will die being a Saints fan! Never mind them nigga's ain't gave us a Super Bowl in years." Dru teased making everybody laugh. I gave him the middle finger.

My cell phone rung and I saw it was my father in-law calling. When I answered he was asking me if he could get Keion ready for bed. He said Kimmora had not picked him up yet. I asked had he called her and he said yea but she didn't answer. I told him to go ahead and I would pick Keion up when I close up shop.

I hung up and dialed my wife cell phone. I t was not like her to not tell me or her dad she was getting off late. She worked at a hospital so I gave her the benefit of a doubt. I called it went straight to voicemail. I put my phone and finished up my customer. Half an hour later it was just me and Kalvin.

"This ain't like Kimmora to not answer her phone," I said out loud but more to myself.

"The hospital probably had an emergancy bro. Just text her what you gotta say." While he talked my cell phone ringed.

"Here she is right here." I said to Kalvin as I answered the phone. I was expecting to hear my wife voice. Instead I heard a white female and the shit she was saying to me had my stomach doing flips.

"What the fuck happened to her? WHAT! Ok I'm on my way!" I hung up and gathered my shit.

"Bro you good?" Kalvin asked as he walked out the break room.

"Naw, Kimmora is in the hospital! She was attacked!" Kalvin didn't hesitate to grab his shit to so we could leave. He locked the shop up while I fled to my BMW.

"Kevin let me drive bro. I got it and I will get us there fast I promise." I tossed Kalvin my keys and we took off into traffic.

"Bro somebody is about to die I swear to God! My wife doesn't bother no fuckin' body so why would somebody fuck with her?" I was so fucking mad all I could do was stare out the window. Kalvin had us at the hospital in no time. He had called my brothers and told them what was going on. I could hear all of them flip out like I did.

Me and Kalvin hopped out the car once he parked. I went through the emergancy doors and went to the nurses station. I gave her Kimmora's name and asked her how severe her injuries were. She informed with a nasty ass attitude that she didn't know anything. Before I slapped her ass to kingdom come. I went to room 60 where she said my wife was.

When I walked in the room Kimmora was laying down watching the TV. She had a black eye, her lip was busted and her nose was bandaged up. When she saw me she broke down crying and I hurried to her and embraced her. I was hugging her so tight as if she was leaving me. This was my boo and I let her down protecting her. Rage and destruction filled my body and I was ready to kill.

"Kim boo I am so sorry I was not there to protect you. I swear I will find out who----"

"I already know who. It was Chrissy's mama and her two girlfriends." Before I could react the door opened and the police walked in.

"Excuse me, Mrs. Royal we need to speak to you regarding your attack. Um can you give us some privacy?" One on the white cops looked at me and asked.

"Hell no! This is my fuckin' wife I'm not going anywhere." I sat down on Kimmora's bed.

"Sir, for her to feel comfortable talking to us we would prefer if she was alone."

"What the fuck you mean for her to feel comfortable? She can speak with me right here. I would never hurt my fuckin' wife so whatever she says I need to hear the shit to." I was looking at the fucking pigs like the trash they all were.

I didn't want Kimmora to tell them who did this to here. I wanted to handle Chrissy's mama myself but in my way and on the right time. Right now, Chrissy's mama knows I will be looking for her. She left Kimmora alive and able to speak on purpose. She wanted me to slip. But I didn't have to tell my wife shit. She knew me well enough to tell them pigs she does not know who attacked her.

She told them her attackers covered there faces and they tried to rape her but heard someone coming. If I didn't know any better I would have believed her story. Once the cops left I went back to kissing and hugging on her. The door opened again and it was my brothers and her sisters. Her dad came in with Keion and six of her uncles. I have never seen my father in-law look the way he looked when he saw his daughter in the hospital. He hugged and kissed her and so did everybody else.

"Kim tell me all what happened boo and don't leave shit out." I asked her while sitting next to her. She held Keion in her arms and got to telling all of us what happened.

All you heard was the TV and Kimmora talking. All the babies were sleeping. While Kimmora told us the story her sisters started crying but I had killing on my brain. The fact that they held my wife down and did that to her gave me anger I had no idea I could have. Her father stood up and looked at me.

"Se non li ottieni vorresti (If you don't get them I will). Kevin I have never doubted you and your brothers when it comes to protecting my girls. But if you do not get these muthafuckas then I will. I don't play fair when it comes to my family. You guys have rules and I respect that but I have no fucking rules. Women, kids, old people, who the fuck ever it is will die. You hurt mines and I'm hurtin' yours. That's my code. I know you gotta move smart that's one of the things I respect about your family. But I need this fixed!" He stood up pointed to me and my brothers.

"All of you have become my sons, even those of you who fuck up." He looked dead at Kaylin and Kalvin.

"But your young and I know real love when I see it because I have been in it. I have had it and I know you all love my girls. Just protect them for me just as much as you love them. Leave all these bitches where they belong. I am trusting you all with my most precious treasure. Please don't disappoint me. I don't think right when I'm dissapointed." He looked at me and my brothers.

Then he hugged his girls and left out. I couldn't say shit but respect what he was saying. Even Karlos had a smirk on his face because he knew what we had to do. After everyone visited with Kimmora for a while they all went home. Keion went back with Kimmora's dad and I stayed with my wife. As we laid in her hospital bed and she slept sound on my chest. I closed my eyes and pictured me killing Chrissy's mom. I already knew the two bitches she was with to. I was going to handle them as well. They fucked up laying a finger on my wife. I kissed Kimmora's face a few times then I went to sleep.

Tony

"Ughhhhh Tiny Wony yesssss! Fuck me like that bae." I was drilling the fuck out of Kylee from the back. Her chocolate ass was moving like waves in a sea.

"Say you love it Kylee. Say you love this dick girl." My sweat was dripping all on her back.

"I love this dick bae. Ssssss damn." Once she said that I spilled my kids all into the condom.

Pulling my dick out I was breathing hard as fuck while I went to the bathroom and flushed it. That right there snapped me out of my fantasy. When I do get the real Kylee back I am never using condoms. I was going to bust in her pussy every chance I got. I wanted to start a family with her. The only thing that was going to be hard was making her forget about her husband. Once I kill him and have his brothers locked up I will comfort her until she sees she still loves me.

"Do you want something to eat?" Kylee came in the bathroom and asked me. I hated looking at her because she looked so much like Kylee.

She reminded me of what I didn't have. But then I also couldn't be mean to her becasue she looked so much like Kylee. She softened me up the way Kylee use to. I ended up paying $15,000 a month to have her with me 24-7. I had this bitch doing all the shit Kylee use to do. I even had her taking Italian speaking classes on the weekends.

I took her shopping for clothes like Kylee and I had her hair twisted like Kylee's. It wasn't as long but the Africans added weave. I even told her to sleep in the same type of shit Kylee would sleep in. Boy shorts and tank top or just a thong. I brought her a Kindle and told her to start reading books like Kylee does. This bitch never complained about shit becasue I treated her right. I spoiled her as if she was Kylee and I fucked her good.

"Yea that sounds good. What are you about to cook." I cleaned off my dick and put my boxers on. I turned to look at her and I was stuck. Her eyes were big and brown and she kept eye contact just like I taught her. Kylee always looked me in my eyes when she talked to me.

"Well what about some fish tacos and peanut butter cookies for dessert." I smiled at her and kissed her on the lips. I told her it sound good and watched her walk downstairs to the kitchen.

Once she was gone I set on the side of my bed and picked up my cell phone. I went to my fake Instagram account and went to Kylee's page. She uploaded some pictures of her baby girl. Her daughter was so pretty. I could not deny that but she had her nutty ass daddy grey eyes. Kylee also uploaded some pictures of her in the gym. Looks like that nigga of hers opened a new gym. Kylee's body was so fucking sexy to me. I use to lick her body from head to toe even her ass. That baby didn't do anything but bring her hips out more.

She always had body but damn she was looking like she needed to be in a Gucci Mane video. Kylee had one thirty second video where she was doing some squats. My dick woke right back up and before I knew it I watched the video sixteen times. Not being able to take it anymore I went downstairs to fuck the shit out of Kylee on my kitchen counter.

But not before I take out my burner phone and try to call her. Lately she was hip to my tricks. She blocked every number I called from . I had brought thirteen burner phones and she blocked all of them. This was a new one I brought so I was going to try my luck. I dialed her number and smiled a little. I just wanted hear her voice.

"Hello. Helloooo." Her soft voice said on the other end of the phone.

"Kylee please don't hang up. I just wanna-----"
Click!

Before I could even say anything she hung up on me. I went to call back and she blocked me again. I was so fucking heated I wanted to break some shit. All I wanted her to do was have one conversation with me. One lunch, breakfast or dinner date so we could talk. She would not even hear me out. Kylee acted as if she never knew me like we never had anything. I was sick of this shit. The longer I set there the more sinister my thought began.

My fucking sister had been acting stuck on some other shit over Kalvin's ass. She thought I didn't know but I went through her phone a few weeks back. This nigga was married and was flirting with my baby sister. Then when they went out he got caught up. Keira and Taylor fought and now Kalvin wasn't fucking with Taylor. Any other bitch I would have killed for touching Taylor. But because it was Kylee's sister I let the shit pass. Besides, Taylor shouldn't have been fucking with a Royal anyways. All of them were poison.

Now that his ass got my sister beat up he was going to die just like his older brother. I would never hurt Kylee but I was getting sick of this shit. I needed her and the fake her was not cutting it anymore. The next time I step to Kylee I was going to make sure she heard me out. I was no longer giving he a choice. I put the burner back in the drawer and went downstairs with Kylee to fuck her and eat some food.

Keira

Two weeks later

"Seems like forever since we been here." I looked at Kelly and said. I had my arm through hers as we walked in the cabin.

After the crazy shit that went down with Kimmora. Kevin decided we all could use a vacation. We all had a ball in the past when we came to Colorado and rented a cabin. All of us came but Kylee and Karlos. That was when they were broken up and keeping far away from each other. Now we were back in Colorado with the snow and cozy little town.

The cabin we rented was bigger then the one we had last time. Kevin wanted it be extra special for Kimmora so it was a cabin suite. It was a seven bedroom, eight bathrooms, fully furnished, full kitchen cabin. It was beautiful with stone detail in the inside and outside. The rooms were huge with California king size beds. The kitchen was wood and chrome with all appliances. There was a beautiful stone fireplace int he living room and all the bedrooms.

"Thank you boo for this. I needed to get away and this was perfect timing. We will still be home for Christmas." Kimmora walked in with Kevin behind her with their bags. She was fully healed which made us all happy. Kevin made sure to pick her up everyday from work. If not him then one of us or our father.

"Anything for you boo." He kissed her as they walked upstairs to the bedrooms. All but two bedrooms were up stairs and two bathrooms.

"This is going to be a nice a four days." I bent down to pick my bag up but Kalvin stopped me and grabbed it first.

"I got it Keira just point me to your room." He followed him into the room I chose with the white fur rug on the floor. He set my bags down by the end of the bed. I was loving the design of the room. The dresser and bed frame were a matching chocolate brown.

"Keira how have you been? You passed the state bar for the braid shop. I'm so proud of you bae like for real." I looked at him standing by the door. Kalvin was so fine and I missed the hell out of him. But he went on a date with another woman and I could not forgive that. It has been three months since we have lived in the same house together. I missed my husband like crazy. I cried myself to sleep every night since I put him out. I wanted my bae love back but I felt embarrassed.

"Thank you Kalvin I appreciate that. So how have you been?" I asked him while I pulled my clothes out my suitecase.

"I been miserable. Keira, I miss you bae. This shit is killing me not being with my wife. I feel suffocated with you away from me. I swear I don't even talk to Taylor----

"Kalvin, stop. I came here to relax and help my sister relax after her attack. This is not about me and you." I stood in front of the dresser and looked at him. He looked miserable but like I said, it wasn't about us.

"I apologize I do want you to enjoy this vacation and be there for Kimmora." He turned around and left while closing the door.

I couldn't help but cry because I knew my pride was in the way. After I put my clothes up I walked out the room. Heading too the living room I noticed Kalvin took the room right next to mines. I smiled big as I headed to the kitchen to get a snack. Kevin had us write a grocery list out of our favorites. He had the kitchen fully stocked with all our food we liked. I grabbed a red Powerade and opened the cabinet to grab some Oreos. My short ass couldn't reach it.

"I got you bae." Kalvin walked over to me and reached his tall ass arm up and grabbed them for me. He gave them to me while still standing behind me. This was the closest I have been to him in so long.

"Thank you." Kalvin smiled and bit his lip making me blush and smile big.

"I don't know why y'all playin'." Karlos deep ass voice made me jump out of Kalvin space. Him and Kylee walked in all hugged up. I smacked my lips and waved my hand at him. Kylee was smiling big at me.

"So, we are about to go down to Over Easy and eat dinner. Y'all coming?" I looked at Kalvin and he was looking at me still biting his lip. I blushed and looked away.

"Why don't y'all just stay here and fuck," Karlos nasty ass said making Kylee hit him in the arm. I laughed and walked out the kitchen. Thinking about fucking Kalvin was making me horny and I knew I didn't need that.

*

We all arrived at Over Easy restaurant and got out limo. Anytime we went out of town we had drivers. Over Easy was a nice laid back restaurant with a bar inside. I kept my attire casual in some True Religion skiny jeans, a cream off the shoulder sweater and my brown Stuart Weitzman boots. I couldn't help but notice how fine Kalvin looked in his Calvin Klein jeans and button-up. He had them black Yezzy's on lookin' like a whole dinner.

Walking in the waiter seated us and we all picked up menus. Everybody must have had a taste for the same thing because we all ordered shrimp, steak and pasta. We talked and had fun as usual when we were together. It felt good to hang out all even though Kaylin was not here. Only I knew why he couldn't make this trip. He swore me to secrecy and I wanted to keep good on that promise.

When our food arrived we all ate and enjoyed Over Easy good ass cooking. After we were done eating and on to dessert I decided I wanted to go to the bar and order a drink.

I excused myself and walked over to the bar. I picked up the menu and looked it over. I decided to order a cranberry martini.

"What can I get you tonight beautiful?" The bartender came and asked me. He was very handsome. He seemed a little older then me and he had a bald head with a goatee. I smiled back at him and told him my order.

"Can I have a cranberry martini please. And thank you for the compliment." I gave him the menu.

"Just stating facts. How long are you in Colorado for?" he asked me while he made my drink.

"Four days. I love it out here in the winter. It's beautiful and the town is so different from the loud city life." I smiled and adjusted myself on the bar stool.

"Well you need to come back in the summer. We have a cherry pie festival and it's fun as hell. There's a parade and you even get to see yours truly dress up as a clown and entertain the kids." I looked at him and could not imagine him in a clown get up. He was a little on the chubby side but his face was handsome. I couldn't help but laugh. Oh Lord I hope he doesn't think I'm being rude.

"I'm sorry I don't mean to laugh. I just cannot imagine you dressed as a clown." He started laughing as well.

"Shit I go all out with it. I make animals out of ballons, I ju ju on that beat and have a funny voice." I started cracking up when he did his funny clown voice. He was laughing as well.

"What's funny? I wanna laugh." Kalvin walked up next to me at the bar. I stopped laughing and looked at him. I did not need him beating up this bartender when he wasn't doing anything.

"Aye my man, you a bartender or a fuckin' comedian?" Kalvin looked at the poor guy and asked. I placed my hand on his arm.

"Kalvin," I whispered his name but loud enough so he could hear it. Kalvin didn't even acknowledge me talking to him. He looked at the bartender like he was prey. His eyes had a look in them that I never seen. My sweet bae love was not present. The bartender looked at him then at me.

"Don't look at my wife nigga. I asked you a fuckin' question." Kalvin's mouth was tight as he talked. My heart was beating fast.

"I'm a bartender sir." The poor guy answered.

"Ok well stick to your fuckin' job and get to back to mixin' drinks. Don't even look at her, keep yo' head down until we leave out the restaurant. If I see yo' head up I'm choppin' that bitch off." I sucked in all the air around me. I could not believe Kalvin just said that to another grown man. I looked at the poor bartender and he had his head down.

Getting mad I walked off and went to the bathroom. I have never seen my bae love act that way. He was always the voice of reason and so sweet. I looked at myself in the mirror and shook my head. I didn't even have to use the bathroom I just needed to get away from him. I washed my hands and dried them. Just as I was about to open the door Kalvin came barging in. He pushed me against the wall and looked at me with his hand on the side of my face.

"Don't do that shit no more." My breath was caught in my chest. He bit his sexy lip and looked at my lips. I couldn't take it any more.

I kissed him and he let me. Our tongues were fucking each other. I had not kissed my husband in months. This was truly missed and I needed more. I guess he knew it because I heard him undo his belt. I undid my pants and pushed them down. Before I could look up he lifted me up by my legs. His dick slid in me and we both paused. I felt like I about to cum already and I knew he felt it. He looked at me with his bottom lip in his mouth. I smirked at his sexy ass face. Then he started moving and fucking me like nobody's business.

"Forgive me Keira. Please forgive me bae love. I fuckin' miss you and I need you. I swear I apologize for that stupid shit. Ughh. Fuck girl. Please love me again Keira. I won't make it if you don't bae." Kalvin's dick felt so good I could not even speak. I just bit down on his shoulder blade as I came long and hard.

"Oh my God Kalvin. I miss you so much bae." I let my words slide on out because it's how I felt. I missed my husband, I just don't know if I can forgive him. Once we were done he cleaned me up and he did himself. I fixed my clothes and helped him fix his. When I was about to open the door he stopped me.

"When you saw me out with her I was dead as wrong. But it took me to sit across another woman to realize I don't want anybody but you. That was lust and I have seen plenty more of it since you put me out. I just don't have the need to go after that bullshit. I don't know what the fuck I was thinking but I promise you this. I have not talked to her since, no text, calls, social media or nothing. I only want you Keira forever and ever bae love." He kissed me and opened the door for me to walk out. We got back to our table and everyone was packed up ready to go.

"Zip yo' pants up bro," Brandon said making everyone laugh. We got up to leave Kelly packed me a dessert to go. When we got to the door I looked at the bartender and his head was still down while he cleaned up. Kalvin gave me a look telling me to put my damn head down as well. I laughed to myself.

*

We were on our last night in Colorado and we have been having a ball. We had a bonfire with roasted marshmallows and hot chocolate. All the guys cooked for us for a change and they actually did good. Although Karlos did all the work on the grill but the guys did good with the sides. I have been sleeping in the same bed with Kalvin since we left dinner. I missed him and we had a long talk. I know I wanted my marriage and with God leading us I know we can get through this.

Now all of us were in the living room about to play a game. We loved doing this like some big ass kids. Tiff went on YouTube and found this game called the 1,2,3, Challenge. We all had a piece paper with each others name written on it. Tiff was going to ask a question. We count 1,2,3 and whoever we thought matched the question we had to hold their name up. The person who's name was up the most each round had to take a shot. It was cold out so we had the fireplace lit and we all had on pajamas.

"Ok, y'all ready?" Tiff asked and we all said yea.

"Ok, who is most likely to cry on a movie?" We all held up Kylee's name and started laughing.

"Shit that was easy. Kylee's ass cries at commercials," Brandon silly ass said. Kylee got up and grabbed her a shot of Ciroc. She was laughing and shaking her head. Tiff went to the next question.

"Next, who is most likely to say the first thing on their mind?" We all put up Brandon's name. He had up Tiff's name.

"Hell naw, my wife is worse then me!" he laughed and took a shot.

"That's why y'all perfect for each other," Kevin yelled laughing making all of us laugh.

"Who is most likely to dance no matter where we are?" Everybody put Kylee's name up again.

"I feel like y'all fuckin' with me and Brandon," she laughed and grabbed her a shot. I was cracking up because my big sis will twerk in church if they playing a good song.

"I got one!" Kelly said. Who is most likely to talk shit first?" It was a tie between me and Kalvin. Tiff did not hold up a name.

"Sorry bro," she said as she held up Kalvin's name.

"Fuck y'all," Kalvin laughed and took a shot. He came back over to me and put his arms around my waist. I was sitting bewteen his legs.

"Let me go. Who is most likely to talk about the damn Saints?" Kylee asked and we held up Kevin's name fast as hell.

"That nigga is a fuckin' fan bitch over them," Karlos said making us all laugh. Kevin gave us the finger and took his shot.

"My turn. Who is most likely to pop off first?"

"KARLOS!" We all shouted out at Kalvin's question. All of us fell out laughing and he got up and took his shot.

"That nigga will kill the doctor that spanked Kylee's ass when she was born!" Brandon shouted making us including Kylee laugh. Karlos couldn't help but laugh to.

"Y'all better leave my baby alone. He gettin' better with his attitude," Kylee said while rubbing the back of Karlos head. He was looking at her with so much love then he kissed her.

"SHITTTT!" we all said in unison.

"Kylee you know you pretty right," Kalvin joked. We knew what he was doing and the shit was funny.

"WHAT NIGGA!" Karlos looked pissed at Kalvin statement and we all fell out laughing. Kylee laughed to as she turned around and kissed Karlos again. We finished that game and played Monopoly, some trivia games and of course UNO.

It was now 2 in the morning and me and Kalvin were laying on the white furry rug in my room. We had the fireplace lit and I had Chrisette Michele-Better album playing on my iPhone 8. We were naked with a sheet wrapped around us. I was loving every minute of it as he kissed all over me.

"Keira, I promise to never fuck up like that again. I don't ever want you to think someone else can get what I give to you. I was on some other shit but I promise I will continue to let God lead me and never stray again. I love you so much bae love." I smiled at him and kissed him deep.

"I love you too Kalvin and I accept your apology." We kissed again. For the rest of the night we listened to music and talked about everything. I love my bae love.

<u>Kylee</u>

"Oh my God Karlos," I moaned with my hands gripping the sheets and my back arched. He was sucking the soul out of me and I was lovin' it. I started grinding my hips in his face. I was about to cum for the third time with him between my legs.

"Shitttt baby! Ugh! I fuckin' love youuuu." I came hard as fuck my heart felt like it was about to beat out my chest.

My back had a permanent dip in it thanks to Karlos. We had been going at it like rabbits lately. He was either fuckin' me crazy or lickin' me like a starved man. After I came he started kissing my thighs making me jerk with each kiss. He kissed his way up to my face. Karlos was so fine and I could never get tired of looking at him. I bit my lip, grabbed the back of his neck and kissed him. I was naked and so was he. I loved making out with him while he was on top of me. His warm skin felt so good on top of mines. Karlos hard chest pressed aginst my titties just made me feel so good. When I felt him get hard and start licking my neck I knew what that meant.

"Oh my gosh Karlos, you are wearing me out." I smiled and whined to him. He started kissing me again.

"I know baby, I'm sorry. You just turn me on so bad I don't know what my problem is. I'm so fuckin' addicted to you." He had his weight on his hands as he hovered on top of me. I looked in his gorgeous light grey eyes and got lost.

"Karols I love you so much baby. I'm addicted to you to just as much as your addicted to me. But baby my pussy muscles are sore as hell." We both laughed and he laid on the side of me.

I looked over at the baby camera sitting on my dresser. Kaylee still was sleep even with the morning light in her room. We had been back from Colorado for three days now. Yesterday I decorated our house gold and red Christmas decorations. Me and Karlos put our tree up and we had so many gifts under it already.

"Baby rub on my shoulder blade. This tattoo is in it's itching faze and it's driving me crazy." I told Karlos. He started rubbing it making me close my eyes because it felt so good.

At Kaylin tattoo party I got my baby girl's name inside of a heart on my back shoulder blade. That way if I have more kids all I have to do is get another heart. Me and Karlos got matching tattoos on our inner wrist. We got crowns and under mines said Queen and under his said King. We both had it bad. I had his name across my left ass cheek. Which he made sure to be there and that it was done by a girl. I had his name on my thigh with a lock and key coming out of it. And on our outter wrist we both had the life line tattoo. His said Kylee and mines said Karlos. It was not healty to love the way we did but oh well.

"You and Kaylee still going to the mall today?" I looked up at him and asked while I was laying on his chest.

"Yea, me and my princess hangin' today. You gone be good without us?" he asked running his fingers through my curly hair. I nodded my head and he just looked at me and bit his lip. I looked down and saw the tent in the sheet that was over us. I looked back up at Karlos and climbed on top of him. Kissing him nasty like always I grabbed his dick and slid down slowly on it. No matter what I always was hungry for this man. Just as I was about to start moving Kaylee began to move and squirm in her sleep. I looked down at Karlos and we both just laughed. I slid off his dick and got ready to get my baby.

"I got her baby," Karlos said as his sexy naked body climbed out of our bed.

He went to the bathroom and washed his hands. Picking up his sweatpants he put them on and walked to Kaylee's room. I picked up the camera monitor, watched and listened to him go in her room.

"Hey my princess Kaylee. You ready to get your day started?" He picked her up out of her crib. Kaylee was chunky all ready at only four months. Her hair seemed to grow every day and those eyes. Oh my goodness those eyes were so big and light grey and made you want to give her the world when she looked at you.

"Come on princess let's change yo' diaper and get some grub in yo' belly." He laid her on her changing table and changed her.

"Daddy gettin' better at this Kaylee? We not gone tell mommy about yesterday when I put yo' diaper on backwards." I laughed when he said that.

"Princess you know don't nobody suppose to see you naked but mommy, daddy and the doctor. When you get older not even daddy suppose to see you naked. Only mommy and the doctor. If any nigga's try to see your body you let daddy know. Cause I got a nice grave waitin' for them. Daddy gone cut they dick off and shove it in they mouth then cut they hands off." He picked her up and laid her on his chest. I swear you could see Kaylee's big eyes light up when she looks at her crazy ass daddy.

"You wanna know why daddy would do that for you? Because you daddy's princess and boys are some nasty, slimy ass creatures. And they are no good for my princess Kaylee. You and mommy gone make daddy get grey hair early as fuck. But I love y'all more than I love breathing and will die protecting y'all." Karlos held her up and kissed her chubby cheeks.

"Come on let's go get some breakfast. Daddy gone burp you and put you in yo' swing. I need you to be a good girl so daddy can climb back in yo' mommy sweet goodness. Ok princess?" He kissed her on top of her head and left out her room. I sat in the bed cracking up at my crazy ass husband. I got up to take care of my hygiene and put a robe on to go join my family for breakfast.

*

Kaylee and Karlos left to got to the mall. They looked so cute in their matching Gucci outfits. I loved the days when it was just the two of them. It gave them a chance to bond and it gave me a chance to have the house to myself. I was cleaning up our master bathroom. I showered put on my black and grey PINK joggers and matching shirt. I put my hair in a high bun and went downstairs to pig out on the couch.

Eating some Pringles and honey bun my cell phone rung. I looked at it and saw it was a number I didn't know. I rolled my eyes because I knew it was Tony. I was so sick of him calling but I knew I couldn't tell Karlos so I just kept blocking him. I hit ignore and went back to watching TV. My hone rung again and again making me finaly answer it.

"Tony stop fucking calling me!" I yelled into the phone and I hung up.

I was getting ready to block him but a text message came through. I backed out of my block list and went to open the text. It was loading and and when it was done a picture of Kimmora with Keion at Barnes and Nobles came to my phone. I was so confused so I looked at the number it came from. It was the same number that called me. Another text came through.

Unknown: If you don't want nothing to happen to them then you better call me. You have five minutes.

My heart was beating so fast I felt it through my shirt. I didn't know what to do as I looked around. I hit my call log and was about to dial Kevin but another text came through. This time it was a picture of Kimmora getting in her car with a red dot on her head. She didn't even know she was in danger. My eyes filled with tears and my hands started shaking. Another text came through.

Unknown: Two minutes.

I groaned as I dialed the number back. It rung two times and then someone picked up. I didn't even give them a chance to talk.

"Please don't hurt my sister or my nephew. I don't know what you want----"

"You Kylee, I want you." My posture changed when I heard Tony's voice. I turned my nose up with tears falling in my mouth.

"Tony? What the fuck are you doing? You no killer so why the fuck are you doing this."

"You made me do this. All I wanted you to do was talk to me but you kept curving me. Now I have become desperate. Get up and meet me at my house. I know you remember where it's at. Kylee do not play with me. If I don't see you in thirty minutes I am killing your sister and her baby." He hung up before I could say anything. I jumped up and put my shoes on, grabbed my keys and was out the door.

As I drove I texted Karlos and told him I was going to get my nails done. I put my phone between my legs and drove through the traffic. I was wiping tears from my eyes as I drove my Escalade. I could not believe Tony would do something like this. This man was not even built this way. Street life was not him at all. He knows how important my sisters are to me. Why would he do this? I never led him on or anything.

I never gave him false hope or played games with him. Now this man who I once loved was putting people I love in danger. I turned down his street and looked for his blue and white house. When I saw his car was in the driveway I pulled behind him. Getting out my heart was beating so fast. If he was home that meant he had someone else watching my sister and nephew. I was so scared but I cleaned my face and got out my truck. Walking to his door way I didn't have to knock. He opened the door for me.

"Glad to see you come Kylee. Please come in." He opened the door wide and I walked in. He was shirtless with some Levis jeans on and no shoes on. I had only one thing on my mind.

"Tony where is my sister and nephew? Are they safe?" He stood in the middle of his living room just looking at me. I began to get frustrated and scared.

"Answer me!" I yelled at him. He chuckled at said.

"Why the fuck do I have to do all of this? Why are you treating me like we were never in love? Like I never used to be inside that pussy driving you wild." He walked up to me until he was in my face. I could not do anything but let tears fall.

"Tony. Please tell me my family is ok. Please."

"Shhhhh. Kylee they are fine. I was never going to harm them. I------"

Slap!

I slapped him across his face so hard my palm was stinging.

"Why the fuck would you do this? Tony, I know what we had but we have been broken up for a while now. I'm married and have a child with someone else. I don't love you anymore Tony. I am madly in love with someone else. Please stop this and just live your life. You were doing just fine and now all of a sudden your doing things that are not in you character." I wiped my face while he laughed and shook his head.

"Kylee you don't even know who your married to. That man is a fucking sick ass monster who kills for fun. He is a threat and YOU married him AND had a child with him. I thought you were going through a stupid phase. Y'all had broken up and you were ready to move on with me again. I saw it in your eyes my sweet Kylee." He walked closer to me and I backed up shaking my head no.

"Tony I was never coming back to you. I met up with you because I was heartbroken. I wanted to see if I could be in another man's company again. I apologize if you thought more. Please please just stop this. You're successful, handsome and have no kids I'm sure you can find you someone else." I looked at him with pleading eyes. I really just wanted this to stop.

"I don't want someone else. I WANT YOU! Kylee I only want you!" I jumped when he raised his voice.

"Tony look at me. Why would you want someone who is scared of you. I do not love you anymore. Please try to understand what I'm saying to you. My heart belongs with someone else. Even if he dropped dead tomorrow I will die with him. Our love is that fucking deep Tony. I have his name tattooed all over me. I will never belong to another man as long as I'm breathing." Tony looked at me and a tear fell from his eye. I had no emotion to him crying. I only spoke the truth and now I was ready to leave.

"Get the fuck out of here Kylee. I will never bother you again." He only had to tell me once before I was hauling ass out of there. I jumped in my truck and flew out of there like a bat out of hell. I could not believe this happened and with someone I thought I knew. As long as my sister was ok. And he said he would stop then I was good. I can go home and put this mess behind me.

*

I arrived home and saw Karlos and Kaylee were home. The whole ride home I had this Tony shit on my mind. I had to pull my shit together before I walked in my house. Karlos and I were so connected we can tell when shit is off with each other. I checked my face and made sure my eyes were not puff or damp. Once I gave myself the ok I turned my truck off and got out. If I'm lucky he might be sleep.

When I walked in the house I heard the TV on in his man cave. I was happy because that way I get to go straight up-stairs and call Kimmora. I just wanted to make sure she was ok even though he said she was. Walking up the stairs I looked in Kaylee's room and saw she was sleeping. He had her baby camera in his man cave with him. I pulled my phone out and Facetime Kimmora. We talked for a few minutes. She was at home with Kevin and Keion. Once I was ok I let her go and told her to put me up a plate of food she cooked. I put my phone on the night stand and closed my eyes taking a deep breath.

"Kylee. Why you come in the house and go straight upstairs?" Karlos scared me with his deep voice.

"Oh, I was on the phone with Kimmora silly ass." I smiled hoping he would not question any further. He arched his eye brow but went to the bathroom. I breathed out a sigh of relief. Karlos came out the bathroom with his shirt off. He walked over to the dresser and took his jewelry off. I was sitting on his side of the bed by the door. I took my shoes off and put them in my closet.

"I thought you were going to get your nails done?" Fuck me Kylee. I forgot about my nails. I had to think quick on my feet.

"Oh um the shop was closed - I mean crowded so I left." I walked passed him and went to the bathroom. Karlos was hot on my tail.

"What the fuck is going on wit'chu Kylee. You come home and don't say shit to me or Kaylee. You ain't even kissed on me or nothing." He stepped closer to me.

"Today is Monday and I know for a fact your shop was closed. So, do you wanna tell me where the hell you were? And why you had to lie to me about it." He looked my in my eyes and the fear I had in me was indescribable. He didn't even blink he just kept his stare. I felt my palms sweat.

"I-I went to another nail shop Karlos." He closed his eyes and I swear I felt him stop breathing. When he opened them they were black and he had veins in them.

"Kylee please do not lie to me again. Talk to me baby and tell me where you were." There was no way I could lie again. Not when he already knew I was lying. I was stuck and as much as I did not want any blood shed I had not other choice but to talk.

Karlos

Kylee had me completely fucked up if she thought I would not catch her in a lie. Even if she was the best liar ever. I still knew her ass better then any fuckin' body. I knew some shit was off when she didn't say shit to me. I don't give a fuck who she is talking to or around. If she enters a room where I am she always comes to me.

Then I looked on Kaylee's camera monitor I had in my man cave. Kylee peeked her head in the room but didn't go in. She didn't pick her up or kiss on her. That alone gave some shit away about her hiding something. Then that nail shop lie was another thing. Kylee would wait hours in the nail shop if she had to. My wife was girly and didn't play about her nails.

But I knew Kylee was so scared that she wasn't thinking straight. When I closed my eyes I felt them muthafuckas turn black. Opening them I was looking for my target but I saw it was my wife. This was my baby, my heart beat, the reason I breath every day right so I knew I couldn't hurt her. But I swear if this girl tell me she is fucking someone else I don't even know what the fuck I was gonna do. I looked at her as she began to talk. I was ready to pop off if she say some shit I couldn't handle.

"Karlos something happened today but I handled it." She began talking. She told me about her being at home and her ex Tony calling her. She said he had been calling her from different numbers but she had blocked them all. Then she told me about the threat he made to Kimmora and her son. She got scared and went over his house to see him. I cannot tell y'all how fire hot I was. Kylee has taken me to another level of anger and rage that I didn't know existed.

"So let me get this shit straight. Yo' ex has been calling you for months even after you told him not to call you. You block all his numbers and he still calls you, threatens our sister and nephew. And you fly over to his house so you can reason with this nigga." She didn't say anything she just dropped her head.

"Why the FUCK didn't you just call me?! Or better yet why the FUCK didn't you let me know weeks ago when the nigga first called?! Why the FUCK are you protecting this nigga?!" I don't even give a fuck that my yelling was making Kylee jump and cry. Her actions were stupid as hell.

"Because Karlos I didn't want any blood shed. If I had told you he was calling me I know you would have-----"

"You damn right I would have killed his ass! I would have killed him with a smile and with my dick hard. Then I would have came home with the same smile and had you suck my dick like the Queen you are! Now what Kylee?" I looked at her with my nose turned up. She had me fucked up!

"I'm sorry baby. I panicked when he sent me that picture and I didn't know what to do. I just wanted him to stop without involving you." She wiped her face and looked at me with sad eyes. I still was pissed off.

"Why the fuck is he doing this shit now? I been in your life for almost three years and his ass was nowhere to be found. When was the last time you saw him?" When she didn't answer and she dropped her head I knew the answer.

"You saw this nigga while we were broken up?! Huh?!" She nodded her head up and down. I almost knocked her ass out but I quickly checked myself. I would never hurt my baby.

"So you jump back on his nasty ass team but you shut my ass out for months." Kylee popped her head up and looked at me like she wanted to kill me.

"Don't you dare go there with me! Had you not FUCKED somebody else I would have never went out with him. And we didn't do shit but go to Starbucks. I didn't run back to him or tell him anything to make him think we were getting back together!" I looked at her with squinted eyes.

"Did you kiss him on y'all date?" Her silence was enough for me. I turned around and punched the bathroom wall. My huge fist put a hole in it and made Kylee scream. I was hotter then a match and gasoline.

"Karlos we were broken up and I just wanted to see if I could be in the company of another man. I was trying to move on from you. I never wanted Tony I swear and I never told him I did." She sobbed and told me.

"What the fuck do you mean company of another man? YOU ARE MINES! You have been mines since I first saw you and you always will be. No other woman will ever have me the way you do Kylee. I cut a bitch baby out of her and killed her whole family over you and I would do it again. So don't ever fix your sexy ass lips to say company of another man. That dread head nigga you called yourself talking to while we were broken up. Where the fuck do you think he is at now Kylee. I don't fuckin'play when it comes to you and yo' ass knows that. You think this is a fuckin' game?" I waited for her to answer but she had my dick between my legs when she said.

"Oh so you was squeaky clean the entire time we were broken up? HELL NO YOU WAS NOT! I know for a fact you fucked other bitches! So you don't get to be mad at me for kissing somebody when YOU are the one who broke my fuckin' heart!" You could have stuck a fork in me because I was done. That shit hurted me to know I was the reasin. But fuck that, my ego and pride wouldn't let me bow down yet.

"I fucked bitches weks after not being able to find yo'ass. Besides I kept them hoes in check. They knew not to come at me talkin' about feelings and a realtionship! You don't see any of them hoes doing the most like that bitch ass ex of yours!" She wiped her face and rolled her eyes.

"So, you mad at me for a punk ass kiss but you get to fuck bitches and expect me not care? Wow! Well then I guess I should have gotten me some dick." She stood there and folded her arms making sure to look in my eyes when she said that shit. I'm positive there was no word in the human dictionary to express how mad I was.

"If you ever in yo' muthafuckin' life say some shit to me like that again. You gone witness first hand why they call me Killz." I made sure to not blink as I said that to her.

"You don't scare me Karlos." She responded to me and I just looked at her and smiled big as hell. I was done talking to her ass. Kylee was on some other shit so I left her standing right where she was at. I knew what I had to go do.

*

I called my P.I. guy and had him do a background check on this Tony nigga. I was so mad when I left I forgot to get his fucking address from Kylee. Now her ass not answering my calls which means she mad at me. But right now I didn't give a fuck about her feelings. She been hiding shit from me for to long. I knew some shit was off with her but I thought I was just being paranoid. What got me so mad about this whole situation is she saw this nigga while we were broken up.

After what he did to her she went crawling back to his dirty ass. Meanwhile I was sleeping outside of her condo for weeks. And this nigga puts my sister and nephews life in danger and Kylee *still* wasn't going to tell me. The more I thought about this shit the more heated I got. Now I was on my way to my P.I. guy to get this information.

Pulling up to Saulet apartments I called my guy and told him I was here. I got out my truck and leaned against it. I called Kylee again for the fifth time but she still didn't answer. How the fuck could she even call herself being mad? I'm the one who had been lied to. I didn't go out with a fuckin' ex her ass did.

All I did was shoot on a few bitches faces when we were broken up. But that was weeks after I couldn't find her. My hoes were trained though, they knew not to try any funny shit. While I waited for my guy to come down some girls walked out the building. They looked at me like they wanted to tag team my balls. The blonde head one licked her lips at me.

"Beat it bitch. I ain't interested," I said looking at all three of there thirsty asses. She smacked her lips and fliped her weave. As long as they got the fuck outta my face they could have broke down crying for all I cared. My guy walked out just as I was about to call his ass again.

"What's good Donny. What'chu got for me." He walked up to me with a folder. Donny had been working for our family for years. There was nothing his ass could not find on a person. The only time he couldn't deliver was when he couldn't find Kylee for me. But her ass had her father help her dissappear and that nigga is old school.

"I dug up a bunch of shit on your college boy. You know he use to fuck yo' wife right? Like they were together heavy." My nostrils flared and Donny threw his hands up in a surrender way. This was my guy but if he didn't shut the fuck up I was going to knock his ass out.

"A'ight good looking on this. I know it was short notice so I threw a lil' something extra for you." I gave Donny two stacks and jumped in my truck.

I needed to know where the fuck I was going so I opened the folder. This nigga Tony was a straight preppy boy. A spoiled ass mamas boy. What I didn't understand was why he was going to an escort service. The nigga was young and had money. That right there was a bitch magnet. Nigga probably was into some freaky ass shit taht only hookers would do. I read on to his family and childhood.

"MUTHFUCKA!" I turned my truck on and pulled off into traffic. I had fire running through my veins. I swear the way this world is set up you can't trust no fuckin' body. I drove through traffic like the crazy ass nigga I was. This shit was starting to piece together and I wasn't likin' it.

SCURRR!

I pulled up at my brothers barber shop not *even* caring

that I took up three parking spaces. I hopped out and walked around to the enterance. Barging in I opened and closed the door so hard the whole muthafucka shattered.

Slap!

Taylor's body flew across the room into Kevin's work station.

"BRO WHAT THE FUCK!" Kevin shouted as he ran to me to block Taylor.

"FUCK THAT BITCH! SHE TONY'S SISTER!" I yelled as Kalvin, Dru and Nick held me back. Melissa went to help Taylor off the floor her lip was busted and she was crying.

"WHO THE FUCK IS TONY?!" Kevin shouted.

"WAIT! WAIT! EVERYBODY SHUT THE FUCK UP!" Kalvin yelled. All you could hear was Dave East-Paranoia album in the back ground.

"That bitch is Kylee's ex sister. The nigga hit my wife up sayin' he would shoot Kimmora and Keion if Kylee would not meet him. He sent a picture of Kimmora and Keion ! I'm tellin' you bro all this shit is adding up. Kimmora getting jumped ain't a fuckin' coincidence! That bitch know what's poppin'!" Kevin turned around to Taylor and grabbed that bitch by her hair yanking her up.

"You better talk bitch! Yo' brother threatened my fuckin' family. If you don't talk you will die right now." I smiled when he pulled his gun out on her.

"Please don't! I didn't know he would take things this far. He just wanted me to get close to y'all so I could find out more about Kylee." My eyes got big and I grew more heated at this nigga. "Where the fuck does he live?" She told us the address and I was ready to roll.

"We comin' wit'chu bro. Dru, Nick close up. And bet nobody say shit about what the fuck they saw," Kalvin said as we were out the door.

"Get that bitch, she comin' too," I told Kevin and he grabbed Taylor by her arm. When I get a hold of this nigga ain't nobody gone stop me from killin' him nice and slow.

*

We pulled up to a blue and white house. I saw a black Jaguar in the drive way that I'm assuming is his.

"That's his car?" I looked in my rear view mirror and asked Taylor. She had that black shit running all down her eyes. She nodded her head and cried harder. Me and my brother's checked our heat and got out the truck. Walking up to the front door I yanked Taylor in front of me.

"Unlock the door and you bet not say shit," I said through gritted teeth. She nodded and did what I said.

When she let us in Kalvin stood behind with his gun on Taylor. You would never know he use to lust after that bitch. The way he was ready to pop her if she tried some shit. I walked through the down stairs of the house with Kevin. We both walked through the kitchen, bathroon and his punk ass man cave. We checked closets and cabinets since there was no basement me and Kevin went upstairs.

There was three bedrooms with the doors closed. We checked two of them and there closets and didn't see shit. The last bedroom had to be where the nigga was at because I heard the TV playing. Me and Kevin had our guns out ready to go in. Opening the door the room was empty with the bed messed up and the TV on.

"Shower," Kevin whispered to me and pointed to the bathroom. I nodded my head and walked torwards the bathroom. I pushed the door slowly open and walked in with Kevin behind me. There was a girl standing with a robe on putting her hair in a high ponytail. My heart fell to my fuckin' feet. I felt my hand grip tighter around the handle and the colors around me turned red.

"Kylee?" I said making the girl turn around. When she saw my gun her eyes got big and she held her hand up.

"No I'm not Kylee. My name is Nina please don't kill me please. I don't even live here I'm an escort." Her tears fell from her chocolate face.

"Hold the fuck up! How the fuck do you look just like my sister?" Kevin asked. I stood there froze just looking at her. Then is dawned on me, this the girl I saw in the gas station.

"I don't even know who Kylee is. All I know is the dude Tony pays $15,000 a month to my escort service for me to be here full-time. He has never told me what his obsession is with this Kylee person. He just tells me how to dress, keep my hair, nails and how to talk. Please don't kill me." I walked up to her.

"Where is he now?" She wiped her tears. I had to look away becasue I wanted to hug her and tell her it was going to be ok. That's how much she looked like my Ky.

"I don't know. He told me he would be right back when he came out his office he looked mad." I looked at Kevin and he ran his hand over his face.

"Bro this is some movie type shit. This bitch looks just like Kylee man and now we don't know where he at." I looked back at Nina.

"Where is his office?" I asked her and she pointed to the closet in the bedroom.

I walked out the bathroom to the closed door. When I opened it he had pictures all over the wall of Kylee. I'm talking about wallpaper of Kylee's face covered the all the walls. He had pictures of her sleeping, eating, in the pool, laughing, and them together. I could look at them and tell they were pictures when they were together.

I had to run my hand over my face to keep from burning this bitch down. To even think of anybody obsessing over my baby was killing me. I was ready to murder somebody. I walked over to the computer screen. The screensaver was a picture of him and Kylee kissing. I moved the mouse and a screen popped up.

It looked like he was emailing somebody back and fourth. Then I seen my address somebody sent to him. They sent it and two hours ago. If you would have touched me you would have burnt yo'self. That's how hot I was.

"Aye we gotta get to my crib. That nigga is going there." I rushed out the room yelling at my brothers. I made it downstairs and Kalvin was still holding his gun on Taylor.

"Come on we gotta go!" I rushed passed them.

"Karlos what'chu wanna do with her?" Kevin asked pointing to Nina.

"Aye how the fuck she look just like Kylee?" Kalvin asked.

"Bring her too! Come on niggas!" We loaded my truck and I pulled off fast as hell to my crib. I said a quiet prayer to God. I know I have not lived and done shit right. But please God protect my wife and baby girl. Kill me and let them live. In Jesus name amen.

I pulled up to my crib and jumped up. My brothers grabbed Taylor and Nina and were on my heels.

"KYLEE!" I called her name. I moved through my house like a burglar in the night. I ran up the stairs three steps at a time.

"Baby!" I went through the bedrooms. I got to Kaylee's bed and it was empty as well. I walked over to the crib and saw a piece of paper in it. I picked it up.

They are my family now.

I balled the note up and squeezed my fist so tight I felt my knuckles stick out like spikes. My vision became blurry like I was about to black out. I closed my eyes and stood there in my princess room. When I opened them I felt the veins in my neck beat like a pulse. My eyes were filled with black and rage. I didn't even feel like myself I felt like a demon had taken over me. Naw, not a demon more like the devil. This nigga had my fuckin' wife and princess. My whole fuckin' world was stolen from me. Naw, this can't happen.

I took a deep breath and walked out Kaylee's room. I walked downstairs where Kalvin and Kevin stood in the living room with Taylor and Nina.

"What's the word bro? Where sis and niece at?" Kevin asked me. I looked Taylor in her eyes and said.

"He took them." I walked over to her and snapped that bitch neck. Her lifeless body hit the floor. Nina screamed and I looked over at her. Her eyes grew huge and tears fell from them.

"Please don't hurt me. I swear I had nothing to do with this. I would never do anything like this I'm only 21. Please." Standing over her looking like the killer I felt took over me I couldn't kill her. My brothers looked at me and nodded their heads.

"Let's roll," I said to them and we left out my house. I texted Kaylin and Brandon 911 the warehouse. I knew exactly what I needed to do next.

"So, wait a fuckin' minute. This nigga gets a hooker to that looks just like Kylee, threatens Kim and Keion, then takes Kylee and Kaylee?" Brandon said as he loaded his heat. We were at our warehouse. I had four of our workers come and clear all work out of it. I told them to do nothing but keep an eye on Nina.

Feed her, let her watch TV but don't touch her. As we stood inside the warehouse loading up Nina sat on the couch. It was hard to look at her becasue she looked just like my baby. That's honestly what saved her life. When we were done I walked over to her. She started breathing hard and getting scared.

"Calm down. Ain't nobody about to fuck with you. You gone stay here where it's safe. These nigga's gone watch you but they won't touch you. If you hungry just let them know. As you already know I don't fuck around so don't try me. Stay here." I looked at her.

"Ok," she responded. I stood up and walked torwards my brothers.

"Shit is creepy as fuck," Kaylin mumbled. We got to my truck and loaded it up. Once we were all in I headed to my destination with black still all in my eyes.

*

We pulled up to a big ass white house with black shutters. There was a black painted fence around it. A white Mercedes and silver Audi in the driveway. I got out with my brothers right behind me. Walking up to the walkway some white neighbors looked at us with there noses turned up. I kept it moving because these problems were not on there Christmas list. Pale muthafuckas.

"Where the fuck are we Killz?" Kaylin asked. I smirked at him and knocked on the door. After three knocks I heard someone coming to the door.

"Can I-----"

"ARGH!" I cracked the nigga in the nose with the butt of my gun. My brother's knew exactly what to do when we got in the house. I had them so fucking trained that without knowing where the fuck we were at they knew what to do.

"Ahhhhh!" I heard a older woman yell. Brandon waited by the door with the nigga I knocked out.

I'm assuming it was the butler since he came to the door lookin' like Jeffery from The Fresh Prince of Bel-Air. Kevin and Kaylin had upstairs and I walked in the basement. I could here Marvin Gaye playing and what sounded like weight lifting. When I got down there I was right. A older nigga was listening to music and lifting weights. I walked over to where he was at and stood over him.

"Who the fuck are you?" he yelled as he tried to sit up from his weight bench. I pushed him back down.

"Where the fuck is your son?" I looked at him with a straight face and black eyes.

"Who are-----"

Punch!

I hit his old ass right in his nose. I don't know why the fuck people wanted to test me today. Old man grabbed his bloody nose and looked at me. I kneeled down and asked again which is something I do not do.

"Where is your son? He has my wife and daughter. Where the fuck is he? And don't say at home because I checked there?" I grabbed his throat with my black gloves on.

"I-I-I dont't know where he is." I squeezed harder making him struggle for air and he hit my hand.

"Think nigga. What other place does he have? I see y'all got a lot of money so I know he has more than one place." I loosened up my grip so he could talk.

"Heee j-j-just brought a place in the French Quarters." He told me the building and apartment number. I stood up ready to take my leave. He started coughing and catching his breath.

"You are no good for her. Just let Tony have Kylee back. You and your family are nothing but cancer," he coughed and said.

I stopped in my tracks and walked back over to him. Standing over him again I smirked and picked up his 45lb weight plate. I held it up in the air with one hand and dropped it on his fat foot before he could react.

"AHHHHHHHH!" He yelled like a bitch in the night. I kneeled down and whispered in his ear.

"Your foot made the same cracking sound your daughter's neck made when I snapped it." I smiled big with eyes black as the night. He whimpered and shaked as tears fell out his eyes.

"I will be killing you son as well. Take it as a lost becasue ain't shit you can do about it." Getting up I walked up-stairs to my brothers.

"Let's roll," I told them as we walked out. Next stop was the French Quarters.

*

"All y'all got y'all safeties on and and gloves on right?" I looked at my brother's and asked. They nodded their heads.

I turned the knob to the apartment and with my luck it was unlocked. When we walked in there were two women on the couch smoking crack through a pipe. The TV was on blast playing Sanford and Son show. They looked like some big dyke bitches. They were so busy getting high they didn't even see us come in. Kevin walked up to them and put a bullet between both their eyes. We all looked at him like he was crazy. Usually it was me that killed on sight.

"Them fat bitches jumped Kimmora," he said. We all nodded and kept it moving. There were only two bedrooms. I pointed to the one on the right for my brothers to follow me.

Opening the door some nigga was standing up getting head by another cracked out looking bitch. She wasn't as bad looking at the other two. She looked like if you cleaned her up she would be a MILF.

"WHA----"

The nigga's words were cut short when I held my gun up. Kevin grabbed the bitch and put a bullet through her head.

"That's Chrissy's mama. And that's Kimmora's ex Tyler the nigga I fucked up. What the fuck is going on here?" Kevin asked with the same look in his eyes as me. I looked at the nigga and he had his hands up.

"How the fuck do you know Tony? You dying anyways so you might as well tell us." We were all whispering because the Quarters were filled with people.

"I was approached by him four months ago. We go to the same escort service place. He recognized me because he was with Kylee when I was with Kimmy." Kevin eyes turned black when he said that. The shit made me smile. Tyler saw his face and cleared his throat looking scared.

"He told me he had a plan to get y'all locked up. I told him I'm down because I wanted Kimmora back." He was breathing hard and he looked at Chrissy's mama dead body.

"How the fuck you know her?" Kevin pointed to her dead body.

"Tish? She works at the escort place I go to. She was cheap not expensive as the one Tony got. She saw a picture of Kimmora on my desk at my crib one day. That's when she told me the two of you killed her daughter. But I knew that was a lie. Kimmy-----"

His words were cut short from Kevin. Tyler's lifeless body hit the bed next to Tish. Kevin spit in his face and I dabbed him up. I told Kalvin, Kaylin to stay in the front in case somebody came. Then I told Brandon to call the clean-up crew. Me and Kevin walked out the room ready to go to the next room. I heard instrumental music playing like the sounds of a piano. I turned the knob and almost threw up. That nigga Tony was over my wife's naked body ready to fuck her.

"THA FUCK!" Kevin yelled making him jump up. He tried to roll over and grab the gun on the night stand. I speared his ass and me and him fell on the side of the bed.

The bitch ass nigga got a hit in my face. But I had so much rage through my body that I didn't even feel it. I stuck my knee in his chest and hit him twice in the face. Because the nigga was almost my size he didn't knock out to easily. I didn't want to pull my heat out on him. I wanted to beat his ass then kill him. He hit me in the side of my ribs but I didn't feel that either. I hit him all my 280lbs weight and hit him in his face three times knocking his as out.

I got up off him and dragged his body from the side of the bed and the wall. Once he was in the middle of the floor I took my size 13 Timberland boot and stomped his face. Each stomp I gave him I saw the image of him and Kylee. I saw him take my two babies out from our home against their will. I saw him touch her, kiss her, talk to her, put fear in her. Touch my princess Kaylee, look at her, talk to her.

"BITCH! BITCH! BITCH!" I stomped his face over and over. I was biting my lip and spit was coming out my mouth.

"KARLOS! KARLOS BRO THAT'S ENOUGH MAN!" I heard Kevin yell at me but I didn't stop. I couldn't stop.

"KARLOS KYLEE NEEDS YOU BRO." The sound of my baby's name made me snap out of it. I looked around and remembered where I was at.

"Where the fuck in my daughter?" I asked looking around. I saw a little crib in the corner. My princess was in there looking around. I smiled at her and she gave me those deep pretty dimples.

"Karlos, Kylee is not moving man." I turned around and walked over to my baby.

Kevin covered her body up. He called Kaylin back to get Kaylee. I climbed on the bed and put Kylee in my arms. I felt like I was dying looking down at her. She was not a heavy sleeper so the fact that she didn't wake up scared me. This same nigga that did not fear shit was scared out of his mind. Losing my mama and pops messed me up in the worst way. If I lost this girl right here that was the end for me. I don't even know life outside of her. How could I be a good father to my princess?

"Kylee, baby get up. What the fuck did this nigga do to you baby." I checked her pulse and it was beating. Her chest moved up and down slowly. She was drugged. I wrapped her up in a sheet and carrind her bridal style out the room. Brandon looked up at me and his eyes grew big.

"Is she—" I shook my head no to his question. He let out a sigh of relief.

"Bro we got to change your boots. You got that nigga's eye balls and blood all on your shoes." Kalvin said to me as I put Kylee in the truck next to Kaylee. I walked back in the apartment and went in the room Kylee was in. I pulled my silencer out, put it in his mouth and pulled the trigger. Smoke was coming out his mouth. I put two more bullets in his heart and walked out just as my cleaning crew was walking in.

*

I set next to Kylee while she was laying in the hospital bed. The doctor said she was drugged with roffies and molly.

She must have woke up when she was with that nigga because he injected her with so much. That's why she was out so hard. The police came and I told them she was missing for some hours. I tracked her phone and it led me to the French Quarters.

When I got there Kylee was passed out and Kaylee was in the crib. The pigs ate that shit up when I told them no one else was there but my wife and daughter. Now they are going to put out a search warrant for Tony. They asses will be searching forever because that nigga will never be found.

That nigga's house was filled with a shrine of Kylee so they took it as an obsession gone wrong. The doctors did and exam on Kylee and Kaylee and said no sexual activity had been done to them. I guess I arrived just in time. I would have went back and killed his whole fucking family if he had touched my wife or my princess. The whole family was in the waiting room. I filled her dad in on what happened. He was ready for war like I was but I told him the nigga was dead. Along with those muthafuckas that jumped Kimmora. He was pleased and thanked us for handling shit.

I held Kylee's hand in mines. Kaylee was in her play pen right next to me. They tripped on me bringing her back here. But I pulled my gun out on the doctor and nurses and they changed their tune quick as hell. I wanted my baby to wake up to mines and Kaylee's face. I wanted to bring that bitch ass nigga back to life and kill him all over again.

Kaylee slept sound in the play pen while I dropped my head in Kylee's hand I was holding. Even though I knew she was ok I just hated seeing her like this. While I closed my eyes I felt a hand touch the back of my curls. My head shot up so quick. Kylee pretty ass was smiling at me with those dimples.

"Ugh Baby." I kissed all over her face and hugged her so tight. Pull my bitch card because I had tears in my eyes. I don't give a fuck I was lost knowing my wife and princess was missing.

"I can't breathe my Los. Oh my God, where is Kaylee!" She sat up looking scared. I got up and picked Kaylee up out the play pen. Kylee closed her eyes and smiled. I placed her little chubby self in her arms. She was only four months but she had some meat on her little body. When she got in Kylee's arms she opened her eyes. Those big pretty grey eyes. Kylee kissed and hugged on her.

"What happened? The last thing I remembered was Tony breaking into our house. He was trying to get me and Kaylee to go with him. He had two big ass women with him. That's all I remember before blacking out. Where are they?" Her eyes filled with tears.

"Handled baby. All of them, Taylor too." She looked at me with furrowed eyebrows.

"She was Tony's sister. You never met her because she lived with there aunt in D.C." I explained to her. She covered her hand with her mouth and started crying.

"He told me about her but I never met her. I had no idea that was the Taylor working at the barber shop. I'm am so sorry Karlos. I'm sorry that I didn't tell you sooner about him calling me. I figured I knew him and he was harmless. I am so sorry I put myself, our daughter and our family in harms way." She broke down and I went and hugged her while she held Kaylee.

"Kylee there was more to this shit then just you baby. It is not your fault at all. I was pissed off at you earlier. But seeing you unconscious made all my anger at you go away. But Kylee look at me." I tilted her chin so our eyes could meet.

"Don't ever keep shit from me again. I don't give a fuck how little it is baby. You have a looney ass husband who will bring the world to it's knees over you and my princess. But you still need to tell me shit." She nodded her head and hugged me again.

"I love you so much my Ky. Don't ever scare me like that again or I'm kickin' yo'ass." We both laughed. She rubbed the side of my face and looked me in my eyes.

"I love you more my Los. Now let me feed Kaylee then you can put her in the play pen. I'm gonna suck yo' dick while you call me your Queen." I bit my lip and nodded my head. I kissed my baby one more time on the lips before she started feeding my princess. I blew a long breath as I looked at my family. I would gladly end my life to save and protect there's any day.

A Few Hours later

I was laying in bed when my cell phone went off. I hurried up and grabbed it so it would not wake Kylee and Kaylee up. I had both of my babies in the bed with me. After the day we all had I just needed them under me. Looking at my phone I saw it was one of my workers.

"What's the word?" I asked while wiping my eyes. He told me them L.A. niggas were outside the warehouse and had there heat out. I was already up putting my basketball shorts, t-shirt and Timberlands on. I told them I was on the way.

"Baby what's wrong? Where the fuck are you going?" Kylee set up in the bed and asked me.

"I'll be right back baby. Some shit is happening at one of our warehouses and I need to handle it. I'm coming right back to y'all. Ok?" She looked at me and nodded her head. I gave her a sloppy kiss and told her I love her. I kissed my princess and walked out the bedroom.

The last eighteen hours have been a fuckin' ride. This shit with Kylee's and Kim's crazy ass exes was enough to make a movie. Now these L.A. niggas were trippin' off some shit that has nothing to do with me. I stand by what the fuck I told them earlier. I ain't payin' shit so if it's war they want then that's what they will get. I don't think I will ever get tired of dropping bodies.

I pulled up to the warehouse and saw the same niggas standing outside. They had there heat out like my worker said. I had my nigga's pull up the same time as me along with my brothers. I hate to get them out the bed from there families. But this was business and if one had beef then we all had beef.

"Why the fuck we back out here? This shit was settled when y'all came to my club. I ain't payin' shit my uncle told y'all." I stood in front of the one I assumed was the leader. He was a slim tall nigga with red on from head to toe. He sucked on his teeth and said.

"Then we have a problem." He stepped to my face. We were nose to nose and that was to close for me. I balled my fist up ready to swing.

"Aye look at his fuckin' leg!" His boy shouted while pointing to my leg. Me and the nigga's eyes never left each other's. That was a smart nigga because as soon as he would have looked away that would have been it for him.

"Rell he got Nina on his leg!" His boy yelled again. This time everybody including myself looked at my leg. The nigga eyes got big and he pulled his gun out on me. I was just as quick because my gun was on him as well.

"How the fuck you know my sister? Where the fuck is she?" he said looking like he was ready to shoot at me.

"Nigga this my muthafuckin' wife. This ain't yo' fuckin' sister. I got that bitch in the basement of our warehouse." He bit his bottom lip and became trigger happy.

"Why the fuck you got here? What you kidnap her for nigga? I been looking for her for months! Let me see her?"

"I ain't kidnap no fuckin' body. Yo sister been hoeing and got caught in some shit. You better be lucky I do have her. The nigga she was with was on some "Get Out" type of shit. Now lower yo' fuckin' gun and I can take you to her," I said with my gun still pointing at him. He looked from side to side and lowered his gun.

I lowered my gun and nodded at my brother's. They knew that meant to stay outside with guns still on them niggas. Me and gumpy ass walked in the warehouse. We walked down the basement and I opened the first door where his siter was at.

"Darnell!" Nina jumped up smiling hugging him. He smiled and hugged her back.

"You good baby sis? This nigga fucked wit'chu?" He pointed to me and I had to laugh.

"No. They saved me from this nigga named Tony. He was obsessed with his wife." She pointed to me.

"He was making me her clone and shit. Then he took her and his baby. It's a whole mess but I'm ok. How did you find me?"

"Aye-aye! Finish this reunion bullshit somewhere else. Yo' sister lookin' like my wife was the only thing that saved her. Now if I give her to you then all this beef shit is settled." I looked at him with a serious face. If he denied my offer then him and his sister was about to die.

"We squared blood. You took care of baby sis." He held his hand out to me. I kept my eyes on him and I shook it. We walked up stairs and I nodded at my brothers thelling them shit was cool. The L.A. niggas hopped in there rides and left. What a fuckin' day!

Kaylin

New Years Eve

I watched Kelly's BMW pull up in the driveway. I became more nervous when she parked and began getting out. Keira told her a client wanted her hair braided. It was early in the day on New Years Eve so I knew Kelly would not think nothing of it. Keira played her role real good and Kelly took the bait. I missed Kelly so much and knowing she was carrying my baby made me love her even more.

I don't know shit about the baby. I didn't know how far she was or who her doctor was. The only thing I did know was she still was pregnant. I made sure to keep tabs of that. Everything else I wanted me and her to experience those things together. I know I fucked up bad but I'm hoping she will forgive me and we can be back together.

Kelly walked up the long walk way of the house I was in. She looked so fucking good in her black short peacoat. She had on some dark fitted jeans and some Burberry rain boots. Her slim thick body was looking so good. My baby was making her hips spread and her skin glow more then it did. He hair was all down and curly and that beautiful ass face still made me smile. Kelly knocked on the door. I took a deep breath and opened it.

"Kaylin? What are you doing here? Where is Keira's friend at?" I smiled at her pretty confused face.

"I'm Keira's friend. I didn't know any other way to get you to talk to me. I wanted to come correct when we finally talked. Please come in Kelly." I looked at her and moved out the way. She hesitated for a minute then she walked in.

"You look good Kelly," I said to her as she walked in and turned around to me.

"Thanks," she said while putting her phone in her back pocket. I cleared my throat and began to talk.

"Kelly I won't even get into how much I miss you. Or how incomplete my life has been without you. Seeing the movers come and move all your shit out of our condo killed me. I won't tell you how I miss your voice, your touch and your presence. I won't tell you how I miss our trips we use to go on. We have been all over the world together and still have more to see. I always feel like Jay and Beyonce when we take our trips. It's like our private world when we are out the country together." She chuckled and so did I.

"Kelly when I found out Kaine was my pops I felt a bunch of emotions. I felt like I was not good enough for anyone. My mama wouldn't get clean for me, my brothers considered me the hoe of the group. The goof ball, my pops didn't even want to call me his son. Then these hoes out here just see money and having a baby with pretty eyes. Then there was you. You didn't want to have my baby or talk about us getting married. I felt like I would always be hoeish Kaylin who nobody took seriously." Kelly looked at me with tears in her eyes. I continued.

"I was drunk as fuck at that bar that night. Emily and her girl's were in there partying popping pills. I was already drunk and high so I popped some E and shit just got out of hand. I was trying to just numb shit. Kelly, I apologize bae. I don't want Emily and I never have. I was fucked up and that bitch is fucked up. I thought me being with you was not my reality.

I don't wanna make excuses because even with all that being said. I still cheated on you. I still fucked that nasty thot. I am truly sorry Kelly. And I promise you that if you let me gain your trust back I will never fuck up again." Kelly took her hand out her pocket and wiped her tears. I stood there looking at her waiting for her to say something.

"Kaylin you hurt me so bad. I only wanted to be there for you and support you. Even though your actions were wrong I have some wrong in it as well. I should have talked to you about me having children. It's not that I don't want to have your child. It's just I am scared of being pregnant. I'm scared of giving birth.

What happened to my mother when she had me and Keira scares me. I look at my dad when he talks about our mother and he has a sadness in his eyes. I never want to have you like that. Marriage does not scare me I just know with marriage comes children. I apologize for not telling you how I felt. I don't ever want you to think I don't want to have your child or marry you. I still love you Kay." That was all I needed to hear before I rushed her and kissed her lips. We kissed long and deep and we started taking off each others clothes.

*

"Kaylin who's house did we just fuck in." Kelly looked up at me. She was laying on my chest while I was rubbing my fingers through her hair.

"This is our house." I looked down at her smiling. She set up with her pretty ass titties bouncing.

"What? How is this our house? It's fully furnished!" She looked around the living room smiling.

"I brought it when y'all were in Colorado. Only person I told was Keira. She helped me pick out the furniture to decorate it." I sat up adn grabbed her hand.

"Come on let me give you a tour." The both of us ass naked I showed her the downstairs first. The kitchen was cherry wood and granite counter tops. I took her to the man cave that I had set up like a theather. There was a 70-inch TV on the wall and all my video games I play. The bathroom downstairs was white and gold with glass shower doors. Upstairs I took her to our master bedroom. The colors scheme was grey and burgundy with a California king size bed. The bathroom had a jacuzzi tub and vanity mirror in it. We had one huge walk-in closet the size of our living room.

"Here is the best part." I opened the door with one of the bedrooms and it was decorated for a baby girl. Keira told me Kelly used to tell her she wanted her daughter to have a Minnie Mouse room. So I had my decorator hook the room up. Kelly's mouth was on the floor. She had tears falling down her face.

"Kaylin it's beautiful." She smiffed and wiped her face. I smiled big as hell seeing her so happy.

I grabbed her hand and took her to the next room. When I opened the door Kelly gasped. The room was decorated for a boy. I chose The Lion King character. That was my favorite Disney movie. I had a brown crib and Simba as a cub all on the walls with Timon and Pumba. Kelly looked around and in the closet. It was filled with clothes and everything a baby could need.

"Kaylin this is fucking amazing bae." She looked at me with teary eyes and a dimpled smile.

"I'm glad you like it baby. This is just in case you have a boy. Then we can try again and put a girl in the other one." I smiled at her and said.

"Well, we may use both when I deliver. I'm having twins Kaylin. Ahhh!" She screamed when I picked her up and spinned her around. I was happy as hell to be having twin! Twins! Oh my goodness. Man you can't tell me God don't show up and show out.

"Bae that shit is so fuckin' lit. I love you so much Kelly. I promise to be a good man to you and a good father to our babies." I smiled big at her pretty and. I picked her up by her legs and wrapped her legs around me. We kissed passionately all the way until I laid her naked sexy ass down on our bed. I stood up over her and looked at her stomach. I bent down and kissed all over it.

"Hey my babies. This y'all daddy talking to you. I love y'all so much and I'm going to give y'all the world. I love you and y'all mommy very much." I kissed on her stmach again. Kelly was smiling while rubbing my head. I reached over her and opened the night stand. I pulled out a small box.

"Kelly can we start completely over bae." I opened the box. Kelly's eyes lit up as much as the 6 karat ring.

"Please agree to be my wife again Kelly Marie Ricci. I promise to take my time and be patient. Just promise me you won't make me wait to long bae." I looked at her and her pretty ass was crying.

"I would love to be your wife Kaylin Deon Royal. I promise to not make you wait long. I love you so much. Just promise to be the man I know you can be. You never have to feel like your not enough to me. Your more then enough bae." I put my finger under her chin and brought her lips to mines. I laid down and made Kelly stradle me. This was my bae and I loved her and our babies so much. It was our turn to be happily married with our babies. Wow! Twins!

Epilogue

(Kylee)
A Year Later

"Happy Birthday to youuuuu." Karlos had his big arms wrapped around my waist kissing on my neck as our family sang happy birthday to us.

With our birthday being a day apart we always celebrated together. This year I wanted a Gatsby theme party. We turned Royalty into a 1920's gold and black event. Karlos looked so damn sexy in his pinstripe suit with bow tie and fadora hat. He let me braid his hair in two big braids. I was so shocked because he hates braids. But he looked so good that I had to have him take me to his office earlier.

We blew the candles out of our four level black and gold cake. There were twenty-eight candles going around the cake. Once we blew the candles out me and Karlos kissed and cut into the cake. Everyone went back to partying and gambling. We walked back up-stairs to the VIP section. I checked my phone to see if my dad called. All the kids were at his house. But with our nonna and millions of cousins there were fine. Kaylee was getting so big now.

Our princess will be 2yrs old this year. She was Karlos weakness and he knew it too. She had him watching My Little Pony and Nick Jr. All day. It was the cutest shit ever. Karlos gym was doing so good. In May he will be going to Miami to open up a second location. I am so proud of my baby. As for me, I put my notice in with Ink.

Although I loved that publishing company it was time for me to go out on my own. Kylee Royal Presents was doing amazing. I had six authors in the top 10 best sellers list. I was still just starting out so it was only me and two other staff members. But we were doing pretty good and in a few years my name will be a household name.

Kimmora and Kevin were doing amazing. Keion kept them so busy with his active ass. His little chubby self with cheeks touching the floor. He use to look just like Kim but the older he got the more you saw Kevin. His big jet black curly fro was bigger then him. Kevin talked about wanting more kids all the time. That nigga was not playing about knocking Kimmora up again. She was 6 months pregnant with there second baby boy.

Kevin wanted a girl but he told Kimmora they would just have to try again. She claimed she was getting on birth control but we all know that's not happening. They decided to name their baby boy Karson Royal. Kevin and Kalvin's barber shop was still doing so well. The Essence Festival brought them major celebrity client's every year.

Speaking of Kalvin, him and Keira renewed there vows last August on there anniversary. Kalvin said he wanted to start over fresh and what better way then to renew your vows. They had a small ceremony in Italy at the house our dad grew up in. The shit reminded you of a God Father ceremony. Kyra was getting so big and she was beautiful. When she walks it was the cutest thing in the world. Her short little fat legs were so little and fast when she ran. Kalvin was such a good father.

Kelly and Kaylin had there wedding on New Years day. It was a beautiful wedding at the Civic Theatre in New Orleans. It was breath taking it should have been in a magazines all over the would. There theme was Winter Wonderland with blue and diamonds everywhere. I got so emotional watching them have there first dance to Jeremih-Love Don't Change. Kelly looked so beautiful in her Oscar De La Renta dress.

Kaylin wanted Kelly to have any and everything she wanted. Between him and our father, there was no limit to what she wanted. I was so happy for my baby sister but more happy for Kaylin because he was actually involved in his wedding planning. The other guys wanted nothing to do with that shit. The greatest thing about there wedding was there four month old twins were there looking so adorable as the Jr. Bride and Jr. Groom. Kelly had a boy and a girl named Kennedy and Kenny after our dad. He was such a proud grand pa.

New chapters were opening for Tiff and Brandon. My sis and brother in-law were moving to Miami. Tiff was going to run Karlos gym which was perfect for her because she loved the fitness lifestyle. Brandon was opening up a car wash inspired by the movie The Wash. The shit was lit and they were so happy to be starting a new leaf. I was really going to miss my sis Tiff. She became part of me and my sisters circle so quick.

Tiff was an amazing mommy and Brandy was the prettiest chocolate little girl. Her long ponytails at only two and a half years old put some grown women to shame. Brandon had her spoiled rotten. There going away party was in a few weeks. It seemed like the more the time came for them to leave. The more nervous Tiff became but that's a different storey for a different book.

*

"She looks so peaceful when she sleeps," I whispered to Karlos. We were in Kaylee's room looking at her sleep in her toodler bed. Her room was still done up with Marie from The Aristocats movie. She just didn't have her crib anymore. When she turned one we brought her a purple princess toddler bed. Me and Karlos kissed her again before walking out her room.

"You have fun tonight baby?" Karlos asked me as he took his suit off.

"I had a fucking ball baby. That Gatsby theme was such a good idea and so fun. You look so sexy in a bow tie." I looked at him and bit my lips. Karlos was taking his braids down and his long sexy hair was all big and curly.

"Thank you baby but you was looking good as fuck in that beaded gown you had on. Givin' me some birthday pussy was the shit." He walked over to me and kissed my lips. I put my arms around his waist once I stepped out out my dress. I had on a black lace panties and bra with a garter belt.

"Happy birthday baby. I love you my Los. Thank you for everything you do baby." I kissed him again.

"Happy birthday to you too baby you never have to thank me for doing my job. I love you more my Ky. But if you keep giving me these weak ass kisses again I'mma kick yo' ass." I laughed while shaking my head at him. I gave him a deep nasty kiss that made his dick hard and my pussy wet.

"You and Kaylee got my heart in y'all hands. You know that right?" He looked at me with those sexy grey eyes. I smiled and nodded my head yes. He picked me up and carried me to our bed. Laying me down his hard tattooed body hovered over mines. Karlos looked at me with love mixed with lust in his eyes.

"What I wanna hear Kylee?" He asked me biting his juicy bottom lip. I felt my panties get so moist at the sound of his voice. My breathing changed and my heart was beating fast. I knew exactly what my baby wanted to hear.

"I'm never leaving you baby. I'm yours and only yours forever and ever." He was removing my panties while I was talking. Once there were off and his boxers were off he slid inside of me.

"Say it again." His deep voice set my body on fire in my ear. He fucked me all night while I repeated over and over how I was his and never leaving him. I meant that shit to. The love we had for each other was dangerous but I dare somebody to tell us any different.

We were all so happy with our husbands and children. It's so funny how life plays out. What you think is about to be a regular moment in life turns out to be a moment that changes your life. Going to the Royal's party almost four years ago led us to being their wives. Taming the hearts of these New Orleans savages was no walk in the park.

Every tear drop, every fight, break-up, was all worth it to get to where we were now. Our men knew what we would take and what we wouldn't take. And to me that's what it was all about. Finding someone who knew how to treat you. I know I was loving every moment of being in love with my New Orleans Savage.

<u>The End</u>

"What up people! This ya' boy Karlos I just wanted to let y'all know that this is the end of our story but stay tuned. Because my boy Brandon and baby sis Tiff got a whole story of their own coming up. The shit gone be lit as fuck!

If you thought we had some drama wait until you read about them. We will have a couple of lines here and there in their book. But it will be all about Brandon, Tiff and my cute ass niece Brandy. Their new life in Miami and the shit brewin' up for them. So stay tuned and be a little patient with my girl Londyn Lenz or I'm comin' fuh ya ass! A'ight I gotta get back to my Ky and princess Kaylee. I'm out!